Praise for *A Killing Gift*

"Nerve-wracking suspense and wry humor . . . a unique narrative filled with sharp dialogue, quirky characters, and shades of oriental mysticism. Glass brings the Big Apple and its inhabitants to life as only a native New Yorker could, and Manhattanites—as well as mystery aficionados—may well find Woo to be one of the most compelling heroines to grace the genre in years."   —*Publishers Weekly*

"The pace is fast, the characters gritty and the intensity . . . grabs the reader."
—*Romantic Times Book Club*

Praise for *The Silent Bride*

"If you haven't succumbed to the Woo/Glass one-two punch, *The Silent Bride* should win you over."
—*Chicago Tribune*

"The author [has a] flair for capturing cultural idio-syncrasies and developing quirky characters. . . . With its rich characterizations and well-drawn setting, this rollicking mystery is a plentiful source of comic thrills and suspenseful chills."
—*Publishers Weekly*

"Excellent. . . . The strength of the series continues to be the characterization, especially the details of April's dilemma in trying to reconcile her Chinese heritage with her American way of thinking."
—*The Mystery Reader*

"Woo comes across as wonderfully human. . . . Plenty of suspense and enough red herrings to make it interesting."   —*Crescent Blues*

coninued . . .

ALSO BY LESLIE GLASS

Leslie Glass

A CLEAN KILL

AN ONYX BOOK

ONYX
Published by New American Library, a division of
Penguin Group (USA) Inc., 375 Hudson Street,
New York, New York 10014, USA
Penguin Group (Canada), 10 Alcorn Avenue, Toronto,
Ontario M4V 3B2, Canada (a division of Pearson Penguin Canada Inc.)
Penguin Books Ltd., 80 Strand, London WC2R 0RL, England
Penguin Ireland, 25 St. Stephen's Green, Dublin 2,
Ireland (a division of Penguin Books Ltd.)
Penguin Group (Australia), 250 Camberwell Road, Camberwell, Victoria 3124,
Australia (a division of Pearson Australia Group Pty. Ltd.)
Penguin Books India Pvt. Ltd., 11 Community Centre, Panchsheel Park,
New Delhi - 110 017, India
Penguin Group (NZ), cnr Airborne and Rosedale Roads, Albany,
Auckland 1310, New Zealand (a division of Pearson New Zealand Ltd.)
Penguin Books (South Africa) (Pty.) Ltd., 24 Sturdee Avenue,
Rosebank, Johannesburg 2196, South Africa

Penguin Books Ltd., Registered Offices:
80 Strand, London WC2R 0RL, England

First published by Onyx, an imprint of New American Library,
a division of Penguin Group (USA) Inc.

First Printing, June 2005
10 9 8 7 6 5 4 3 2 1

For the Home Team—
Jim, Alex, Lindsey,
Rocky, and Julius

ACKNOWLEDGMENTS

Thanks to all the police officers who have shared their stories with me over the years. It is always an honor and a privilege to work with them. They are the heart of all my NYPD stories. I take my liberties with the geography of New York City, but not with the Department. I do my best to get it right. Cheers to all my friends at the New York City Police Foundation, and to all who work so hard at NAL to make my books look so good.

One

Everyone has a favorite place and a favorite time of day. For Madeleine Wilson, mornings in her private spa in the garden at the back of her town house were her salvation. Every day that she had to endure the pressure of living in New York with her famous husband, Wayne, and two hyperactive little boys, she spent the hours between eight and eleven in her private gym to get away from them.

At thirty-four, in the prime of her life, Maddy had never experienced violence in any form or wished real harm on anyone. All she wanted was the kind of peace and contentment that she felt working out in her spa. Never in a million years would she have believed that a bloody fight to the death would occur there, and that she would not emerge the victor.

Madeleine, known to everyone as Maddy, suspected that Wayne had built the gym for her as a salve to his guilty conscience for ignoring her exactly the same way he'd ignored his previous wife. The gym had a glass-roofed exercise and massage room, a hot tub, and a fabulous shower with a bunch of pulsing jets that could also be used as a steam room. She went there every morning, and often she slipped away there in the afternoon, too. The spa was her haven, the only really private place she had to indulge herself and soothe away the nagging irritations of a glamorous existence that had come with a very high emotional price tag.

On June 4 her morning started in the usual way, with a spike of rage. In his typical hurry, Wayne had inched out of their bed long before she'd begun to stir. Every morning she tried to be in sync with his demanding schedule, but every morning she woke with a jolt to realize he was already gone. Today, as usual, she reached for his spot to see if the sheets were still warm and she was disappointed that they were cool.

She felt logy, not quite herself, and was annoyed anew that her husband, a restaurateur of some renown, had the ability to slip in and out of the bed they shared without her being aware of it. He never woke her when he came home from work very late. But even on those rare occasions when they went to bed at the same time, he was never there when she awoke in the morning. This was a chronic hurt. So was the fact that he could eat and drink all night and still be up before Maddy, hungry for more, while she worked hard to avoid food and needed her full eight hours of sleep.

In the early days of their marriage, Maddy had considered his stealth in the bedroom a blessing. She'd thought it was nice of him not to bother her with the demands of his job—all that coming and going for the early staff meetings and the endless round of late-night parties. She hadn't wanted to give credence to the myriad bitter complaints of his first wife, Jenny. First wives were by definition evil hags. Jenny still harassed him, and often her, as well. It wasn't a pleasant situation. She used to think Jenny was just crazy, but now she was more sympathetic to her former rival. Wayne's bedroom stealth was just sneaking around, a trick he must have mastered with her, or even before, to confuse all his victims. Well, maybe that assessment was a little dramatic. She was hardly his victim.

Maddy had been twenty-seven when she'd met the handsome forty-two-year-old. They'd both been part of a daredevil trip in which a group of wealthy friends flew in small planes to a remote area way in Canada to ski fresh deep powder on a virgin slope. Like numerous women before her, Maddy had been attracted to him right away. She had appreciated his appetites, and she'd ended up pursuing him as much as he pursued her. At the time, he was backing out of a failed marriage, the father of two nice children, and she believed every word he said about Jenny's failures as a wife.

Maddy had been certain that she was a woman of the world, game for anything. She'd been a champion skier, after all. All legs and pretty enough to be a model. With her huge blue eyes and blond hair, she'd been photographed many times for ski magazines and had plenty of boyfriends in the sports crowd. Her past popularity and athletic prowess were painful to remember now because Wayne did not turn out to be interested in sports at all. He was just a very handsome foodie. Seven years ago she didn't even know what a foodie was. Now she was buried in the type—that special breed of human being who devoted his (or her) entire life to the art of the meal.

Never mind what meal, where or at what time of day it had been eaten, how, or what year. A foodie could spend hours discussing the merits and demerits of a meal consumed a decade ago in a country that had since been annihilated. Breakfast, lunch, dinner, even tea—it didn't matter. All kinds of meals were worthy of lengthy savoring and even longer debate. It wouldn't affect Wayne's conversation one bit if the restaurant, or indeed the whole city, he might be praising had been totally destroyed by a war in which poison gas was used to exterminate half its citizens. Its demise wouldn't be the point. It wouldn't be mentioned. Events and the passage of time had no relevance whatsoever to the memory of an excellent meal.

When the two handsome people had met in a tiny plane in a very cold place where Maddy certainly felt very much at home, she had no way of knowing that history, even Wayne's own personal history, was significant to him only in the context of some dish or some ingredient of some dish. He remembered Jenny through the itinerary of their meals.

A gastronome had an encyclopedic mind in one area only, and that didn't even hint at the depth of knowledge about food possessed by a true foodie. Wayne was a true foodie. Other interests, like skiing or skydiving, this wife or that one, would come and go in his life, but food would always dominate. Maddy had learned that to her deep chagrin. For him every country had a terrain and a cuisine built on the ingredients cultivated there. Every cuisine had its history and its traditions, its utensils and vessels for presentation. He could write books. He did write books, or rather someone wrote them for him and let him take the credit.

And then, almost worse than foodies, Wayne's friends were winies, too. Or maybe *winos* was a more fitting description. When wine was added to the menu of foodie conversation, they talked all day and all night, as well. They knew which wine went best with each and every course, which slopes and caves in every country were best for the grapes, which years were the best vintages, and when every vintage should be drunk, as well as the perfect temperature to serve it. Not to mention the shape of glass required to give every wine the very best nose.

Maddy Angus Wilson was raised in Jackson, Wyoming, where she grew up on Cherry Coke, beef, antelope, venison, french fries, and not a lot else. They certainly didn't have mâche lettuces, baby vegetables the size of an infant's pinkie, and free-range chickens in her family's kitchen. Maddy preferred a different kind of physical life. Her friends were skiers, skaters, sailors, golfers. They were not much in attendance at places where foie gras was served with kumquat coulis. Unfortunately, however, there were a great many women who shared Wayne's passions. Maddy had become an angry woman, but who could blame her, she asked herself. This wasn't what she'd signed on for.

At seven thirty she dragged herself out of bed and studied herself critically in the mirror. She was still beautiful, but for some reason not as sharp this morning as she should be. She washed her face, brushed her hair, dressed in sneakers and almost see-through pink leotards that showed off her magnificent figure. Then she hurried into the kitchen, where Wayne was already having breakfast with the boys. They were having a feast without her. Her exclusion from that special ritual hurt, too.

The presentation had included fresh homemade sausage patties; whipped cream; a huge bowl of blueberries, raspberries, and strawberries; apricot preserves; three kinds of honey; thin, rolled pancakes filled with fresh raspberry jam that had been made only yesterday. Maddy had seen four jars of it cooling in the kitchen last night before she went to bed. Not much was left of the meal now, and Maddy's eyes widened with further distress to see that Remy, their supposed nanny, was sitting at her table with her one big and two little men, enjoying her share of the feast as if she, not Maddy, were the lady of the house.

"Remy made pancakes, Mommy. They're sooo yum." Bert was five and a half. Towheaded and smiley all over, he was a happy boy who looked just like her. At the moment, the bottom half of his face was smeared with bright red raspberry jam, and so were two of her favorite French blue toile napkins with the idyllic rustic scenes from the eighteenth century on them. Maddy's mouth tightened.

"Hi, Mommy," little Angus chirped from his special high chair. He was three and a half but still had a throne of his own, and he, too, was covered in red, likewise his napkin.

"Hi, sweetie," she cooed, then gave both boys careful kisses on the tops of their heads. She did not kiss Wayne, but he was busy with a sausage and didn't seem to notice.

"Hey, they're not just plain old pancakes, boys.

They're crêpes. Didn't Remy do a great job?"
Wayne said.

"Yea Remy," Angus said.

And that did it. Maddy wanted that woman out
of her house. Out of her life. Today. She was gone,
fired. Maddy didn't care that they had the special
bond of growing up in Jackson, and both had escaped to the city for a better life. She didn't want
Remy stealing *her* life. She picked up a jam-
smeared napkin. "You ruined the napkins—" she
snapped at the young woman.

Wayne jumped in before she could go any further. "Oh, don't be an old silly. Who cares about
napkins when the meal is terrific? Come on, honey,
try one of these patties. Oh, wait. I forgot, you
don't eat before noon." He finished off the very
last bite and dabbed at his lips.

Shit. Maddy's blood boiled at the insult. He put
her down and insulted her every chance he got,
always looking like an angel with his bland expression. *An old silly?* Now she was a freak who didn't
eat? Now she was old? Maddy flushed angrily, trying to hold her rage in check. "The boys are going
to be late," she said coldly.

Remy checked her watch and jumped up. "Do
you want me to get out the car, or wash the boys'
faces?" She directed her question at Wayne, as if
he was the one in charge of the troops.

Wayne knew what he wanted and tilted his head
in the direction of the garage. "You go get the car.
I'll take care of the boys."

But he disappeared instead. Maddy was the one
to hoist her little Angus angel down from his chair
and to take both boys to the downstairs bathroom,

where she removed the kid-sized chef's aprons that had been protecting their clothes and got them washed up for play school. She gathered up their backpacks, walked them through the hall to the front door and out to the curb where she was more than a little surprised to see that Wayne was in the passenger seat of the Mercedes. He rolled the window down when she indicated she wanted to talk to him.

"Where are you going?"

"I'm taking them to their first day. Then Remy's driving me to work," he said.

"I thought you weren't going in until noon." Maddy frowned. He was wearing a polo shirt, no jacket. He never went to work that way, never took them to their first day of anything. She glanced at Remy, busy strapping the boys into the back seat. She didn't have to wonder what was up. She knew this was Remy's doing.

Then she saw Leah, the redheaded girl who hung around all the time, tagging along with Remy wherever she went. Leah often walked to play school with them. She clearly expected to do so today. Remy chose that moment to ignore her friend, and Leah had a spacey, left-out expression on her face. She stood there like a spurned lover, or a beaten dog that didn't know enough to get out of the way. In fact, she looked as hurt as Maddy felt herself. Comparing herself with the rejected friend, however, was too painful a thought for Maddy to linger over.

"Well? What's going on?" she demanded of her husband.

"I need to take care of something," Wayne told

her, scratching his nose, which was always a clear sign of a lie.

"Well, I have to take care of something today, too," she replied. She leaned in and spoke softly in his ear so that he could not mistake her meaning or her intent. "I'm calling the agency for another girl. I've had it with Remy and all her little pals. Say good-bye, Wayne. She won't be with us tonight."

"We'll see," he replied genially. "We'll just see about that."

Two

Fifteen minutes later Derek came into the gym from the garage entrance and frowned when he saw Maddy. "You're in a funk today. What's the matter?"

"Does it show that much?" Maddy was clutching the first early-blooming iris to open in her garden. It was deep purple, one of her favorite colors. She held it out for his inspection. "Pretty, huh?"

He nodded.

Then she shook her head sadly. "The spring flowers are the one thing I love about New York. Everything else sucks," she muttered.

"What about me?" he demanded.

She kept shaking her head. He cost her thousands of dollars a week in vitamins and tonics and physical therapy—not to mention the love she didn't get from her husband. It made her want to laugh out loud that he pretended to be her friend while bleeding her dry for his services. Only the abundance of spring blooms in her tiny garden could cheer her today.

"Oh, oh. Maddy as a hatter today," Derek remarked. "Let's get started. I know what you need."

She made a face and dropped the iris on the bench by the door.

"Maddy as a hatter," he repeated teasingly.

"Stop it," she said automatically.

He was appraising her in the way that made her uncomfortable sometimes, though she didn't know exactly why. He was big, big enough to break every bone in her body. Sometimes that bigness was comforting, but sometimes it annoyed her. He knew far too much about her. He also had far more control over her body than her husband did, and today she didn't want that intrusion on her life. She made another face. She was upset about the argument she'd just had with Jo Ellen Anderson from the employment agency. Jo Ellen was not sympathetic about her very genuine complaints about Remy's flirting with her husband. Sometimes she wondered about them all. Why couldn't they just be happy?

"Now, settle down there." Derek spoke to her as if she were Angus's age. Then he laughed. He was six four, had blue eyes and a wide sensuous mouth, close-cropped, wheat-colored hair, and the kind of body that was displayed on the covers of romance novels. They were about the same age. Derek was a man who knew the power of his looks just like Maddy was a woman who knew the power of hers.

He'd started out as her trainer to keep her weight down, to help with some chronic pain she had, and to keep her strong for skiing, but he turned out to be as good as any chiropractor on her spine. He knew where weakness lurked in her muscles, and she had to admit that his vitamin packets and greens were fantastic. Unlike Wayne, Derek was a health nut who shunned animal fat and carbohydrates, but he had some weaknesses of his own. He talked nutrition all day long, and kept Maddy's weight off with vitamins and cocaine. He'd become much more than her trainer, but Wayne let her have all the money she wanted and didn't seem to mind the relationship.

Now Derek dropped a hand to her shoulder and scooted it across her back, then started rubbing at a tight muscle in her neck.

"Oh, we're in big trouble," he said.

"Yes, we are," she agreed.

Maddy was five ten. With high heels, she was a big girl. But Derek's hands on her always made her feel petite. He always told her she was too beautiful and smart to put up with a disrespectful husband. Maddy didn't like to think Wayne was slipping away, but what could she do? Divorce was out of the question. She had two small children—and worst of all, she still loved him.

"What happened today?"

"When I came down for breakfast, that little bitch was sitting there in my place having breakfast with Wayne and the boys. I could kill her."

"My, my. Here, start with the Precor. I'm thinking we shouldn't do too much today, just loosen you up and stretch."

"Guess what she served them," Maddy went on while he programmed the machine.

He shook his head. He didn't want to guess.

"Crêpes with homemade raspberry jam. The way she stuffs my boys with all that sugar makes me want to puke." She hopped on the Precor, fuming.

"You shouldn't let it happen. They'll be hyper all day," he agreed.

"I fired her," Maddy said exuberantly.

"Wow! Good going." Derek patted her on the back. Then his hand wandered, down to her butt and stayed there.

"I won't have her back in the house—don't do that, Derek."

"What?"

"You know what."

"Oh, Maddy, Maddy, Maddy, aren't I always good for you?"

"Not today," she said angrily. "I'm in a firing mood."

"Don't be silly—you'll never get rid of me. Okay, okay." He backed off the ass-patting when she shot him an angry look. "Do ten minutes. I'll be right back." He drifted out into the garden with his cell phone in his hand, and she got to work.

After her session was over, Maddy felt a lot better. That day Derek was good to his word: she did only the ten minutes of cardio, twenty minutes of Pilates mat work, and finally he stretched her out and gave her a quick massage. At nine she kicked him out abruptly. She wanted to be alone, had stuff to do. "Be sure the door is shut when you leave." She turned her back on him, closing him out.

"Jesus, no one likes a party pooper," he muttered.

She didn't see him go. After drinking a glass of water, she took a quick shower with the glass door closed and only two of the six jets on. Before going in, she'd put some eucalyptus oil near the steam jet, and hit the power button. In six minutes the heat and aroma in the handsome pink marble room that served as both shower and steam room would be exactly the way she liked them. While she waited for the steam to fill the room, she downed another glass of water. She did not bother to check the door to the gym. She came in here every day. The door had an automatic lock. She trusted Derek to do as she asked. She felt refreshed and safe, ready to do what she had to do.

Outside her sanctuary the day had started. Her husband was at one of his restaurants—who knew which one? Her boys were at play school. Maddy glanced at her watch. Jo Ellen had promised that she would talk with Remy and get her out of the house by noon. She planned to oversee Remy's packing to make sure that the girl didn't steal anything from the house when she left. Those Culinary Institute people had proved unreliable in the past. The last one had left with the Cuisinart, half the silver, and a bunch of expensive knives. She wasn't going to let that happen again.

Then Maddy thought of her children. She was looking forward to having the boys to herself again, picking them up and giving them a healthy dinner. She told herself she didn't really need a nanny. Why couldn't *she* be the only mom? She watched the steam build and tallied her tasks. Then, when the pink marble walls were gone and everything was white, she went in and inhaled the eucalyptus-scented steam. Delicious. She closed the glass door and lay down naked on the fragrant teak bench. She was not going to let anxiety about Remy and her husband ruin her day. This was not the first time she'd been forced to take action when

Wayne's affection appeared to wander, and it probably wouldn't be the last. She stretched her body out on the bench and succumbed to the soporific power of steam.

The steam hissed, and she became soothed and dreamy. She did not hear the outer door to her spa open. She did not hear someone come in and move around in her private gym. All she heard was the soft *ssss* through the pipe. Her body was relaxed, her eyes closed; and for a brief moment her soul was at peace.

When the first blow came, it was only by chance that she had raised her arm to wipe the sweat from her forehead. The attacker lunged, and the point of the knife was deflected by her elbow. She yelped as the blade sliced into the muscle of her upper arm, and the person staggered off balance.

"Bitch!"

"What—!" Maddy jumped up. In the fog she could see only a thick shape and the yellow rubber gloves from her own kitchen sink. She was shocked. It looked like Remy.

"Remy!" she screamed. "Don't!" Blood poured out of her arm, but oddly, she did not feel fear. She was at a disadvantage without a weapon, but she was in her own space, her own house. She did not expect to die. She expected to live a long life, keep her husband, raise her children. No one could take that from her. Rage pumped her full of adrenaline. She wasn't going to let anyone hurt her.

"Get out of here." She kicked out with a bare foot and hit plastic, sturdy plastic. She screamed. What the—? It wasn't raining outside or in the shower room. She realized it was a raincoat, and the person inside of it seemed stronger than the reedy, thin Remy Banks. But she couldn't be sure.

Oh, shit. The knife came at her again. Now she could see it. It wasn't a very long knife, and she still was more angry than afraid. She kicked again. This time she missed the target and lost her balance. As her foot came down on the marble floor, she slid through a puddle of her own blood and fell hard. She thrashed on the slippery tiles, trying to get up as the ghoulish form covered in plastic came at her again. Suddenly her vision was impaired and she couldn't tell if it was one person or two.

She screamed as the knives jabbed at her from both sides—at her hands, her feet, her knees. She fought to protect the soft targets, her breasts, her vital organs, and was struck in the chest over and over as she moved from side to side, trying to get away. Then she started begging for her life.

"No, please!" She didn't want to die. A roar filled her ears as the knife made contact with her forehead, slicing away the scalp over one eye and entering the eye.

Her hands jerked up to the place where her eye had been and finally opened a clear path to her chest and belly. The knife struck her belly button. She screamed one last time as the phone rang. As she turned toward the sound, one of the knives sank into her chest and found her heart.

Three

Alison Perkins watched the numerals on the clock by her bed change from 9:31 to 9:32 as she listened to Maddy Wilson's irritatingly long voice message. Maddy wasn't picking up. She rolled over on the big bed she shared with Andrew, Floyd, and Roxie, waiting for the message to end so she could speak her mind into the void. She was annoyed and wanted it to be known. Just a little while ago Maddy had called her in crisis, demanding instant attention. She'd had it with Remy, had it with poor Leah. Even Derek was pissing her off. Alison couldn't talk to her then because Andrew was having his ten minutes of the day with her and didn't like to be interrupted. Now Andrew was long gone, and it looked as if Maddy was gone, too.

Alison hated that. Everybody was so demanding! Andrew worked all the time, never came home, but had to have her early in the morning, the one time the whole family was together and the kids needed attention, too. Then Maddy *had* to meet with her about the *same old thing,* but only after she'd finished with Derek. She expected Alison to wait around for her. Alison's whole life had turned into a waiting game. She'd waited for Andrew to marry her, and now she was trapped with two little kids, always waiting for him to come home.

She'd retreated to bed to count down the minutes to the end of Maddy's session. Floyd and Roxie had followed her. For more than an hour they'd lazed around together. Now they were all up. The black standard poodle was lying on his stomach as close to her as he could get without actually lying across her lap. His large head was propped on crossed front paws. Roxie, the long-haired Chihuahua, was nosing her phone arm, wanting attention. Maddy's message ended, and the beep sounded.

"Maddy, I'm here. You *said* you'd be done at nine thirty. It's nine thirty-two. Where are you? I have a thousand things to do. I don't have all day to wait for you."

Alison hung up and put the phone back on the night table. Roxie was now running through her bag of tricks. Without waiting for a command, she rolled over. Then she rolled over again and bumped into Floyd. He growled. She twirled again and bumped into the huge poodle a second time. He growled louder, but she had no idea how small she was next to him. She wasn't afraid. She knew what her job was, and she performed it well.

Give me some food. Give me some food. Attention, attention. Alison was distracted from her perpetual feeling of discontent, and smiled at the little dog. "Hi, cutie! You beautiful baby."

Despite her claim of business to attend to, the truth was, Alison did have all day. Except for her early lunch with Maddy and her one o'clock appointment with Derek, she didn't have a single thing to do. The girls were gone for the day. They had playdates after play school. Lynn, the nanny, would go get them, escort them to their appointed rounds, then feed them dinner. Alison would put them to bed around eight o'clock, before Andrew would even begin thinking of returning home. She had no idea when he would get back. He'd blown off their Easter vacation and now expected her and the kids to hang around all summer while he did whatever it was he did. To appease her he'd promised to spend a month on the Vineyard in August. But last year, she'd been stuck up there all alone practically the whole time. He'd come only for one weekend. She was still angry about it.

Now she didn't bother to get dressed. She lay in bed, running through her list of grievances, playing with the dogs, waiting for her best friend—who happened to be in pretty much the same boat—to call her back. But Maddy never did.

Four

When the homicide call came in, Lieutenant April Woo Sanchez, commanding officer of the Midtown North Detective Unit, was about to go on vacation. It was Monday. She was leaving Friday. Her mind was on cleaning things up at the shop so she could bolt, and never had she wanted to escape work as much as she did now. She was excited, almost vibrating with vacation anticipation as she rode in an unmarked black Lumina with her driver, Detective Woody Baum.

She was on her way back from a meeting with the chief of detectives, Chief Avise. He'd called her downtown, and as was common with his meetings, they'd met at police headquarters, which was near Chinatown where she'd grown up and begun her career but worlds from where she lived and worked now. From her West Fifty-fourth Street precinct, she and Woody had traveled downtown on the West Side Drive. An hour and a half later they were returning the same way.

At ten a.m., they were circling the tip of Manhattan where the Statue of Liberty could be seen in the bay, holding up the torch of freedom. April's thoughts were crowded with the ten thousand tasks she had to accomplish at Midtown North before leaving for her first real vacation ever. She and her new husband, Captain Mike Sanchez, were off on the honeymoon they'd already postponed two times since tying the knot in a big Chinatown wedding the previous fall.

Twice NYPD business had gotten in the way, but not like in the old days when Mike had been head of the Homicide Task Force. Back then, they'd often worked together on cases, and it was murder that wrecked their plans. Now things were different. Mike had been promoted to captain. She'd been promoted to lieutenant. They'd moved up in the food chain, had become bigger bosses, and didn't have time to get hitched, move from Queens into their house in Westchester, and take off on a honeymoon all at the same time. So they'd married, moved into their dream house, and gone back on the job a week later. Honeymoon postponed. Then an orange alert at New Year's postponed it again, and something came up again in the early spring.

Nearly nine months had passed, and there had been no exotic location, no sitting on the beach, no mai tais or piña coladas. Still, April considered herself more than half lucky. In normal times a promotion would have required her to leave the Detective Bureau and go back into uniform as a supervisor, or an administrator, like Mike.

But nothing post-9/11 would ever be normal times again. The bureau had lost so many ranking officers to retirement and to special counterterrorist units that experienced detectives were at a premium. Mike had left homicide to become commanding officer of the Seventeenth Precinct. But

April remained in the bureau assigned to the commanding officer slot at Midtown North after her boss and nemesis, Lieutenant Arturo Iriarte, retired. It had seemed like a good thing at the time.

The advantage of rank was that she could come and go without anyone yelling at her. The problem was that freedom was limited by responsibility. All the crimes that occurred in her precinct were on her shoulders. A lot of activity occurred in midtown on the West Side of Manhattan. She was in charge of every complaint—every mugging, theft, break-in, assault, homicide, missing person, whatever. She assigned the detectives in her unit, oversaw every investigation, and followed each case to arrest, prosecution, and trial. Every day, whether it was quiet or busy in the precinct, she had the job of juggling schedules, skills, personalities, and personal problems. She was buried deep in administration, and her head was lost in process almost 24/7. But this time she was determined to make her precious escape.

It was a June morning, weatherwise a perfect New York day—neither too hot nor too cold. The sun was on high. The squawk box was on low. Officers' conversations with the dispatcher were further muted by Woody's whistling through his teeth. It wasn't a real whistle, more like a tuneless little hiss. Usually it bothered her enough to tell him to shut up. Today she paid no attention to it. She was thinking about how every time she went downtown, the rules changed just a little, and change always caused chaos for somebody. In this case it was a big problem. It was a sad thing, but something she shouldn't be handling at all.

Strictly speaking Vice should be in charge of the strip clubs. Vice or DEA. Her task should be limited to preparing her new second whip, Sergeant Eloise Gelo, for taking command while she was gone. The trouble with Eloise was she looked like a lap dancer with a badge. That gave the male officers who dominated in the caveman detective unit an excuse for staring at her with drool hanging out of their mouths rather than taking her seriously. A male problem in a circular kind of way that was not unlike what called her downtown to Chief Avise's office. Girls distracting boys caused disorder at every level of society.

In this case the young son of a U.S. senator from another state had squandered his entire trust fund (she was surprised that this particular senator's son had a trust fund) in some local strip clubs, and he wasn't even twenty-one. So he shouldn't have been served the alcohol, much less the cocaine, that caused him to lose all sense of reason. On top of that, young Peret's cocaine overdose had landed him in a psych ward, where last night he'd been a raving psychotic. Chief Avise was taking the case personally as a serious embarrassment to New York City. He wanted war on the clubs that served underage customers, and the strippers who pushed two-hundred-dollar bottles of champagne, as well as ecstasy, methamphetamine, weed, and cocaine, on boys (and men) who wanted to touch their bodies.

It was a tall order since strip clubs had gotten very popular again. This was a sad irony because free sex was available everywhere. Thousands of single women thronged to the bars every night to drink themselves silly on exotic martinis and try to get laid. Free sex, though, posed the problem to men of having to relate. They had to make strangers like them and hope for a real connection when they had no interest in that at all. At the strip clubs, customers didn't have to make friends. The strippers came to them and would do anything—for a price. The oldest con in history was alive and well. Clientele seeking excitement mingled with naked lap dancers who primed them for bigger things. Sometimes, in the private rooms, the girls got the out-of-town customers wasted, then lifted money and other items from their wallets. At four in the morning a lot of things happened.

The descent into hell was always worse for the kids. In three months Justin Peret had gotten addicted to thrills he couldn't get anywhere else. He'd squandered a hundred grand and was working on reducing his nostrils from two to one. Still, he was one of the lucky ones. ER rooms all over the tri-state were jammed with ODs every weekend, and sometimes they couldn't be revived.

April brooded on the problem. Her unit didn't have the manpower (or womanpower for that matter) to do undercover work in the clubs. And the precinct captain, who was in charge of reducing crime in his area, should be relying on the Conditions Unit—the detectives in charge of monitoring unusual criminal activity in the precinct—to take care of these problems. Vice and DEA should also be involved. The captain should do the mopping up, not the detective unit that was responsible for all other crimes. April wondered what Avise was up to, asking her to go around the end zone on the precinct captain. In any case, the assignment was a threat to her honeymoon.

She wished she didn't always have to pay such close attention to her boss. When she was little, her old-style Chinese mother had to yell to get her attention. "You stupid, *ni*? You blain go on vacation, Howaday Inn?"

Before she was a cop, she didn't listen to anything she didn't want to hear, and she blew tasks off whenever she felt like it. For the police, however, every incident could have life-and-death consequences. Even though she wished her brain and her body could go on vacation to Holiday Inn, she couldn't ignore an order. The parent she called Skinny Dragon Mother still had a name for her: worm—triple stupid for being a cop, and a thousand times stupider than that for marrying another cop, who wasn't even Chinese. And ten thousand times stupider than all the previous stupids, for letting a bunch of white ghosts boss her around. Sometimes she was right.

"Homicide in the Seventeenth," Woody said, breaking into her reverie.

"What?" Reluctantly, April tuned in.

"Female, Fifty-second Street, town house, four hundred block. That's way east."

"Shit," April muttered. The Seventeenth was Mike's precinct. The last thing they needed was a homicide now. Her cell phone began to ring in her purse. She plucked it out and saw that caller ID was blocked. That meant it could be anybody in the Department, or even her Skinny Dragon Mother.

"Lieutenant Woo Sanchez." Sometimes she called herself Woo and sometimes Woo Sanchez to distinguish herself from her husband, the former Lieutenant Sanchez.

"*Querida,* where are you?" As usual Mike's voice was calm in the eye of a storm. But she could feel his tension just the same.

"Just heading up the West Side Drive, *mi amor.* What's up?" April already knew what was up, the new homicide. She glanced at Woody.

"I want you to take a look at a body," he said quietly, then gave her the address.

She heard the name. It was familiar, but she couldn't quite place it. Didn't matter. Someone was murdered. That always changed everything. "I'm on my way," she told him.

Five

Homicides always caused a peculiar vibration in April's body. She could feel it start as the car changed direction and they headed east to look at the victim, instead of uptown to deal with drug-dealing strippers. April had been planning to put Sergeant Gelo, who'd fit right into the club scene, on the Justin Peret case. In the old days she used to drop her vacation plans and take care of everything herself, shut down whoever needed to be shut down. But now she had to get used to being a boss, and was trying to learn to delegate responsibility. She couldn't personally take on every single problem that came her way. Still, it didn't matter whose problem rogue strippers should be; when Avise told her to jump, she asked how high. She was a loyal officer, who always did what she was told. Almost always.

Murder was the ultimate crime that pushed everything else onto the back burner. Each time it happened April was jolted into high gear. The harmony of life was shattered, and she wanted to jump out of the car, race after the perpetrator, and catch him quickly before he had a chance to escape. Or she did—whoever it was. Each time she was

overwhelmed by rage at the wrong that had been
done and felt an urgency to correct it. But this
wasn't her case. She shouldn't be thinking about
this. She didn't want to be involved. She just
wanted the world to be safe for once so she could
go on her honeymoon.

And something else bothered her. She and Mike
hadn't worked a homicide together in almost a
year, not since she and her parents had been attacked by a murder suspect in their home in Astoria, Queens. After that case, they'd moved on in
separate jobs; and they had an unspoken rule to
keep it that way. Mike's call both surprised her and
made her anxious. She had other plans. She had to
get Sergeant Gelo on track. Then they were taking
a plane to paradise. She didn't want anything to
interfere with that. Even as she was thinking this,
she knew her feelings were entirely selfish and felt
bad about them.

"What's up, boss?" Woody tried to make conversation, but she wasn't in the mood.

Her mood darkened even more when they got
there. Two Hispanic male uniforms manned the
blue barricade that partially blocked Fifty-second
Street on the east side of First Avenue. As Woody
drove across the street, the taller one tried to wave
them north. Woody kept going until the uniform
could see the ID clipped to April's new purple
spring jacket.

"All right. You can put it there." He pointed to
the last open slot in a long line of blue-and whites
and unmarked Department vehicles that reached
down practically to the river.

Woody pulled into the spot, and April was out

of the car before he'd even killed the engine. "Boss?" he called after her. *Don't I get a look?*

No.

He didn't have to say it, and neither did she. Like old partners who'd been through it all dozens of times, they communicated in shorthand. She patted the air over her shoulder as she walked away. *Stay here. Make friends with the neighbors; start asking questions. Shoot some candids with your little digital camera. Figure it out.*

"Whatever you say, boss." The preppy-looking cop who didn't always get things right had his uses.

She hurried down the tree-lined street past the clots of dog-walkers and gawkers. Like an old beat cop, she found herself sniffing the air. After another long frigid winter, the sun had finally returned to warm the city. Trees dressed in lush new leaves lined both sides of the street. Greening ivy trailed out of the square tree plots, which were enclosed by little iron fences with spokes to keep the dogs out. Details like this made the difference in a neighborhood.

This wasn't a commercial area like Midtown North. This was a high-priced residential East Side neighborhood where order was required. When violence shattered that order, the status of the residents alone demanded something be done about it. April didn't want to get entangled in the kind of politics she knew would be involved in a case like this. Mike was not asking her to take a look, then walk out like the other brass, who left the job of investigation to others. She'd never been able to do it anyway. Like a reporter or a first responder to a catastrophic event, once she showed up at the party she had to stay to the end. She was thinking, *Be smart this time. Walk in and walk out.*

She saw two reporters talking earnestly into video cams outside the yellow police lines that roped off the sidewalk. They were on opposite sides of the street, and their mouths were moving before they even had a story. She crossed the street, praying for a reprieve.

"Captain Sanchez," she told the sandy-haired officer at the door. He glanced down at April's ID. LT. APRIL WOO SANCHEZ.

"Yes, ma'am. He's waiting for you in the kitchen, first left."

"Thanks."

She went in and started mapping the place immediately. An old habit. The place was an elegant brick house, four windows wide across the front. The foyer was all marble with a circular staircase hugging the wall around it, except in the middle where it made a bridge into the sleek modern living room behind it. The living room was decorated in shimmering silver and black. And behind that, all the way through, the back wall was a bank of French doors that opened on a garden. A blond girl wearing jeans and a sweatshirt leaned against a huge grand piano, talking with a detective April immediately recognized from Mike's description of the CO of his bureau. The detective was called Sergeant Ed Minnow, and everyone called him Fish. As directed, she turned left at the first door and went in. Oops.

A surprised Chief Avise broke off a conversation to stare at her. *What the hell are you doing here?*

She shook her head. He'd given her an assignment less than an hour ago and didn't expect to see her again so soon. But news of homicide traveled fast, and April had a long history of serving on homicide task forces outside her own precinct. He shouldn't be surprised that Mike would call her in for a look-see.

As he turned away, she was distracted by the splendor of the kitchen. The place had more stainless steel appliances and sinks than she'd ever seen outside a restaurant kitchen. Three sinks, three dishwashers, a huge restaurant stove, a wine refrigerator, two other refrigerators—wow. Pots, pans, and bunches of dried herbs hung from beams in the ceiling. What kind of private home was this? A large glass dining table was surrounded by modern tub chairs. And there was a high chair. She stared at the high chair with dismay. Children always changed the story.

And then she was aware of Chief Avise moving purposefully in her direction and braced herself for a chewing out.

"She's with me." Mike said, cutting him off before the tirade began.

Saved by the cavalry. Her lips curved in a tiny smile. She couldn't help being impressed by her husband in uniform. No longer the swaggering detective with the flashy mustache and slicked-back hair who'd worn cowboy boots and cologne stronger than any tart's perfume, Mike Sanchez had cleaned up amazingly well. His black hair was short now, his mustache clipped, his aftershave subtle. He'd always been a handsome man, but in uniform he ruled. Next to him, the chief of detectives with his large belly and wrinkled brown suit looked downright sloppy and peevish.

"Don't push, Mike," the chief threatened, making it clear that April was his detective, not Mike's, so he was the one who decided where she worked.

"You want a quick resolution to a homicide, you know where to go," Mike replied. He smiled at his gorgeous wife, and she knew he was appreciating her new short haircut and stylish spring suit. She was a willowy five feet five, had delicate features in a classic oval face. Mike's smile told her that she was caught in the political web again, and she knew why.

The last two murders in this precinct had been solved by Mike and detectives under his old command at the Homicide Task Force. Now that he was no longer in the Detective Bureau, he couldn't call on Homicide Task Force detectives without messing up protocol. If he didn't trust the detectives in his own precinct to get the job done, he couldn't disrespect them by bringing in his old people. Furthermore he couldn't take on the task himself. Precinct captains did not investigate homicides. They were supposed to walk in, look around, and walk out just like the other brass.

Good going, Mike—just call in the little woman to take care of things. April kept a straight face and let the former boss and his underling figure it out. Mike and Chief Avise were pack leaders with the same goal but different teams and agendas. One of them had to back down. Finally the chief shrugged. "Fine, let her take a look. Then she goes home." He moved away.

That's how it was done. Although it didn't appear as if the chief had given in, Mike clearly thought she was in on the case. "Sorry, *querida*," he mumbled.

"Who's the victim?" she asked, getting to the point.

"Madeleine Wilson, wife of Wayne Wilson. Remember him?"

Oh, God. Suddenly it all clicked. That explained the kitchen and Mike calling her. "Oh, that's *terrible*. Where is she?" April felt bad for Wayne Wilson. He was such a nice guy and had a great young family. And, it was going to be a big circus.

"We better go this way."

Mike opened a door that led into an exceptionally neat garage, where no fancy car was parked at the moment. Right away April noticed the little blue bicycle and the even smaller tricycle up against the back wall. Two expensive mountain bikes hung on a hook above them. Leaning against the far wall was an assortment of skis in various sizes. Oh, God, these were rich people. Really rich people who had a house in the middle of Manhattan with a garage all its own, and they skied down mountains. She hated this already. Not that rich made any difference to her at all. Any family with little kids mattered. But it always bothered her that money never saved anybody. It never really helped, and surprisingly often money made things worse.

Holding her breath, April followed him into a gym that looked new. The floor was polished wood, a light color. Exercise machines filled the space. She didn't recognize some of them. Pilates was the brand on the side. She looked up. This room was obviously an addition. The ceiling was made of slanted glass. Billows of white linen, like upside-down umbrellas, shielded the room from the sun and people looking in from the windows in the apartments above.

"She's in there." Mike stopped short at the door to the shower and moved aside.

April looked in, and her eyes flickered as she adjusted to a horrific scene. Even after years of experience, she never expected to see a mutilated person in a serene setting, a rich setting like this. Or indeed any setting at all. Violent death was always a surprise, but the remains of Madeleine Wilson were particularly shocking. April had seen her photo in the social columns of the newspapers, in an oil painting on the wall in the living room. She knew the woman had been beautiful and those were the images she held in her mind. Mrs. Wilson had been the American ideal, tall, blond, well built. The machines in the gym indicated that she cared about her body.

That was what made it so difficult to look at her now. Naked and sitting on the teak bench of her shower, Madeleine Wilson was as spooky a ghost as April had ever seen. Her long hair was plastered on her neck and shoulders, darker than in her photos and soaking wet. Her skin looked waxy and gray, and was just beginning to pucker. One of her eyes was open, the other a pulpy mess. A gash had opened her forehead, and there were stab wounds all over her chest. It wasn't clear whether she had been sexually assaulted or not. The ME would have to determine that.

And there was more. The perpetrator hadn't just run amok and then split. He'd handled the body. From the number of wounds, it didn't seem likely that the victim had died sitting up. The killer must have picked her up, arranged her on the bench, and then turned on the shower to wash all the blood down the drain. The lack of blood was the eeriest thing. Not a drop was visible in the shower, on the victim's body, or on the floor of the gym. Mrs. Wilson had defense wounds on her arms and face and hands, even on her feet. She'd fought for her life. April guessed she might have kicked at the knife, but all traces of the fight had been washed away. The bathroom floor was clean. The sink was clean. The blond wood floor in the gym seemed unmarked. Crime Scene was going to have a lot of work to do. They'd have to take the place apart, open up the drains, to find anything.

She swallowed and turned away. "She was attacked in the shower and arranged that way after she was dead, right?"

Mike nodded. "Looks that way."

"Was the floor dry when you got here?"

"Yes."

"What about towels? Someone must have mopped up."

"*Querida,* we just started," Mike said.

"Did you find the murder weapons?" She went on as if he hadn't spoken.

"Weapons?"

"Looks like more than one size wound to me," April murmured. She couldn't see the woman's back but didn't want to get any closer. The CSU team would scream if she touched anything. They were going to scream anyway. A lot of people had been in here.

"Maybe, maybe not."

April squinted at the eye and the chest wounds. One wound seemed bigger than the others. There wasn't that much damage to the face, if you didn't count the forehead and eye. It looked as if a thinner blade had done that damage. Maybe a boning knife or an ice pick. Certainly not a butcher knife. April's father was a chef. Her first important gift had been a cleaver. She knew her knives.

"I'm guessing two," she said.

"Perpetrators?" Mike looked surprised.

"No, knives. What have you got on the knives?"

"Nothing yet. We're checking with the nanny to see if any are missing from the kitchen."

"Is she the young woman in the living room?"

Mike nodded a third time.

"Who found the body?"

"She did. The nanny. Name's Remy Banks."

The girl in the living room might be the killer. Was she big enough to attack a larger woman, then move the body? April wondered about that, then told herself not to jump to conclusions. Everybody at a crime scene looked guilty. She backed out into the gym area, studying the floor. Not a footprint, not a gum wrapper. Nothing. Except a purple iris lying on the table. April's glance swept over it out to the garden, where other irises were growing in a patch. Someone had come in here from the garden. Maybe the victim, maybe someone else.

"Where's the husband?" she asked.

"He's on his way."

"From where?"

"One of his restaurants. I don't know which one. He has an alibi. He was with a chef."

April didn't respond to that. She knew chefs were notorious for saying anything that came to their heads. Her father and his cronies could lie like rugs. "Mike, I don't want to start anything I can't finish," she said slowly.

"Look, just help me out for an hour or so. Talk to the nanny and check back with me, okay. I won't embroil you, I promise."

April shook her head. They both knew that wasn't the way it worked. "Okay, I'll talk with the nanny," she said.

Six

Remy Banks was still shaking. She'd seen plenty of dead people and dead animals in her time, especially in her childhood in Wyoming. Gruesome things. Cattle and dogs that had their intestines ripped out by wolves. Once she'd seen a video of a grizzly bear mauling a human being. The whole thing had been caught on tape. A stupid tourist had thought he could chase a huge bear away from his campsite with some pot-banging, and then a few potshots from his rifle. The bear retaliated by trying to eat him. It seemed there was always someone around to photograph a freak thing like that. She'd seen the video back home, but the bear mauling could now be found on the Internet. A cautionary tale.

Remy had also seen kids who'd frozen to death. When she was a teenager, two ten-year-olds had broken through thin ice on the river in late winter and gotten stuck. A freak thing. She went through her list of accidental deaths. In summer people used to die by drowning even in the shallows, on raft trips, probably still did. Queer things happened. Out West there were a lot of unnatural ways to meet one's maker. Everybody had guns. Remy was used to guns. Every year there'd be shootings, accidental and otherwise. And then, there were the kitchen accidents. When she'd worked as a line cook in a steak house in Salt Lake City, she'd seen really bad cuts, bad burns. Bleeding into the hamburgers on the grill, a line cook would just keep on getting those orders out, or lose his job. But Maddy's face . . . the place where her eye should have been . . . Remy couldn't stop shaking.

"You gonna be okay now?" The detective called Minnow who'd been questioning her closed his notebook.

Remy stared at him. Anybody could see she was not okay. He looked like an actor on one of the cop shows, somebody's idea of a cop. He had a round face and pasty skin, a bulging stomach. If she'd been in a better mood, she would have analyzed his diet by how he looked. She thought of things like that. How people ate. He was clearly way past forty, which was the same to her as being a hundred.

"Roomy?" He missed a lot of things, couldn't even say her name right.

"Fine. I'm fine." Remy's head bobbed up and down. She could tell that sergeant didn't believe a word she said. She turned toward the garden, toward the gym where Maddy—where the body— still was. She wondered where Wayne was. Poor Wayne was going to freak out. But she was freaking out, too. Neither of them deserved this. The boys didn't deserve it. No one did. She didn't want to tell the police that she was having a relationship with her boss. They wouldn't understand how it really was. Jo Ellen had already chewed her out for what she called "alienating" Wayne's affections. She told Remy to keep quiet about what occurred in the privacy of her clients' homes. Shit, how could she be private about this?

Remy's thoughts drifted back to the early morning when she'd gotten up so happily to make the pancakes, and Maddy's outrageous reaction. Then Wayne told her in the car that she'd have to try to make up with her if she wanted to keep her job. But when she got back, she couldn't smooth things over with Maddy because Maddy was dead. What was she supposed to do now? Remy wasn't aware that time was passing. She was thinking about her life out West, about what had made her move East, about her uncertain future here in New York. She retreated deep inside herself and didn't realize Sergeant Minnow had been replaced.

"Remy? I'm Lieutenant Sanchez."

Startled by the soft voice behind her, Remy turned around to face a woman about her own size. The woman was wearing a deep purple pantsuit and a gun in a holster at her waist. She didn't look like a cop, or Latina, for that matter. She looked like a model, or a talk-show host. Glamorous. Remy's spirits lifted at the sight of her. "Hi."

"I'd like to talk with you for a few minutes."

Remy was still shaking. She had no place to go. The boys wouldn't be through with play school until three. She wondered what would happen to them. Her thoughts started drifting again, and tears filled her eyes.

"You were the one to find Mrs.—?"

"I called her Maddy," Remy said, wanting to set the record straight. She wasn't a maid.

"Okay." The woman took out a notebook.

Remy was distracted by it. Minnow had had one, too. It seemed so old-fashioned. "What do you want to know?" she asked meekly.

"Pretty much everything. What happened today. What the family is like. Your role here. Anything you can think of."

Remy nodded and tried to remember what she'd already said. "I already told—" Remy looked blank. Suddenly she couldn't remember his name.

"Sergeant Minnow. I know, but maybe I can help you." The woman smiled as if they were girlfriends.

"Help me?" Remy swallowed. How could anyone help her? The whole thing was a big mess.

"We'll work together. We'll figure it out, okay? Why don't we sit down?" The glamorous lieutenant led the way to a silver sofa.

Remy shook her head. Maddy didn't like her or the children sitting in the living room. Then she remembered that Maddy couldn't tell her what to do anymore. Still, she felt uncomfortable sitting there in her kitchen jeans. She tried to focus on the first question.

"Did you like Maddy?"

"Of course, I liked her. Everybody liked her. She didn't have any enemies." That was what people said on TV. She said it without thinking.

"You two got along pretty well?"

"Yeah. She was a dream to work for. What will happen to the boys? I'm supposed to pick them up at three." Remy knotted her fingers together.

"We'll see about that later. Tell me what happened this morning. Anything out of the ordinary?"

"Not really. Maddy had her usual temper tantrum. Wayne and I took the boys to play school at quarter to eight. I didn't see Maddy after that. Alive, I mean."

"Why did she have a temper tantrum?"

Remy sighed. "She was upset because I made breakfast."

"Why would that upset her?"

"I don't know. It's my job. I guess she was jealous because she can't cook." She shrugged.

"You said she was a dream to work for."

"Most of the time she was." Remy rubbed her nose.

"Then what happened?"

"Oh, it was nothing. She made a fuss, and then Wayne and I took the boys to play school."

"Do you and Wayne always take the boys to play school?"

"No. Usually I take them. But today was the first day of the summer session."

"And Maddy didn't want to go?"

"She has her trainer at eight. She never misses that."

"Every day?"

"No, three days a week." A muscle jumped in her eye. Remy blinked to stop it.

"Uh-huh." Lieutenant Sanchez wrote that down and moved on. "What happened in the car?"

"Wayne told me she would calm down by the time I got home and not to worry about it."

"Did he say why not?"

She made a face. "He told me to make up with her."

"Did you come right back to the house to do that?"

"No. Wayne took me to Soleil first. He wanted to show me some new equipment he'd gotten."

"Soleil?"

"That's his new restaurant. It's only a few blocks away, so I walked home afterward. I wanted to give her time to cool off."

Remy studied the lieutenant's face. The features were empty, blank of all emotion. It was a little unnerving the way it went flat. She opened her mouth to ask another question.

"Did you think Maddy would calm down?"

"Yes, she was a nice person, really." Remy looked down at her hands.

"What time did you get back?"

"Just before I called 911, whenever that was. I have a class at ten." She was sweating now. She wanted to go to her room and hide.

"What kind of equipment was it?" The questions kept coming.

"Ah." Remy turned to stare out the window. There were so many things she didn't want to think about. She didn't want to think about the dead woman who'd gotten so mad at her because she'd made a wonderful breakfast. Maddy had no right to be jealous, especially when she was sleeping with that creep Derek. She tried to concentrate on the question. What was the equipment in the restaurant that Wayne had wanted her to impress her with?

"An oven," she said after a pause.

"Did you see the trainer when you got back?"

Remy's attention wandered. Suddenly she knew

what bothered her about the Latina lieutenant. She looked Chinese. And now she'd changed the subject again. She wanted to know about Derek. "No, I never see him. He doesn't come into the house."

"What's his name?"

"Derek Meke."

"How does Derek get in? Did she let him in?"

"No, he has the code for the garage door," she said.

"Can you hear him coming and going?"

"Sometimes, if I don't have the music on."

The Chinese lieutenant with the Spanish name gave her a hard look. "Did you have the music on today?"

"No, but I know he was gone when I got here."

"Did you hear the garage door?"

"No."

"How did you know?"

"When I went into the garage I could hear that the shower was on. He never goes into her shower."

"How do you know that?"

"I do the laundry. There's never more than one used towel." She looked at the ceiling.

"What about today, Remy—what made you go into the gym if you knew she was in the shower?"

There, the lieutenant did it again. She changed the subject. Remy's heart thudded. "What made me?"

"Yes." The pen was moving across the pad. The pages were filling up.

Remy spoke in a small voice, a little-girl voice. "I wanted to make up. I was sorry she was mad at me. And I had to go to class. I wanted to make everything right before I left."

"What school do you go to?" the detective said abruptly.

"The Culinary Institute."

"Ah, that's a good school. I thought of going there," she said.

Remy was startled. "Why?"

"My father's a chef. Why don't you show me the kitchen? You do the cooking, right?"

Remy nodded. "But I'm not the maid," she said firmly. "I was just supposed to be here in the house until the new restaurant opened. I have strong restaurant credentials. I'm going to be the sous-chef there, Wayne promised. Very soon . . ." Her voice faded off. "Are we finished?" she asked after a moment.

"No," the lieutenant told her. "We're just beginning."

Seven

April's eyes dropped quickly to the page. She was surprised by what she'd written. Back in the day when she'd been a young detective in Chinatown and even in her old precinct the Two-Oh, on the Upper West Side, where she'd met and first worked with Mike, she used to piss off her bosses by taking notes in Chinese. She hadn't done that in a long time. Now some unknown force caused her to sketch out *yang,* the Chinese character for "sun." She stared at the long unused calligraphy. Sun. Wayne Wilson's new restaurant was called Soleil—"sun" in French. Doodling, April had translated it into Chinese.

To April, doodles mattered in the same way that body language mattered. Remy's body language betrayed her in every way. The way she stood, the way she rubbed the side of her nose when she answered questions. Both were sure signs that she wasn't telling the truth. Now she was caught in a lie for sure, and April had recorded it in the Chinese character for "sun," the name of Wayne's restaurant. *Yang,* which was the spoken word for "sun," also meant male energy. Action and aggression. The opposite of *yin,* the symbol for female passivity.

Even though April was an ABC, American-born Chinese, the teaching of ancients—Huangdi, Tao, Confucius—was in her blood and often guided her thinking without her even being aware of it. She'd heard the ancients' voices through many tutors in her Chinatown childhood. Those long-ago lessons had been impossible to evade then, and were no easier to escape now.

The root of everything was the duality of yin and yang, earth and heaven. Female and male. Dark and light. All the qi (energy) in the universe was connected to the primal yin and yang: the four directions, the five earthly transformative elements, the six atmospheric influences. In the human body there were the nine orifices, the five organs, and the twelve joints. The ancients believed that balance in all elements of the universe was achieved only in the proper alignment of yin and yang. When male or female dominated the other half, trouble followed.

What did it have to do with the murder of Maddy Wilson? April had no idea. But it came to mind because sun was the ultimate yang. Clearly Wayne Wilson identified himself with the sun qi, the heavenly energy that surrounded and protected the earth. He was the very epitome of yang.

April hadn't let on to Remy that she knew all about Wayne Wilson and his new restaurant. The new bistro Soleil happened to be nearby in Mike's precinct. Wayne had invited the precinct captain to its opening night, and feeling very special, April had gone with him. That was how she'd met Wayne Wilson. And that was how she knew that the woman who'd discovered Maddy Wilson's body had probably never been slated to be a chef at that restaurant. The restaurant was not going to open. It had already opened, and it was going strong. It was, in fact, a big hit. So Remy was either confused or betrayed—or lying.

Furthermore, April knew all about chefs. Her father had held on to his job for thirty years. They were going to have to carry him out of the upscale Chinese restaurant where he still worked five days a week. Mike's father had also been a chef. He'd died at his station in a West Side Mexican restaurant a decade ago. Since Soleil already had a chef and a sous-chef, Remy's story didn't play. She had restaurant experience and was going to cooking school, but was working as a nanny? Why? But before April could explore that question with the young woman, there was a commotion at the front door. Wayne Wilson was home. Remy jumped to her feet.

"Maddy!" Wayne stared at Remy as he said his wife's name. "What happened to my baby?" he cried.

The girl cringed as he said the word *baby*. April watched their exchange.

"Remy! Tell me it's not true!" He looked shocked.

Remy opened her mouth, but nothing came out. Then Sergeant Minnow came out of the kitchen and stopped the interaction before it could go any further.

"I'm sorry, sir. I need to talk with you," he said.

Wayne spun around. "Who the hell are you?"

"I'm Sergeant Ed Minnow," he replied almost apologetically.

"You've got to be kidding." Wayne made a move to brush him aside.

"No, sir, I'm not kidding. I'm in charge here." Minnow lowered his voice so April couldn't hear him.

It was that terrible moment that April had lived through many times when she had to tell a family member of a murder victim that his life was no longer his own. His house was no longer his house. His secrets were no longer his secrets. All would be revealed in the name of justice. Yangs like Wayne didn't do well in the role.

Wayne's personality had been clearly displayed at the Soleil opening. He'd been wearing black slacks and a black shirt with a black jacket. Very chic. The only color relief had been his gold-on-gold tie with a big sun in the middle of his chest. The brassy color splashed down the front of his shirt and spiked out in all directions. That same logo was on the cocktail napkins, the matchboxes, the dinner plates. Tiepins in the same shape had been the party favors.

He'd moved around the three large rooms of his restaurant, like the Sun King himself, encouraging guests to try his Godiva chocolate martinis, lime martinis, mango martinis—every kind of martini a fan could dream about. Glasses of pink champagne circulated on ever-full trays. A wine bar offered glasses from the bottles on the wine list, and the finger food was exceptional. That night no one went home hungry. Or sober. The crowd swilled the alcohol at a frantic pace. The celebs and models who were invited and photographed at so many events like this all over the city were there. Wayne had been particularly gracious to his precinct captain, singling him out and introducing him around. It was New York, after all, where cops were celebrities, too.

Wayne was not going to let Sergeant Minnow finish his spiel. "It's my wife, my house. I want to see her. That's my right."

Sergeant Minnow tilted his head to one side, sweat gleaming on his forehead. April knew he was sizing up Wayne, trying to figure out how to control the situation. April did not intrude. Mike would have told the sergeant that April would be "helping" him. But he didn't have to tell April to be discreet about it. She already knew the sergeant would not be wanting any help from her.

Minnow lowered his voice even more. April could hardly hear a murmur. She guessed that he was explaining the procedure. Mr. Wilson could not see his wife's remains. The Crime Scene Unit had arrived and was now working in the gym. No one could go in there. Wayne interrupted with a cry of horror.

"She died in the gym? Shit! I built that gym."

Minnow tried to say more, but Wayne couldn't listen. He turned to Remy and saw April. Relief flooded his face.

"Oh, thank God. Lieutenant Sanchez, come over here." He wagged his finger at her.

April almost turned around, thinking Mike was behind her. Most people still called her "Woo." Not "Sergeant Woo" anymore, but "Lieutenant Woo." Or just "Lieutenant." Or even "ma'am." Then she remembered. *She* was Lieutenant Sanchez. "Stay here for a moment," she told Remy.

"But I need to talk to him," the girl protested.

April shook her head. They could not speak to each other.

"Please!"

"No."

"But I *have to*," she pleaded.

"Look, Remy, you discovered the body. That puts you in the hot seat. Remember what I told you. If you want my help, you have to do what I say."

"I would never hurt Maddy. Never. I couldn't do that." Remy looked like a zombie when she said it, though, devoid of emotion.

"I'm talking about something else here. You've seen things no one else has seen."

Remy pressed her lips together.

"What you saw has to stay secret. You can't tell anyone. It's a big responsibility, okay? Only you know what she looked like. It has to stay with you."

"Jesus." Remy sniffed.

"Lieutenant," Wayne called. "You're needed here."

"I didn't hurt Maddy. Please tell him that," Remy begged.

April didn't take the time to reply.

Eight

Awkward, awkward. April hated the jockeying for position at the beginning of cases. And in the marble foyer the feng shui was as bad as it got. All the brass who'd come for their look-see had melted away. Those left behind were standing under the curve of the stairs in such a way that the energy could flow neither out the front door where the press had gathered, nor into the living room where the French doors led to the garden. The energy was trapped, stuck in a funnel like a twister, so no one could easily take the leadership position. Mike was outside, suited up in Tyvek with the Crime Scene Unit, and April felt herself being sucked into a tug-of-war.

Wayne started talking right away, his tone instantly modified. "April, April, thank you for coming so fast," he said as if she were a close friend he had summoned to the scene himself.

April was surprised by the effusiveness of the greeting, and even the fact that he had remembered her name. They'd met only for a few moments, and she had been just one person in a huge crowd. "I'm so sorry for your loss," she murmured, then quickly introduced herself to Sergeant Minnow. Right away she wanted to put some distance between herself and her husband. "I'm Lieutenant Woo."

"I've heard of you," he replied with a smile.

"I've heard of you, too," she said graciously.

Wayne ended that exchange, putting her right back in her place. "April, your husband told me you were going to take care of me. Now, I want to see my wife."

April blushed. She doubted very much that Mike had said any such thing. "Sergeant Minnow is in charge of the investigation. He'll help you with the process," she said smoothly. She wasn't going to let herself get sucked in.

"Now, now. There's no reason to be so nice. That's not what I heard." Wayne touched her arm in a familiar way.

April felt the heat in her face. Wayne was manipulative; he just kept on talking.

"I might as well be open with you. Commissioner Avery called me on my cell phone as soon as he heard. He told me you were heading the investigation."

That was highly unlikely. The police commissioner happened to be in New York Hospital that morning having double hernias repaired. April knew for a fact that he wouldn't be conscious until sometime in the afternoon. Furthermore, he didn't call people on their cell phones to tell them who was handling the case when their wives were murdered.

Wayne was completely unembarrassed about lying. "So let's get started. I want to be involved with this thing every step of the way. I want to see the scene. I want to talk to Remy. She's my right-hand person here. What did she tell you?" He asked this with an open expression.

April glanced at Sergeant Minnow, who was listening to all this very quietly. Now that the police commissioner's name had come up, he began to look worried. It was clear he didn't know the PC's schedule.

"I can't talk about confidential information," April replied after a moment.

Wayne ignored the slight. "Look, this is obvious. We all know who did it. He killed her in my gym, for Christ's sake."

"Sir?" Minnow interjected for the first time.

"He's probably at Workout now."

"Who?" Minnow locked eyes with April. She realized that he hadn't heard about the trainer yet. She didn't say anything.

It had become stifling in the foyer. Wayne actually seemed to have pumped heat into the space with all his bluster. He'd tried to pit the two detectives against each other. He'd pulled rank, dropped names. And as he did it, his color returned. April guessed that he felt better with the upper hand. Finally, he wagged his finger at Remy to join them. He thought he'd put them all in their places.

April had been at many murder scenes. Every single one had been sad and upsetting, but this was the oddest. What struck her the most was that Wayne Wilson had invited Mike and her to his party a few months ago. Now he acted as if they were friends and expected them to overlook the fact that he was a suspect. She had to nip this little hubris in the bud. Murder suspects were not friends. She lifted her chin to give Minnow the heads-up. *I'll take care of this.* He nodded slowly and tipped back on his heel to give her the lead.

"Mr. Wilson. Would you step into the library with me for a moment?" She hadn't seen the whole house yet but figured he had a library. An office, something.

"Of course. Follow me."

Wayne went up the stairs without a second glance. She could see in his back that being in control meant a great deal to him. Outside in the gym, his wife's body was being photographed, videotaped, examined by someone from the medical examiner's office, and slowly prepared for removal. He had given up trying to see her in situ. He was moving on. At the top of the marble stairs he entered an octagonal room filled with books. The sun streamed in from a leaded bay window that completed three of the eight sides. It was noon.

April felt the power of the room with its unusual bright orange Oriental carpet, unusual windows, leather desk, armchairs, and computer hooked up to a large-screen TV. Wayne sat down in his desk chair and leaned forward.

"She was only thirty-four, a beautiful, wonderful woman. A terrific mother to our boys," he said heatedly, riding up the roller coaster of emotion again.

April nodded. Of course she was. The dead were either saints or devils. She was beginning to think Maddy had to have been a saint to put up with him. Or maybe a devil for wanting him in the first place, but it wasn't her call and it didn't matter one way or the other.

"This is why I asked you up here. I want to get

this over and done with right now. Get everything on the table," Wayne said, ignoring the fact that it had been April's idea to find a private place to talk.

April wished she had a tape recorder with her. She had a feeling this was going to be a good one. Wayne's expression was open. She knew his type. He was a liar who deeply believed he told only the truth.

"I'm a man. Once in a while I fucked other women. It didn't mean anything. Maddy was my wife, the woman I loved." He looked to her for the reactions he was used to getting: understanding, applause for the performance, pity. Whatever.

"I'll need their names," April replied stoutly. Out came the notebook. Wayne stared at her as she wrote *player*.

"What?" He sounded startled.

April brushed her fingers against the buttery leather on the back of the closest club chair. "The names of your girlfriends," she prompted.

"Wait a minute. They're not *girlfriends*. You're not listening to anything I said. I thought we were friends. Don't go cop on me," he said in an injured tone.

"Mr. Wilson, just give me a moment to tell you how this works. And then we'll have everything squared away."

"Just a minute—"

"I know this is very painful for you, but friendship doesn't enter into police work," April said firmly, cutting him off. "It's the same for everybody. What's going to happen here is this. You better look for another place to stay for a few days. We'll be going through this house, looking at your wife's things, her notes, her telephone calls, her appointment list. Her friends, her employees—all the people who knew and worked with her will be interviewed. In addition, we'll put everyone in this household under a microscope. It's not optional."

He shook his head. "But this isn't necessary. I can tell you everything you need to know."

"Well, maybe, but maybe not. Did she know everything about you? Did she know about your girlfriends?"

His face hardened. "That's not the point."

"We're going to catch her killer. Trust me on that. You can help us by letting us do our job."

"Well, that's exactly what I'm trying to do," he said benignly. "Help you do your job."

"Good, then we'll get along fine. By the way, all the officers you see here are a team. Sergeant Minnow is in charge, so why don't you tell him what you just told me."

Nine

April found Mike sitting on a stone bench at the back of the garden still wearing his Tyvek suit. As captain of the precinct, he should have been gone a long time ago. He was on his cell phone and gestured for her to come over. Then he abruptly ended the call.

"What do you have?" he asked.

"You first," she said.

"Fish's boys found knives in the babysitter's knapsack. They were wrapped in today's newspaper."

"Oh, gee. Which one?" April asked to lighten the mood.

"The *Times,* does it matter?" He lifted an eyebrow. "What do you think of her?"

April cocked her head to one side. As she considered her answer, she caught sight of a large gas grill in an outdoor kitchen. It was quite a patio out there, a nice leafy bower surrounded by ten-foot brick walls topped with a cap of iron spikes. She wondered who else had the code to the garage door, if anyone could have come over the walls. Who had brought the iris into the gym? She had a lot of questions.

"Where was the knapsack?" she asked first.

"On her bed."

On her bed, right where anybody could find it. Humph. This was how people jumped to conclusions and convicted the wrong suspect. "Well, she goes to cooking school. They use their own knives," April told him.

Mike's eyes narrowed. "Did you see her picture?"

She knew whom he meant. "Mrs. Wilson? Yeah, she was a beauty." And she happened to have a husband who cheated on her. Maybe with the nanny to whom he'd promised a job he hadn't delivered.

"What does the presence of the knives mean to you?" Mike was still on the knives.

"Oh, please. Don't jump to conclusions. For a cook, they're tools, like drills and hammers are for carpenters. She paused, then continued. "It's a guy kind of crime. All that violence and lack of control—male."

He made a face at the gender putdown. "She had opportunity, and it took organization to clean up. That's a girl thing."

"Well, sure. But I'm thinking it was a man," April insisted. "The knife only proves it was spur-of-the-moment. The killer grabbed whatever came to hand—"

"How could a knife come to hand in the gym?" Mike interrupted.

"I don't know. Maybe it was scissors. Did you see the flower? Maybe Maddy brought the knife or the scissors in herself to cut flowers."

"Could be." Mike looked doubtful, though. "The

killer was definitely in the shower with her. Maybe *she* turned on the water to wash herself off, not the victim."

"I don't see the killer as a woman," April insisted, knowing what that meant for Remy.

"It had to be someone with access to the knives, to the gym, someone who was angry enough to keep stabbing after she was dead—"

"Like a lover, or a husband," April said softly.

"Or a jealous babysitter. Someone who knew how to clean. She's the maid."

"Oh, I see. You've been talking to Fish. Okay, my turn. Remy told me Wayne promised her a job at Soleil, and she was only supposed to work here until it opened. She still seems to think he'll give it to her eventually. We know she didn't get the job, but I wouldn't call that a motive." April spoke passionately. She didn't want a lynching.

"Maddy had a trainer, name of Derek Meke, who was with her after Remy and Wayne took the kids to play school. After they dropped the kids off, Remy went to Wayne's restaurant to look at an oven, then walked home from there. We'll have to get confirmation on that. She said that after she got back, Derek did not come into the house, that he never came into the house."

"You know where to find him?"

"I can find him. One more thing." April had kept the best for last. "Wayne told me he fooled around."

"Ay caramba." Mike sighed. "That's too bad. I liked him. Do you have a name?"

April shook her head. "Apparently it was more than one woman. He didn't want to name names."

"Well, if it was the babysitter, there's your motive." Mike stood up. "I have to get going."

"Me, too. What do you want me to do, *chico*?" April said, rising from the bench. "I have a bunch of people waiting for me in my shop. Avise has another job for me. If you think Remy did it, tell Fish to go for it. It's your call."

"Uh-uh. I'm not convinced."

"That's good, because all we have right now is a body."

He ignored the sarcasm. "What I want you to do is put Gelo in charge of your shop and take this case on. You can mop it up in twenty-four hours."

April shook her head at the difficulty of the politics. She got the feeling that he didn't want to step out on a limb on this one. She also felt manipulated. She didn't like either of the feelings one bit.

Since becoming a captain, Mike was a different guy. He had to appear at COMSTAT meetings with all the top brass once a month at headquarters to run the numbers in his precinct. Crimes and arrests, where they occurred, what was being done about it. Every single event had to be accounted for. Responsibility had given him a sharper edge, and his expectations for others in his command had risen proportionally. Fine for them. But April was not in his command. And even if she were, twenty-four hours would not be enough time to mop up any homicide. They wouldn't have a death report, or any crime scene analysis, for days. Even the clear-cut cases took weeks to process. She thought longingly of her honeymoon, less than a week away.

Mike pulled off the protective suit. "I'm done

here. I've got to go. I spoke with Avise. He says it's okay. He'll give you thirty-six."

Thirty-six hours? Were they crazy? April kept her back to the house, where people could be watching. She was fuming and didn't want anyone to see them fighting. "Mike, we agreed that we weren't going to do this anymore," she said.

"Come on, *querida,* think of her kids. It's probably a simple thing, boyfriend/girlfriend thing. You could do this case in your sleep."

She shook her head. "If it's such a simple thing, get someone else to do it." Then she thought of the cute little boys, who now had no mother. What was wrong with her? Not long ago she would have schemed to get on a homicide like this. She'd always been driven to be the one who nailed the killer. Now she was identifying with the babysitter who kept butcher knives in her knapsack. She was worrying about Sergeant Gelo's dress code, and she was thinking of her honeymoon. Not good. Skinny Dragon Mother used to say she had too much yang for a girl. She'd never find a man to marry her. Now she was married and had softened up, and sometimes she wondered if she had enough yang left to be a good cop.

"Mi amor," Mike murmured, "do the right thing."

Shit. Usually he was urging her to do the right thing and stay out of it. Now he wouldn't *let* her out of it. It was tough. She hated to think that the babysitter who wanted to be a chef could have killed her boss over a cooking job. It was hard to imagine anyone having a strong enough motive to stab a young mother to death a dozen times in her own shower. But early this morning someone had done just that.

She sighed. If she identified the killer fast, she could go back to the strip clubs and Fish could make the arrest. It was ironic how yin she'd gotten. She was more interested in sitting on a beach far away with her honey than in getting the credit. It almost made her laugh.

Ten

"Eloise, it's me. What's going on?" Woo was on the phone.

"Boss." Sergeant Eloise Gelo was parked at her desk, but not alone. Sitting across from her, Detective Charlie Hagedorn had been filling her in with some background information on the senator's kid who'd overdosed at some club, and ended up ten hours later in psych lockup at St. Luke's. She'd been listening to Charlie, studying a spot high over his head, and occasionally taking a mental note.

The lieutenant wanted to know what was going on in the squad room. Gelo ran through the list in her head. A drunk who'd exposed himself one time too many on Broadway had been brought in by two uniforms and was now in the holding cell, sobering up. Three detectives were out on cases. The unit secretary was yelling at someone on the phone in Spanish. And Hagedorn, making a pitiful attempt at some form of human interaction, was staring at her breasts. Everything was copacetic.

"It's quiet, boss. Where are you?" she replied.

"We've got a homicide on Fifty-second Street," the lieutenant replied.

"We do?" Eloise was shocked. No one had called it in.

"Yeah, East Side."

"Oh." Maybe somebody's homicide, but not theirs. "Who is it?" she asked.

"A young mother. Madeleine Wilson, that restaurant guy's wife."

"Oh fuck. That's too bad."

"Eloise, the language," Woo retorted.

"Sorry, sir," Eloise replied cheerfully. April Woo was a *sir* to her.

"Look, I'm going to be stuck here awhile," Woo went on.

"Are you working the case?" Eloise took the chance of asking something her boss might not want to tell. She'd never heard of a detective unit CO working a homicide in another precinct.

"No, no," the lieutenant said easily. "I'm just on a look-see."

"Uh-huh." It still didn't sound right to her, but she knew things were not exactly regular in this particular unit.

Eloise tapped her fingernails on the table, and Hagedorn chose that moment to lift his eyes from her breasts to her face and stretch his goofy mouth into a lopsided grin. She rolled her eyes. "You there, boss?"

"Yeah, I want you to work on the Peret case. Find out where the kid went, who served him booze, where he got the drugs, the whole thing. Check his credit card records for that. He may have charged it. Then talk to the girls."

"Sounds good to me," Eloise said.

"I'll fill you in later. Call me if anything comes up."

"Sure thing, boss."

The phone went dead, and Eloise hung up elated. This was the kind of thing she'd returned to the bureau for. If she couldn't be in a counterterror unit, at least she could do something useful until she got what she wanted. "The boss is working a homicide in the Seventeenth," she told Charlie.

Hagedorn mugged surprise. "No kidding."

"That a usual thing?" From the moment that Gelo been assigned this unit, she'd been anxious about working for Woo/Sanchez. Her boss was famous, but not exactly known for being a team player. Going in, she knew that she had a lot to live up to. Charlie took a minute more to stare at her before giving her a serious answer.

"Her husband Mike is the precinct CO; he probably asked for her."

"Of course, I knew that." She knew they were married, anyway, and that they'd worked together in the past. What it all meant for her career, however, was still the big question.

Eloise Gelo had moved up and was in her first few weeks of having an office with a door to call her own. She was still basking in the glory of the promotion, and simultaneously disappointed not to be playing a role in defending the city against the biggest bad guys. The door was nice, but the top half of it was glass, so anyone could look in and see what she was doing at any time. Sometimes the males in the unit stood around, pretending to be having a conversation, but actually gawking at her.

What was the big deal? She was a female, but Woo was a woman, too, and they didn't gawk at *her*. Eloise looked for a pen to jot down her orders. "Damn." Her pen was missing. She was sure she'd been using it only a few minutes ago.

"Did you take my pen?"

Hagedorn snorted.

"Give it back."

He laughed, but not in an unfriendly way. "I didn't take it. Here, use mine." He held his out, but she ignored the offer.

"Somebody did." She rooted around in her drawer for another one. She'd bought a box of pens only last week, but people seemed to enjoy taking her stuff as a kind of joke. She kept some red nail polish in there to annoy the alternate second whip, an asshole by the name of Tony Bobb, who couldn't seem to get over her being his equal. Tony Bobb was an anal kind of guy half her size and twice her weight, who didn't want to be perceived as a nelly. She always left a lot girlie stuff around in her space to bug him. The red nail polish was still there. It distracted her as she searched for a pen and worried about not being able to fill her new boss's shoes.

Gelo had worked for a lot of male officers, but had never worked for a woman. April Woo Sanchez was unreadable, quite the opposite of herself. Eloise was out there, a straight-up kind of person. She talked out of the side of her mouth like a tough guy, had a conspicuous mane of blond curls, which she piled up on the top of her head, wore bright red lipstick and clingy clothes. She had the figure for it and a name to make a girl cry. Wherever she went, in the department and out of it, she got attention. A lot of it—particularly the kind from asshole officers of every rank—was unwelcome. Eloise Gelo had her own philosophy about her style: *I ain't changing for no one. I am who I am. Get used to it.* Both the attitude and the name caused her a fair amount of grief from people she didn't give a shit about.

From time to time, however, she got the attention of someone worthy of her respect. Back in '97, when she'd been a detective third grade, her path crossed with that of Lieutenant Steve Whipet, a former marine who was CO of the chopper unit. She was smitten by him right away. Maybe it was the marine thing, a cowboy kind of allure—the short blond hair, the ramrod posture. The take-charge, I-can-get-it-done attitude. Whatever.

Their paths crossed when she was on a team that needed a bird in the sky to reach a suspect up in the Bronx. Whipet also had a name to contend with. She liked that about him. He was introduced to her as the guy who'd rescued a bunch of people from the roof of the World Trade Center. Back then, there had been only one World Trade Center bombing. And taking a pregnant woman off the tower had been a big deal.

Whipet recruited her from the Detective Bureau and challenged her to take flying lessons. She became the first female copter pilot in NYPD. A lot of people weren't too happy about it, but she never let negativity get in her way. She was good at whatever job she had, and she and Steve had some fun for a while. But he changed after the Fire Department made a rule to shut down access to all tall rooftops in the city. He became a worried man.

After the first tower bombing, the powers that be had decided it was too hard and too dangerous to evacuate people from above. So, in a massive sweep, they'd locked all the roof doors of the office towers in the whole city. Whipet feared that an event on a lower floor anywhere could create a death trap for those working on the higher floors. And that was what happened in the second World Trade Center attack. Everybody above the sixty-fifth floor had no exit. Eloise had been in one of the birds, hovering just out of reach of the hundreds of people frying inside. She hadn't been at the controls, but she'd been there.

In the forty minutes before the first building collapsed, she'd seen the faces of desperate people as they broke the windows to jump out eighty, ninety, a hundred floors above the street. Whipet knew the building well, and it drove him nuts thinking of the dozens of people trapped on the stairs leading to the roof—locked inside where he could not get to them. His unit had been warned off by the FD and by his PD bosses. They didn't want those choppers to burst into flame, trying to save people they felt couldn't be saved. But Steve had believed that he could have rescued some people. While he'd been in the air, he'd shot a bunch of photos. He had his opinions about what he could have done if they'd been allowed to land on the roof.

Afterward, he'd come down to earth to work the site and deferred his retirement for months. Even after he was out, he returned there from time to time. And he still believed that more could have been done. Both he and Eloise continued to have nightmares about it, and the relationship ended. Two years ago Steve bailed for good. He retired from the Department and went somewhere far away with the wife he always said he'd never much liked. He and Eloise didn't keep in touch anymore.

After a fruitless search in her drawer for the missing pens, Eloise finally gave up looking. Hagedorn was still offering the one from his pocket, so she took it. "Thanks."

"What does she want?" he asked about the Woo conversation.

"Oh, she wants us to investigate the Peret case, find out where he went, how he got in, who served him booze. And of course where he got the blow."

"This doesn't sound like our kind of case. Are we going after the clubs?" Charlie said excitedly.

"Not clear." Eloise didn't know what else to answer.

"It sounds pretty clear to me. Lieutenant Woo went downtown this morning. The chief has her on something." He rubbed his hands together. "This is great. We've been too easy on these creeps. The plastic trail should make a good start. We could shut them down."

"Right," she said quickly. She was new to the job. She had no idea what he was talking about. Did precinct units do club raids?

"Also his cell phone. His incoming and outgoing calls might place him inside one of the clubs, or more than one. We could get lucky there." Hagedorn was already on it.

"Check," she said. "You work on the credit cards, and I'll see what we can do about that phone."

Charlie returned to his computer, and Gelo tapped her fingers on the pen, wondering when Woo might get back to the shop and tell her what was going on.

Eleven

"Come on, little girl. Make it easy on yourself. These are your knives, aren't they?"

Remy shook her head. The detective with the crappy diet was now calling her "little girl." She hated this guy. She'd already told him they weren't her knives.

"They belong to the kitchen," she said wearily.

"Cam-onnn." His New York accent was an assault from which there was no retreat. "Cam-onnn, answer the question. Are they all here, or are there more?"

"I . . . don't . . . know," she said very slowly. "This is Wayne's kitchen. I don't keep track of everything he brings home."

And that was another thing that was upsetting her. Why wasn't Wayne here? Why wasn't *he* answering these questions? A pile of plastic bags covered the long kitchen counter. Each one had a knife in it. There were seven cleavers of varying sizes, ten butcher knives. Six carving knives of different lengths, some of them very long. More than a dozen paring knives, with and without serrated edges. They were his knives, so why did she have to answer for them? Frankly Remy was shocked by how many there were. She'd known there were a lot of knives in the house. It was certainly clear that Wayne was a fanatic about them. He had his own sets, one at home and one in his car, that he wouldn't let anyone else use. In addition to those, manufacturers sent him new knives to test out in hopes of getting an endorsement. Sometimes he brought these home, too. Altogether it turned out to be a big number to account for.

She made a disgusted noise. Until today the knives had always been beautiful tools to her. Just that morning after she'd washed up the breakfast dishes, the stainless steel blades had been shiny and the handles as dry as she'd left them the night before. She liked things clean. Since then, all the knives had been removed from the various drawers and locations where they were kept. They'd been labeled and bagged, and she knew they were headed for a laboratory somewhere to determine who had touched them and if there were traces of Maddy's blood on any of them. They all had Remy's fingerprints on them—that was a given.

"I told you I was in here the whole time. No one would have been able to come in and put them back," she said irritably.

Sergeant Minnow cleared his throat. "What did you say your duties are, little girl?"

"I told you a dozen times. I'm the cook." Remy wasn't changing that story.

"I thought you were the babysitter."

"I look after the kids sometimes, but that doesn't make me a babysitter."

"You took them to school this morning."

"Yes."

"Did you do that to be with Mr. Wilson?"

"Please." She made an impatient gesture.

"I asked you a question."

"I went with him because he asked me to," she said sharply.

"Do you do everything Mr. Wilson asks?" Minnow said this with a straight face and a suggestive tone.

Remy didn't see it coming. She didn't see a lot of what he said coming. She closed her eyes.

"Would you do anything he asked you?" he repeated.

She scratched the side of her nose. "No," she replied.

"Oh, what wouldn't you do?"

"He wouldn't ask—" she started to speak, then shut her mouth. She didn't want to say any more about what Wayne wouldn't ask. He'd asked her to make up with Maddy and to keep quiet about their relationship. She didn't want to talk about him.

"Okay, little girl, play it your own way. But we're going to find out everything anyway. We're going to rip this thing wide open, so you might as well come clean."

She didn't say anything.

He softened his voice. "So you're the cook and you don't know how many knives are in your kitchen. Cam-onnn. You expect me to believe that?"

Finally Remy spoke. "Look, this is a kitchen for a bigger staff. There are duplicates of everything. Wayne brings knives and other equipment home to test. We got a lot of stuff here." She shrugged.

He wanted to talk about knives. She could talk about knives.

"Well, look at them carefully."

She looked at the awesome array. "I've never seen some of these," she murmured truthfully.

"Which ones?"

She sat back, putting distance between them. She didn't want to poke at the blades inside their little plastic cases. She wished she could shut down against this whole stupid barrage. Her body ached to close in around itself and seal off the trauma. Her eyelids drooped. "Give me a break," she muttered.

"A nice lady died here in a very shitty way. She fought hard for her life. Nobody gave her a break." The detective started cracking his knuckles loudly. He sounded mad enough to start breaking hers.

"I found her. I wish I hadn't. But I don't know anything else." Remy held back her tears.

She'd been dog-tired a thousand times in her life. Fatigue was an old enemy. Anybody who'd ever manned a grill or a fry station during peak hours in a popular restaurant knew the dangers of fatigue. People got hurt when their attention wandered. Every line cook had to fight it, and everyone had his own way to cope. Cocaine, alcohol, amphetamines were the commonest combatants. Or coffee. Diet Coke, Cigarettes. They were all addicted to something. Remy's thing was Coke, the liquid kind. Since the cops started taking turns with her hours ago, she'd swallowed down almost a case of Diet Cokes. But the caffeine hadn't helped her. She didn't feel a kick, a buzz, anything. The questions kept coming, and she didn't want to give in just because she was tired. She knew Wayne hadn't done it, and didn't think Derek could have, so who else was there?

"How about these?" he demanded.

White lights flashed in her eyes as Minnow pushed the plastic bags aside and added six more to the collection on the marble counter. These, Remy knew, were hers. Her precious knives, which she'd bought before she met Wayne, had cost over a hundred dollars each. They'd been removed from their newspaper wrapping, and like the others, they'd been bagged and labeled. The sight of her beloved tools, hostage to a murder investigation, was more than a little frightening. She had a sinking feeling that she wouldn't be seeing them again anytime soon. "They're mine," she admitted miserably.

Behind her, the wall phone kept ringing. She'd been told not to pick it up, but she wished someone would. Her head was spinning with all the noise and activity in the house. It made her so nervous how police were working the house, packing things up in boxes and taking them out. She didn't know what they were taking. They kept moving her around so she couldn't see what they were doing and took turns talking to her. Sometimes there were two of them, sometimes one. The Chinese woman who'd been nice to her earlier was gone. Several men in civilian clothes looked as if they didn't have anything to do. They stood around talking on their cell phones. Nobody asked her the right questions.

"What were they doing in your knapsack?" The annoying detective forced her to pay attention to him.

What were her own knives doing in her own knapsack? What a dumb question. Remy drew in her breath. "I had a class," she said.

"Oh yeah, what kind of class?"

"I *told* you I go to cooking school. We use our own knives there."

"You carry them back and forth?"

She nodded.

"What class did you have?"

She took another breath. "Butchering."

He let out a nervous giggle as if it were some kind of sick joke. "No kidding. What kind?"

"All kinds. I could butcher a cow if I had to. A pig, a lamb. A chef has to know the cuts of meat." She knew her cuts.

"You know what I think? I think you know a lot more about this murder than you're letting on, little girl."

"I know a lot about food," she said miserably. She glanced at the wall clock, wondering who was going to pick up the children. "Can I go now?"

He shook his head. She sighed and asked for another Diet Coke.

Twelve

By the time April emerged from the Wilson house, the number of Department vehicles had diminished and the number of eager reporters had grown. It took her a few seconds to locate Woody in the crowd. He was buried in a clot of bystanders across the street, talking with a pretty, dark-haired girl in charge of a heavily laden stroller. The stroller was stuffed with a wild-haired toddler eating raisins out of a plastic bag, a plastic tricycle, and a net sack filled with sand toys. April hurried toward them.

Questions barraged her from all sides as she dodged through the crowd of reporters.

"Do you have any leads on the killer?"

"Is Mr. Wilson a suspect?"

"Was the house broken into?"

April didn't let anyone catch her eye. It wasn't her case, and she wanted to avoid attention.

"I'm not the go-to person here. Try DCPI," was all she said.

"They never say anything," someone grumbled.

"April, what are you doing over here?" A female voice screamed over all the others.

April grimaced and turned her head away. It was

someone she knew. Lily Eng, a Chinese TV reporter who'd done a story on her last year, was elbowing through the crowd. "Out of the way, she's my sister," she cried. "April, April."

Woody raised his head at the sound of her name and quickly ended his conversation with the young woman.

April couldn't avoid her. She paused in the street just long enough for Lily to charge. Lily's hair was longer than April's, cut in a shag. But they were both about the same size with delicate oval faces, almond eyes, and bee-stung lips. They were also wearing the same purple pantsuit and did indeed look like sisters.

"Hey, cutie, nice suit," April said, walking quickly to the car.

Lily grabbed her arm to slow her down. "Can you give me some background on the case?"

"No."

"Nothing confidential," she wheedled. "Please. Just background. I won't quote you."

April shook her head. "I don't know a thing about it, sis."

"Fine, I get it. I'll call you later. Hi—Woody Baum, right?" Lily's voice turned to honey.

"Hi, yourself," he said, dead meat for the second time that day. He was an easy mark.

"Woody!" April barked.

He jumped to open the passenger door, shut her safely in, then ran around to the driver's side.

"Was that work or play?" April asked about the girl with the stroller.

"Work. She's the next-door nanny, knows that Wilson babysitter well. There's a gang of them that hangs out at the Boar Park together to complain about their lives. I have some names and addresses." He fired up the engine and backed out.

"Good going. She have anything useful to say?"

"Six months ago the babysitter was hired to be a cook in a restaurant, but Wayne put her on house detail instead. She's pretty pissed off about that."

Interesting. That was not the story Remy had given her. Maybe she didn't tell the truth to anybody. "Anything else?"

"She's worried that a psycho's loose in the neighborhood. Apparently there have been some rapes around here."

"Really?" Mike hadn't mentioned that.

"Uh-huh, do you have a hypo yet?"

"No." April did not have a hypothetical on what had come down here. She turned away from the vultures huddled around the door of the deceased. They were part of the territory, but she never got used to them.

"Well, do you have any ideas?" Woody pressed.

"Uh-huh." But she wasn't going to share them.

"Where to?"

"Five six between five and six. A studio called Workout. Maddy Wilson's trainer owns it."

"Nice address."

"Very nice." The location of Derek Meke's studio happened to be in the very heart of midtown, on the west side of Fifth Avenue, so it was in their precinct. She gave him the number on Fifty-sixth Street, and within fifteen minutes they were driving along the block she called Restaurant Row. Fifty-sixth Street between Fifth and Sixth Avenues consisted mainly of not-very-high old buildings with restaurants and stores on the first floors and small businesses—hair salons, couture dressmakers, shirt-makers, used-book dealers, galleries, and the like—on the upper floors. Workout turned out to be on the second floor of a rundown four-story building in the middle of the block.

At six minutes after one p.m. Woody left the car in a no-parking zone. By then April had filled him in on a few key details of the case, and he was good to go.

"You think we need backup?" Woody asked as they entered the building and pushed the button of a very sorry-looking elevator.

April didn't reply. Two of their prime suspects were already being questioned. If it was a boy-friend/girlfriend thing, as Mike seemed to think, most likely the killer would be Wayne or Remy—or possibly a combination of the two. Maybe it was a love triangle. Babysitter/wife/husband, or even love square: Babysitter/husband, wife/trainer. But never in her memory had a square resulted in a murder, nor could she think of an instance in which a trainer had offed a customer. Why kill a golden goose?

"I think we're good," April assured him.

They had rules about risk-taking. Derek might have been the last person to see Maddy Wilson alive, but different kinds of suspects required different methods of approach. The armed and dangerous, crazy-rabbit killers without much organization or control had to be approached with extreme caution. The careful killers, who took their time at the scene of a crime, then walked away in broad daylight, were likely to return to their lives as if nothing had occurred. Those sociopaths killed without shame or remorse and lied, thinking they were telling the truth. Their mistake was in believing they could get away with it. If Derek was their suspect, he wasn't going to be waiting for them with a carving knife.

The elevator showed no signs of movement, so she tilted her head toward the stairs; they started up. At the top, the only door on the second floor was open to a gym that looked like dozens of others all over the city. April had even trained in a few. A couple of people who'd taken a few courses somewhere and called themselves trainers got together, rented out a place, and set up shop, charging a hundred an hour to people who didn't know any better.

Far from the big trendy exercise facilities with dozens of treadmills and TVs, along with saunas and juice bars, each of these little gyms had its own specialty and loyal following. Interactive stretching, massage, second-stage physical therapy, Pilates, hot yoga, aerobics. There was a long list. April had been a martial-arts practitioner herself in the past. Now that she had the rank to get her way, however, she no longer felt the pressing need to throw large people to the ground.

Workout was a loft space with two massage tables, pulleys attached to the wall, and three area rugs for mat work. The equipment was limited to one Precor, one treadmill, a StairMaster, and some Pilates equipment similar to what April had seen in Maddy Wilson's gym. None of the machines were in use at the moment. The massage tables were occupied by a tall woman with huge breasts, and a tiny brunette with only slightly smaller breasts. Both were having their limbs yanked in all directions. From the description given of him by Remy, April guessed that the bulked-up blond male stretching the brunette's leg way past her ear was Derek.

He paused to look them over. "Can I help you?"

April hauled her gold shield out of her purse. "I'm Lieutenant April Woo Sanchez," she said, rattling out the whole mouthful this time. "And this is Detective Woody Baum."

Woody nodded his hello. "We're looking for Derek Meke," he said.

"That would be me," the trainer said easily. He didn't pause from his task of pulling the leg of the brunette on the table high enough to make her squeak. "What can I do you for?"

"Is there a private place where we can talk?" April asked.

"I'm in the middle of a session here. I have a break at three. How about then?" he said with a smooth smile.

"It won't wait. This is about the murder of Madeleine Wilson," Woody blurted.

"What!" The brunette wrenched herself out of Derek's grasp, and sat up.

Derek looked skeptical. "I saw Maddy a little while ago. She was fine."

The brunette lost it. "Oh, my God. She never returned my calls this morning. Oh, God. She wasn't putting me off." She coughed and started choking. "Oh, my God. I feel sick." She jumped off the table and ran to the bathroom.

"She's like that," Derek explained. "You're putting us on, right? You two don't look like cops."

April didn't ask what cops were supposed to look like.

He made a face. "Come on. You really upset Alison. She's Maddy's best friend. What's going on?"

"Mrs. Wilson was murdered in her gym sometime between seven forty-five and nine fifteen," April told him.

"What?" His mouth dropped open.

"Did you kill Maddy Wilson?" she asked.

"What?"

He didn't seem to have much of a vocabulary. He moved toward the window, where the sun slanted in from the west, and collapsed in one of the three hammock chairs circling a glass table littered with fitness magazines.

"Jesus. I can't believe it." He shook his head. "She was fine when I left."

Woody hunkered down in a second chair. April took the third. "Where do you live, Derek?"

"In Queens." He licked his plump lips. "Is this the third degree?" He looked from one to the other as if he couldn't decide which one to address.

"I don't know what the third degree is," April replied.

"You were the last person to see Mrs. Wilson alive. That makes you very important," Woody interjected. He knew what the third degree was.

"Oh, Jesus." Derek paused to consider that, then said, "How do you know I was the last one? Maybe someone came in after me. They might have a security camera. They talked about getting one," he said hopefully.

That was a pretty good return from a guy who

looked like a meathead. Unfortunately, Wayne had already told them he hadn't gotten around to getting a security camera. "How long have you known Maddy?" April asked.

He was still shaking his head in disbelief. "I don't know, a long time. Three or four years. Sometime after her second baby she had a bad ski accident and needed rehab. She's a champion skier, you know."

April whipped out her notebook and wrote down *Champion skier, bad fall.* "Did she come here for her rehab?"

"No, I didn't have this place then." Emotion finally flooded Derek's handsome face. Tears welled up in his eyes, and his shoulders shook with sobs.

April didn't give him long to grieve. "Where did you meet?"

"Crunch. I was there at that time. Everybody went there. Alison, Maddy, all the girls." He pulled himself together.

"Is that where Alison and Maddy met?" April asked.

"I don't know. I think they've known each other longer."

"What was your arrangement with Mrs. Wilson?" Woody broke in.

Derek found a handkerchief in his pocket and blew his nose. "My arrangement?"

"What did you do with her?" Woody asked.

"I helped her set up her gym, did her nutrition, advised her on spiritual matters."

"Really." Woody snickered.

Derek glared at him. "The body animates the spirit. A healthy person needs both body and spirit to function well. I went to her house three times a week for an hour in the morning."

"Was Mrs. Wilson a healthy person?"

"Yes."

"Did you have an intimate relationship with her?" Still Woody.

Derek was unfazed by the question. "Of course."

"Did anything out of the ordinary happen this morning?" April asked.

He turned to her, blowing air out of his mouth noisily. "Maddy was in a bad mood."

"Was that unusual for her?"

"She has a temper. Today the babysitter pushed her over the edge, so she fired her. It happened just before I got there at eight."

"You were on time?"

"To the second."

"Okay, now, what's this about Remy?"

"Maddy told her to be out by noon. It was about the fourth babysitter in a year, so she was really ticked. I got her feeling better by the end of the session, though."

"Then what happened?" April asked.

"I left," he said simply. "Maddy wanted to oversee Remy's packing to make sure she didn't take anything when she left. Some of them do, you know." Tears pooled up in his eyes again. "How did she die?" he almost whimpered.

"She was attacked in her shower," April said.

"Oh, shit." Reflexively his hands shot up to protect himself from Maddy's attacker. "Wayne finally got her," he sobbed. "He must have come back after I was gone, the jealous bastard!"

April glanced at Woody. *You.* He nodded and

started firing off questions while she kept her eye on the bathroom door. She figured that between the trainer and the best friend, they might actually get the whole story.

Thirteen

It took Alison Perkins forty-five minutes to pull herself together. After nearly choking on the table, then vomiting her entire lunch in the grungy toilet, she washed up as well as she could in Workout's horrible shower. This was the first time she'd ever gone into the moldy old cubicle. Having to get naked and go into that disgusting place almost made her sick again, so she took a tiny bump for the courage to do it.

After she got out, she was so excited and eager for more cocaine that she had to counsel herself to slow down and check herself because she was in the spotlight now. Like a girl already planning her wedding after a first date, she couldn't stop her thoughts from racing ahead to her celebrity. She was thinking a full hour on *Larry King Live*. She was thinking Diane Sawyer, Barbara Walters—all the media shows that would ask her to share with the world her extensive knowledge of Maddy and Wayne Wilson. She and Maddy were best friends. Their husbands were close. The children were close; the nannies were close. She had visions of the instant fame that came to the best friends of murdered people. Maddy and Wayne were top-of-society people.

La crème de la crème. She knew it was going to be big, and she'd finally get some of Andrew's attention. She had no sense of time passing as she dressed by rote, hardly aware of pulling on her tights and wiggling into her leather pants. She didn't remember zipping them up, or grabbing the pink cashmere sweater set, putting it on, and adjusting the plackets of the cardigan just so. She took another bump, just a teeny one, and didn't examine herself in the mirror too closely. It upset her when the capillaries around her eyes burst in fireworks of tiny red spots as happened so many times in the old days when she was bulimic.

She kept telling herself she was cured of all that. She couldn't stand to vomit or hurt herself in any way. She'd had self-esteem coaching and knew she was a stunning woman, small but perfectly formed. She'd gotten over the fact that pretty much everybody preferred blondes. She'd learned that people were stupid, and she could deal with that now. Public opinion held that blondes were more beautiful than dark-haired girls. It didn't matter whether or not they were true blondes or really pretty. It was just a miserable fact, like cancer or war. There wasn't a thing Alison could do about it. Hair as dark as hers couldn't be lightened enough to make her blond. It was just lucky for her some men weren't attracted to the chilly Nordic types like Maddy Wilson. Lucky for her Andrew was one of those. She had big boobs, nice legs. She was cured.

When she was all dressed, however, she felt sick again. She chided herself for throwing up and taking cocaine with a cop in the other room. What was she thinking? Her stomach still heaved and her head hurt like hell. It felt as if pieces of her skull were about to crack off like the iceberg they'd seen breaking up on that cruise they'd taken to Alaska three summers ago. She hadn't enjoyed the trip very much, but she remembered that ice floe. Maddy was dead, and she couldn't come down just yet; it hurt too much. She took another bump. Just a teeny-tiny nothing of a bump, almost nothing at all, and she felt a little better again. She knew she had to be careful. She didn't want to freak out and trigger old behaviors—too much vomiting, too much coke—just because she was upset.

As she walked back into the gym, the first thing she saw was Derek sitting in one of the hammock chairs by the Fifty-sixth Street window. His habitual jauntiness was gone. She was shocked by his posture of complete dejection. The wide shoulders she'd always so admired were slumping forward, and his big handsome face was cradled in those gifted hands. As she headed for the elevator to escape, she actually caught the gleam of tears on his fingers and was horrified. The thirty-four-year-old looked crushed, absolutely devastated. His expression of what appeared to be very real grief set off a searing flash of jealous rage in Alison.

Maddy was the chilly blonde, the one who always seemed in control of her emotions. Alison was known as the hot-blooded one. Sometimes she flew off. Right then she was in danger of completely losing it. Maddy was dead, and Derek cared more about himself (and Maddy) than he did about her.

This total selfishness of his tore her apart because she, not Maddy, had bought his equipment, had cosigned his lease, and taken the time to listen to his woes. She was the one who comforted him when things got bad. She could go on and on, but she needed to run. Even though it was June, definitely in the summer zone, she hadn't given up her snakeskin boots with the three-inch heels. She always dressed for attention, and she got it as she dashed to the elevator. The detectives who'd been listening to Derek so attentively suddenly turned to her. *Don't say a word,* she told herself as the female detective got to her before the elevator left the first floor.

"Feel better?" she asked.

"I'm all right. I just swallowed wrong. I have a strong gag reflex," Alison said.

"That's too bad. How about a cup of coffee?"

"No, thanks. Look, I can't talk about Maddy right now." Alison reminded herself that she'd made a vow of silence.

"Don't worry, it won't take long."

Alison felt the acid rise again in her throat. What should she do? She started calculating. If she talked to the cop, could she still be on *Larry King Live*? She had no idea about these things. Did CNN pay? CBS? NBC certainly did. Her mind raced. She could be on *The View.* How much could she get for her story? She could donate it to charity; that would enhance her image. She liked to think she was smart.

"We could go to the station, if you prefer."

"Oh, gee." Alison forgot about the little bag of powder in her gym bag. She also forgot how much worse she was going to feel in a little while if she didn't get more. She was thinking that she'd never been in a police station, that for once she had the power to help her friends. She had no idea who murdered Maddy, but she was certain that if she put the right spin on their story, Andrew would respect her. Wayne would respect her. Derek would thank her. It seemed like the right thing to do at the time.

"Okay," she said calmly.

Fourteen

Sometimes it was hard for a detective to know what to do with somebody. Alison Perkins presented such a problem. If her name had popped up in Derek's conversation as the victim's best friend, April would have put her on the to-see list and tracked her down some time down the road. She would have visited the woman in her home. If Alison had been a suspect she wanted to shake up, she'd have taken her to the task force headquarters, where Minnow would be setting up his detective team.

Instead she'd found Alison with the last person to see Maddy Wilson alive. That knocked her up to the top of the must-see list. But where should they go? April's personal relationship with the precinct commander complicated the use of the Seventeenth Precinct's interview room, and the press would be watching there. April wanted to keep Alison away from the Minnow crowd and the media spotlight. That left Alison's home or Midtown North. She thought it wouldn't be a good idea to let Alison return to her home, where the telephone would distract her and she could show April the door at any time. In the end April opted for her own shop at Midtown North.

Two separate cars brought her and Alison, Derek and Woody, into the precinct, where no one knew they were coming. April and Alison got there first. During the ride in the unmarked car Alison's mood changed. She clutched her gym bag nervously and fussed with her long, unbrushed hair. Her eyes were red and her pupils seemed larger than before. She talked nonstop.

"Wow, is this where you work?" she asked as they went through the precinct door. "This place needs work."

"Home, sweet home," April said cheerfully, nodding at Lieutenant Lester at the desk. He shot her a look that said *cranked-up hooker*.

She shook her head. *Not even close.* "This way," she said, leading the way to the stairs. It was faster than waiting for the elevator.

"Okay, no problem." Alison clattered up the stairs loudly in her high-heeled boots.

At two thirty the squad room was empty except for a grizzled man, dressed in many layers of stained clothing and snoring loudly in the holding cell; Dominica, the secretary; and the new guy, Barry Queue. Barry was a cool-looking African-American with a bit of an attitude, six one, shaved head with a few days' growth coming in. He'd been in Intelligence for a while and was unusually secretive about everything. He was on the phone, talking softly. When the two women came in, he swung around to stare, then slowly raised his hand in salute.

"Wait here for a second, will you?" April told

Alison, pointing to the visitors' bench near the door.

"Where's Derek?" Alison asked anxiously. "I need to talk to him."

"Soon." April stopped at Dominica's desk. "Where is everybody?" she asked.

The secretary of the unit was nearly forty now. She was a single mother who knew everybody's backstory and was helpful to the detectives she liked. She'd slept with a bunch of them over the years, took care of things when they were sick or needed cover. Those who weren't her darlings got the shaft.

"Sergeant Gelo and Charlie are looking for strippers from Spirit," she reported.

Gelo and Hagedorn out together? April's brow furrowed. Hagedorn never left. The man had an unnatural relationship with his computer, and since they made a pair of aces, no one wanted it any other way.

"Yeah. That Gelo has him eating from her—"

"No kidding. What else?" April didn't want to know where Eloise had him eating from.

"The senator's son was released from the hospital a little while ago. His mother got him out. Senator Peret was at a summit in the Middle East. He's flying in tonight. The clip has been on TV about five times. They're not making any statement until tomorrow." She rattled off the names of other detectives on the first tour, where they were. April listened, but she was thinking about Senator Peret, another high-profile humiliated parent with a kid on drugs. It was tough.

"You want tea, boss?" Dominica finished. "I'll

get someone on it." Not her job, but she was a nice person.

"Yes, please. And a coffee for the lady out there."

April smiled, then went to check her desk. There was a pile of messages from people she wished she could avoid. A stack of files of ongoing cases that needed to be addressed. Some directives from downtown. Five minor complaints had come in since morning and were waiting for assignment. Wanted posters. Personnel schedules. April did not bring civilians in here.

She left her office and went through to the back where the picnic table, the TV, and the lockers were. A quick glance at the interview room discouraged her from taking Alison in there. The wastebasket was overflowing and some take-out cartons and empty cups were on the floor. The mixed odors of spoiled food and sweat were particularly offensive. Too bad for Woody. He was going to deal with it, get a uniform in to clean up. She wasn't doing it. Then she stopped at Dominica's desk. She couldn't help herself. She was the CO. "The interview room needs a cleanup."

"Don't look at me," Dominica said. "Cleaning that room isn't my job." Then she relented. "I'll ask someone to take care of it."

"Thanks. I'll remember you on your birthday."

"You always say that, Lieutenant. But this time it happens to be Friday."

April grinned. "I knew that. I won't forget you."

"See that you don't," Dominica shot back.

Back on the visitors' bench, Alison Perkins was

shaking her foot and beginning to look scared. "You can come in now," April told her. She'd opted for classy and took the woman into her office.

At her desk April set up her tiny tape recorder. "I'm going to tape this," she said, and told the machine who was there, where they were, and what day and time it was. Then she asked Alison her name, address, and phone number.

Hugging her bag, Alison responded, then added, "I have to go in a minute. I don't feel well."

"Okay. Alison, I'm going to ask you some questions about Maddy Wilson."

Alison swiped at her nose. "I think I have the flu."

"Maddy Wilson was a close friend of yours?"

"Yes," Alison said, looking at the machine.

"How well did you know her?"

"Better than her fucking husband did. She was my best friend. We talked every day, usually more than once."

"When was the last time you saw Maddy?"

"Yesterday. We went shopping." Alison glanced at the Wanted posters on the wall and grimaced. She made a little whimpering sound. "I feel bad."

"Where did you go shopping?" April asked.

"Yesterday? Bergdorf's. They're having a great sale." She didn't look too enthusiastic about it.

"Really?" April was surprised. She had no idea that rich women went to sales. "What did you buy?" she asked, curious.

"Jesus, this isn't anything like *Law and Order*," Alison erupted.

"No, this isn't a TV show," April chided gently. "Now, Alison, you know Maddy really well. What was she was like?"

"Oh, she was great. Didn't you see the pictures of her? Great legs, great hair. Great taste. You saw the house, I'm sure. Maddy was just great."

"Uh-huh. Beyond her looks, though. What kind of person was she?" April had patience—she'd dealt with people like this for years.

Alison thought for a moment. "She was into health and fitness, of course. *Very* into maintenance. She took care of herself really well. We both do. You know how important maintenance is."

April smiled. She did indeed.

"Men get distracted easily," Alison said, shaking her foot, pretty distracted herself. "You know, successful, rich, always making a new deal. The older they get, the younger they like their women."

"Did Wayne like them young?"

Alison frowned. "And she was *funny*! She could do Donald Duck at the drop of a hat. It always cracked the kids up so much." She looked up at the ceiling, stuck the bag behind her in the chair, then leaned against it, covering it with her body.

It was clear she realized that she had something in common with the men on those Wanted posters. April made the decision not to nail her with the substance abuse right off the bat. "What about Wayne? Did he fool around?" she asked again.

"Oh, sure."

"Did Maddy know?"

"She worried about it practically constantly."

"Was he sleeping with Remy?"

"Oh, of course. Maddy told me many times that

Remy was trying to take over. I told her what to do." Alison scratched her neck somewhere behind her ear. "I wouldn't put up with that kind of shit in my house."

"Did Maddy take your advice?"

"She called me early this morning very upset. She left a message for me to call back at nine. I called her back but she didn't pick up. Now that I think of it, she might have been on the line with Jo Ellen."

"Who is Jo Ellen?"

"Oh, Jo Ellen places people." Alison reached for the bag, then thought better of it and shoved it back behind her butt. "Aw, shit. This is horrible. Do you have a bathroom here?"

April ignored the question. "What agency does she work for?"

"Anderson. Jo Ellen Anderson. It's her own."

"She placed Remy with the Wilsons?"

"Of course, and the last girl and the one before that."

"How many have there been?"

Alison shrugged. "I don't know. A lot. They never work out. It's always something."

"Tell me about Remy," April said.

"What's there to say? She comes from Wyoming. She doesn't know how to dress and she doesn't know how to clean."

"Can't clean?" April said. Somebody cleaned that gym pretty well.

"Oh, no, she's a terrible cleaner. The place was always a mess. All she cared about was food and Wayne. I have to get out of here."

"Did Remy have any special friends?"

"She and Lynn, my nanny, are very close. Our kids are close. They all spend time together. And there's another girl in the neighborhood, Leah. I don't know who she works for. She hangs around a lot. There are others. You'll have to ask them."

April changed the subject. "What about Maddy's husband? Has he ever hurt her?" April asked.

"Wayne? No! He gave her everything, wanted her to be happy. He built that gym. Wayne would never hurt her."

A uniform called Ulla came in with a mug of hot water and a cup of regular coffee from the deli down the street. She handed the coffee to Alison without asking if it was for her. "You need anything else?" she asked.

"Do you have Sweet'n Low?" Alison asked.

"I could look downstairs," Ulla offered.

"Here, I have some." April reached in her desk and passed two over.

"See, you know about maintenance. Are you married?" Alison dumped the powder in her coffee, stirred, sipped, and was distracted. "Ugh. This is terrible coffee. Do you have anything stronger?"

"Sorry about the coffee." April returned to the subject. "Would you say the Wilsons were a happy couple?"

Alison shook her snakeskin boot. "What's a happy couple?"

"I think you know what I mean."

She dipped her head. "Well, they're totally famous. He's a busy man. I have one like that, too. You have to watch them all the time." She glanced at her watch. "I could use a drink. Oops, I didn't

say that." She glanced guiltily at the tape machine.
"Don't tell my husband I said that."

"Alison, did Maddy use, too?"

"Excuse me?"

"Alcohol, cocaine, other drugs?" April said as if
it were a given.

"Uh, no. Of course not."

"It'll show up in the autopsy if she did," April
told her.

Alison looked scared. "Why are you asking me
that? I wouldn't know something like that."

"You were her best friend. You did everything
together, shared the same trainer, the same employment agency. I think you shared a lot of things.
Did Derek sleep with you both, supply you with
your drugs?"

"Oh, God, no! Don't drag Derek into this,"
she wailed.

"No to which?" April asked innocently.

"Jesus. You're intimidating me."

"This is a murder investigation. The truth is
going to come out, Alison."

"Well, he didn't sleep with her. I know he
didn't."

"How do you know?"

"He liked her, but it wasn't like that. She
wouldn't give him the money for his place. It was
strictly, and I mean strictly, business with those
two!"

"That's not the way I hear it," April murmured.

"Well, let me put that rumor to bed. It was him
and me," she said angrily. "Not her and him. *Me.*"
Then she realized what she'd said. "Oh, God.

Don't get me in trouble. My husband would kill me."

"Alison, where were you at nine o'clock this morning?"

"I told you. I was at home waiting for Maddy to call me. Jesus, are you crazy?" She pulled her bag back onto her lap, clutching it tightly. "What are you saying?"

"Just wondering how angry you would be if you found out Derek was having an affair with Maddy."

"But he wasn't."

April didn't say anything for a while.

"He didn't tell you he was, did he?" she asked in a small voice.

"What about the coke? Where did she get it?"

"I don't know anything about any coke."

"Don't lie to me, Alison. I can see it in your eyes."

"It's not a big thing. I had a bad day."

"You had a bad day?" April repeated.

"Yeah, my best friend was killed."

"But you didn't hear about it until we came to the gym, right?"

"So?"

"Then where did you get the coke? Was it at the gym?"

"No, I had it with me. . . . Shit." Alison pulled on her ear. "It wasn't about cocaine. Don't make it about that. It's all over the place in the restaurant business. Modeling business. Advertising. Wayne had it around. Believe me, no one would murder anybody over that."

"Somebody's dealing. Who is it?"

"Don't make it about that," Alison begged. "If

you go there, you could arrest the whole fucking city."

"So you don't think your boyfriend, the coke dealer, killed her?"

"Shit, I never said he was a dealer, and he would never hurt anybody."

"So you think maybe Wayne got angry when Maddy fired his girlfriend?"

"No! I never said anything about Wayne, either. Maddy's fired girls before, lots of them. It wasn't a big deal. If Wayne liked one of them, he'd give her a waitress job. Nobody lasted long," she said furiously.

"But Remy probably didn't know that," April murmured.

Alison started sobbing. "If Remy did it, then I'm really upset. I can't take any more of this. I have to go home now." She looked as if she might be sick again.

"Well, who else could have done it?"

"I don't know. But Lynn is Remy's best friend. How can I have her in the house now? I'm afraid," she said.

"What are you afraid of?"

"I could be next," Alison cried. "I need protection."

"Why? Who would want to kill you?" April asked.

"They hate us. They wear our clothes. They steal our things. If they can get our husbands, they'll steal them, too," she ranted.

"Are you really at risk? Is Lynn having an affair with your husband?" April asked, wondering at the whole thing. The husbands with the nannies, the wives with the trainer, and cocaine abuse in the mix. How did it all fit?

"What? What? Is Andrew having an affair with Lynn?" Alison said, sounding panicked. "Are you sure?"

"It was just a question."

"Jesus." Alison broke down sobbing. "Jesus. You got me all mixed-up. I don't know what I'm saying."

April turned off the tape. "I think you need help, Alison."

"No, I'm fine. I'm having a bad day. Please, don't drag me and Derek into this. We didn't do anything wrong."

April didn't make any promises. One thing she did know was Alison's cover was blown on the dope. Derek would flush his stash before they got to his place with a search warrant. But the case had just gotten a little more complicated.

Fifteen

April called Mike late in the afternoon. "What's up, *chico*?"

This time he was the one to say, "You first." She could hear his desk chair creak as he sat back to listen.

"Well, Maddy was sleeping with her trainer, Derek Meke. He didn't tell me. Woody got it out of him."

"Good old Woody. What kind of guy is Derek?"

"About what you'd expect. Big guy, bulked up. Looks like he's on steroids. He has no cuts or bruises on his hands, face, or body. Woody checked him out."

"He get permission for that search?"

"Everything on the up-and-up. Derek volunteered to show everything, his body, his clothes, his locker at Workout. No wet clothing. We took some wet towels from the bathroom. He was there at nine twenty. A trainer he works with says he was there when she came in. He said he left the house at nine. Anybody in the neighborhood see him?" April asked.

"So far we do have one hit on that. He stopped for a Snapple at the corner store at about five past nine. He's in the neighborhood often so the woman there knows him. She says he seemed fine, looked the way he always does—very good."

April made a noise.

"The detective who interviewed her said his hair was dry. She has a crush on him, so she'd notice. What about you, *querida*? Do you have a crush on him?" Mike asked teasingly.

"Not my type," she said with a little smile. "But dry hair doesn't mean anything. If he killed her, he could have been wearing a shower cap. And there was a hair dryer in Maddy's gym."

"And he could have been wearing a whole plastic suit, like the Tyvek we wear. We're searching garbage cans."

"What do you think?" April asked. "Think he did it?"

"If he killed her at the end of the session, the time frame wouldn't fit. If he killed her at eight a.m. when he first came in, the whole family would have been gone. He would have had an hour and five minutes to make a bloody mess of her, clean up, and get that Snapple."

"That would work. He had opportunity and time to do it, but what about motive?" April said slowly.

"Maybe they had a lovers' quarrel. What's your take? Is he an angry person?"

"Mmmm, I'm not sure. He's a good actor, has that soft and touchy demeanor that works with women. He's a con type. Really sincere. Looks you straight in the eye. You'll see. He's definitely a player of some kind. He also slept with Maddy's best friend, Alison Perkins. She didn't know he and Maddy had a thing. She was pretty freaked-out to hear that. And there's a cocaine element here. Alison's a user. Maddy may have been, too. It's not clear how it fits. Alison's pretty paranoid. She doesn't want to get anybody in trouble."

"Derek has no record of violence, not even a speeding ticket." Mike put his hand over the receiver and spoke to someone, then came back on the line. "You were saying there's a coke connection."

"Woody searched the gym pretty well. He came up with a lot of vitamins and stuff but no illegal substances. But he didn't take the place apart, of course. Alison said Wayne had blow around and she admitted she had some in her gym bag. I could see her killing Maddy out of jealousy—she certainly has the rage. But she's very small, less than a hundred pounds. Anything on Maddy's finances yet?"

"Minnow has someone working on the bank statements. Looks like Maddy used her ATM with unusual frequency. The lady dispensed a lot of cash."

"I can see a justification for that. It would prevent her husband from knowing how she spent her money. I guess you're following the case pretty closely," April remarked.

Mike was quiet for a moment. He didn't need to say that homicide was his area of expertise, and never mind the protocol of the situation. He was going to work the case his own way, and she was going to work it with him because that was how he wanted it. Since he'd chewed her out pretty fiercely in the past for similar independent action of her own, she almost had to laugh. As they say, "What goes around, comes around."

"What about the incoming and outgoing calls this morning?" Mike asked.

"We have the outgoing numbers. One was to Alison Perkins. One was to Jo Ellen Anderson. That's the employment agency," April told him.

"I know. There were messages from both of them as well. Jo Ellen Anderson, at five to nine, confirmed an interview at her office at two p.m., a new girl to replace Remy. Message from Alison, at nine thirty-two, wondering where she was. Maddy was probably dead by then."

That meant Remy lied about making up with Maddy. Maddy had already fired her. Or else Wayne had underestimated his wife's resolve in the matter; April thought it through.

"So, where did you talk to Derek and Alison?" Mike asked, breaking into her review.

"I took them to my place," she said after a beat.

"You better share, *querida,*" he warned.

"Oh yeah," she promised.

"What's going on with the senator's kid?" He changed the subject.

"I guess you've seen it on TV. His mother got him out of the hospital. No one's saying anything about it. The senator is flying in tonight."

"How's your sergeant doing?"

"She and Hagedorn are working on it," April murmured.

"How do you feel about it?" he asked.

Oh, he knew her so well. April sipped from her latest mug of cold tea and took a second to think about it. When she was coming up, her boss was one Sergeant Margaret Mary Joyce. At the time, Sergeant Joyce was fat as a sausage, wore her suits too tight, and had coffee stains down the front of her blouse almost every day. The woman was as mean as a whip and took the credit for every case April and Mike solved. "Get out of the way" was her motto. April had been a detective second grade and Mike a sergeant. Both had chafed under her rule and conspired to work around her.

Now they were the ones who had to delegate. Captains didn't investigate homicides. Unit COs weren't the legs on even their most important cases. They were supposed to bully other people into doing the work, then take the credit. But assigning Gelo the Peret case was like Mike's allowing Fish to do his job on the Wilson homicide without interference. It wasn't so easy to let go.

"I feel fine. What's the latest on Remy and Wayne?"

"They're standing behind each other. Wayne says there's no way Remy could have hurt his wife. He's keeping her on to take care of the children. He's moved the family to a hotel."

"What's on your plate tonight? Do you feel like having a good dinner in town before heading home?"

"Oh, God, I don't know, *querida,* I've got a lot to do."

"How about a really good dinner at Soleil? I happen to know it's open," April wheedled. "We can ask a few questions."

"Ah, *querida,* now you're cooking with gas."

They set a time and hung up.

Sixteen

Swallowing down sixteen cups of China tea a day was a firm requirement for Chinese good health. April got her seventh cup at six p.m., and reviewed her conversation with Mike.

He seemed to think Derek could be the killer, and if the ME set Maddy's time of death to some time between eight and nine a.m., he would certainly have had plenty of time to commit the murder and go out for a Snapple before meeting his next customer half a mile away at nine thirty. But what would be his motive? Even if, in an amazing coincidence, Maddy had told Derek to get lost the same morning as she'd fired Remy, too many things didn't fit. Unlike Remy, he wasn't into butcher knives as toys, and his place was hardly spotless. April believed that cleanliness was a factor here, part of a bigger picture. Call it intuition, whatever.

Outside of her office, the second tour in the unit had replaced the first tour and begun their tasks. Some detectives were at their desks; a few had already gone out. April was aware of Alison's perfume, still lingering in her office, and recognized it as Beautiful. She put her finger to her lips, mulling over everything she'd seen and heard that day.

Every case started in the same fog. Above, the air was thick with possibilities. Below, a swamp of deadly quicksand. Sometimes the fog cleared quickly, and sometimes it didn't. April's mother, Skinny Dragon, was terrified of that journey to the dead and back again. Ghosts didn't always depart their human bodies right away. Sometimes they became attached to the person most interested in them. And ghosts meant bad luck. Each of April's cases brought the possibility that a ghost might make her sterile, give her cancer. Maybe both. Ghosts ruled the world and could do anything they wanted.

Although her mother believed this, April didn't. For nearly fifteen years she'd wanted nothing more than to succeed in the Department. That meant being closer sometimes to dead people than to living ones. She'd never had much faith in the other facets of life. For her there had been no glitter— no sparkling diamonds, no weekend getaways with ardent boyfriends, no bubbling champagne. For pleasure she'd run her legs off around the neighborhood in Astoria, Queens, where she'd lived in her parents' house until she was way over thirty. She'd knocked people down on sparring mats. She'd kept to herself. It was only after she fell in love with Mike and married him that life began to take on a rosier aspect.

Now she liked driving north on the Hutchinson Parkway, home to her brick house with its pleasant leafy trees and backyard barbeque in Westchester County. She'd enjoyed choosing curtains and bathroom accessories and linens. Curling up on the soft sofa with Mike in front of a real fire on all those frigid nights the winter before had been a major highlight of her life. She liked cooking in her almost-new kitchen with its very nice GE appliances, and even a washer and dryer in their own tiny laundry room. She'd never had the best of everything. In the Woo house, there had been only a human dishwasher.

In fact, April Woo had become so intrigued by the unexpected pleasures of her home life that sometimes when she was at work she wished that domesticity would reach out somehow, and intervene to give her a break from death and the other miseries caused by crime. What would happen to her, she asked herself, if she let ambition go for a while?

Sometimes Skinny Dragon was right. A cop could not avoid being touched by evil. Death did get in the way of living. There was no way to wall it off, take a weekend and forget about it. Each time April walked into someone's murder, the killer grabbed hold of her, too, and wouldn't let her go. Even after the puzzle was solved and the perpetrator was nailed, she played the murders over and over in her head—every single piece, every little fact she uncovered. Every sad particle of chaos that murder created stayed with her. When the cases went to trial, she had to live them again—what she'd done, what she'd seen, what she'd learned. She could write a book.

And the crime scene always told what happened. What had gone wrong, how the perpetrator and the victim had come together, how the victim had responded, whether the body was hidden or flaunted. Even the span of time that passed before the victim was discovered told a story. The killer sent a message whether he meant to or not. The message in the act was more than "I hate you," or "I'm going to annihilate you." The way it went down told a whole narrative in code, each one like a Rosetta stone that had to be interpreted. The story only lacked the who and the why, and sometimes it was simple enough to point right at the who as well.

In any case, Maddy Wilson didn't go out to lunch and disappear, only to be found days later floating in the East River. She wasn't pushed out a window, run over, or shot in the head. She was murdered in her shower and discovered within minutes by a woman who had reason to hate her. Her trainer had been with her just before she was attacked, and maybe her husband, too. But Remy was the one who "discovered" the body and called 911. With all those people so close to the victim in the time frame, it could not be murder by a stranger. The killer knew what Maddy's window of vulnerability had been.

Images from the crime scene kept replaying in April's head. Something had been going on when Maddy was discovered that no police officer had seen. And that might be the most important element of all. No one saw the jets in the shower shooting water at Maddy Wilson's body. Remy said they had been on when she got there. But the shower had been turned off by the time the police arrived. How many jets had been on? Only Remy knew that. Only Remy knew whether the water had been on at all, and although April had asked her those questions, she wasn't yet fully satisfied with the answers. If the shower had kept the body warm for an hour or more, would the ME still be able to ascertain the time of death? She didn't know.

April was not a religious person, not religious in the usual way. She did not go to church, or light incense sticks for her ancestors, or keep a shrine to Buddha. Her parents held deep beliefs and ancient superstitions, but she did not. How could she, in the twenty-first century, still interpret the wishes of people who had died a hundred years ago in a very faraway place, she asked herself. She tried to explain her reluctance to follow the ancient traditions of ancestor worship by the passage of time. But still, she felt guilty for letting the traditions go.

Although sin, as such, was not a part of her own belief system, no one in America could fail to be aware of Christian dogma on sin—original and otherwise—and redemption. She didn't know why, but the thought of baptism and the lamb kept running through her head. The killer washed Maddy's blood down the drain, but maybe there was a message in the water left running after all the blood was gone. Maybe Maddy's *sins* were being washed away.

She shook her head at the confusing picture. Derek, Remy, Wayne, Alison. They were all closely connected. What bothered her the most was that Maddy's killing looked like a man's murder, but not a man's crime scene. She had some time to brood about that and enter her notes into her laptop before hurrying to meet Mike at the Seventeenth Precinct.

Seventeen

Alison didn't go right into the house after the police car dropped her off. She stopped on the sidewalk and called Derek. His phone was off, and she didn't want to leave a message. Then, still lingering outside the modern renovated brownstone with its circular staircase and entrances on two levels, she called her husband on his private line. "Have you heard about Maddy Wilson?" she asked as soon as he answered.

"Where the hell have you been?" he yelled into the receiver. "I've been calling you all day. Oh, Jesus, Alison. Why didn't you call me?"

"They took me to the police station," she told him meekly.

"Why, are you hurt?" He sounded frantic.

She yanked the cell away from her ear. When he ignored her, she was miserable. But when he spoke to her, he was always yelling, or screaming. He didn't have a soft tone in his entire voice repertoire. She could imagine him pacing around his office with a headset on. Wherever he was, he had that phone pasted to his head, and he yelled at everyone. She had to take a pill whenever he yelled at her.

"No, I'm not hurt. If I were hurt, they wouldn't have taken me to the police station," she replied impatiently. "That's the hospital." He knew nothing about real life.

"Oh, stop. Maddy Wilson was murdered and you're always with her. . . . I thought . . . I was afraid . . . I didn't know what to think. Why didn't you call me?"

"They were asking me questions, honey. I couldn't get to a phone."

"That's a crock. What do you know about it?" he demanded.

"Shh. Don't *yell*, Andy. I don't know anything about it. I was at the gym, and they came for Derek."

"Who the fuck is Derek?"

"My trainer."

"Oh, yeah, him." Reference to his wife's trainer stopped him, but only for a second. "Don't tell me that guy who steals your money killed Maddy!" he shrieked. "Jesus, Alison. Now you've done it."

"No, he didn't kill anybody. You're not listening. He was Maddy's trainer, too. They had a session together this morning. And he doesn't steal my money." This offended her. She leaned against a tree, which was missing its little iron fence to keep the dogs away, in front of her house. She was still reeling from the news that Derek had been unfaithful to her.

"You two did everything together. I'm freaked out by this, I really am."

"He doesn't steal my money," she protested again.

"Oh, I forgot, you just give it to him. You know what? I don't want you seeing that guy anymore."

Alison flushed angrily. Why were they arguing about Derek again? "I'm not *seeing* him, Andy. He's my trainer. He's done wonderful things for me. I'm completely straight now."

"Then why did you end up at the police station?" Andrew demanded.

Alison didn't answer the question right away. She was thinking of Maddy. She and Andy lived only two blocks away from the Wilsons. Their houses both had southern exposures and the same address. They'd thought it was such a wonderful coincidence, to be so close in such a safe neighborhood. Very little crime, and the United Nations was not far away. A lovely, lovely neighborhood. They had pretty views of the East River where the sunrises were amazing every morning. And Saks Fifth Avenue was nearby. They could walk there every day if they wanted to. The two women had been in each other's kitchens daily and drunk their afternoon white wines in each other's bedrooms. And they'd shared the same lover. Alison wanted to cry.

In fact, they'd shared everything except the gym where Maddy died. Maddy hadn't allowed Alison in there. That was the reason Alison had helped Derek set up his own studio. Crunch had been too crowded and noisy for her. If Maddy hadn't been so selfish, Alison wouldn't have had to give Derek so much money and gotten Andrew angry. But now she knew that Maddy had betrayed her in a bigger way than that.

"For Christ's sake, Alison, are you there?" Andy screamed into her thoughts.

"I'm upset," she said in a little-girl voice.

"Fuck that. What did the police ask you?"

"They wanted to know about Maddy's life," she whimpered, wishing he'd stop yelling at her.

"Jesus Christ. What did you tell them?" Andy demanded.

"Nothing. Why are you so angry about it? I didn't do anything wrong. I lost my best friend."

"Wayne called me. He's very upset."

"Well, I'm upset, too," she whimpered. "I was so upset I threw up."

"I know, Al, but you can't just blab off to the police."

"I wasn't blabbing," Alison protested. Why was he making this her fault?

"Honey, the police get things all mixed up. You can get seriously embroiled."

"I don't know what you're talking about. My friend was murdered."

"What did you tell them? Wayne wants to know."

"I told you. Nothing. We talked about shopping and the girls who work for us. That's all. We also talked about Derek. They're interested in Derek."

"Really." Derek's name stopped him every time.

"When are you coming home? I'm so scared," she said.

"Oh, for Christ's sake, Al, I'm very stressed right now. I have things to do. Are you going to call on Wayne?" he replied impatiently.

Alison hesitated. That sounded like a terrible idea. Why would she want to call on Wayne? He'd be stressed, too. "I think they kicked him out of the house," she said slowly. She didn't feel up to calling on anybody.

"Well, of course, they kicked him out of the house. He couldn't stay there. He's at the Plaza."

She shuddered at the thought of Wayne and the two boys at the Plaza. It wasn't a low-key place at all. She knew she should help Wayne with the boys. Maddy would want her to take care of things. That was a new stress. Bertie and Angus needed a new nanny, and Wayne couldn't hire one himself. And he certainly couldn't look after the boys on his own. She had to call Jo Ellen about a new girl. Better than taking them herself, she thought. She couldn't handle that. "Why did he go to the Plaza?" she asked.

"I don't know. Look, stay home. Don't go out. Don't call all your friends. Be discreet for once. Do you hear me?"

"How could I avoid it with you yelling in my ear?"

"Don't start with me, okay? I'm trying to earn a living here. I'm doing the best I can."

"But you told me to go see Wayne. I can't go see him. I have to get him a new nanny for the boys."

"Keep out of it. Remy's staying on."

"Remy's staying on?" Alison screamed. "Oh, Jesus, Andy. No!"

"She's with them at the Plaza. She's staying. Now, I have to go."

He hung up, and Alison leaned over to gag in the little plot of unprotected earth around her one lonely tree. She didn't like throwing up anymore, but sometimes life made her sick. The horror of the situation washed over her. Remy had killed her friend, and now the woman was ensconced in the

Plaza with Maddy's husband and two children. It was just too much. She tried to throw up, but she was completely empty inside. Nothing came out. She stopped retching and dabbed at her mouth and eyes with an old tissue from her pocket. She was crashing now, and felt the bad that was like no other low.

Remy had tortured poor Maddy for months— Alison knew that for sure. And when Maddy fired her, Remy killed her. The certainty of that sequence of events terrified her. She stumbled across the sidewalk to the curved staircase embedded in a stucco half wall that curled up to the second floor, hiding the service entrance into the kitchen below and creating an alcove for the front door above. Alison had always wanted to remove the solid stairway and replace it with wrought iron steps that would leave both doorways open to full view. But Andy liked the austere look of the heavy facade with its two hidden doorways.

She didn't like going under the stairs into the kitchen, so she climbed up to the second floor where the living room was. As soon as she opened the door, she knew Jill and Jessica, who were the same ages as Angus and Bertie, were downstairs in the family room watching *Finding Nemo* again. Same DVD over and over. That meant Lynn was doing absolutely nothing to stimulate them. She wasn't reading to them, playing with them, teaching them something on the expensive computer they'd bought. Nothing.

Alison stood inside the front door, listening to the loud movie music that filled her house. She was hurting badly now, and this affront was the last straw. Those nannies were all the same. They moved in and acted as if the house was theirs. After a few months, they didn't want to do the work they were paid in excess of six hundred dollars a week to do! Alison was outraged. She marched down the stairs to confront the girl.

The kitchen was a mess. The family room was none too neat, either. Toys were scattered all over, and the remains of dinner had yet to be cleared from the children's table. Lynn was nowhere to be seen, but Jill and Jessica were curled up on the sofa.

"Mommy!" they cried and jumped up to hug her.

Everything horrible fell away from her. "My babies," she cried, rushing to greet them.

Eighteen

Wayne had given Remy her orders while the police were still in the house.

"Don't tell the boys what happened," he said. "Just get them settled in the hotel room. Give them dinner, put on the TV, and tell them we're on vacation." His expressive face was doing funny tics, and she gathered he didn't want her talking.

"And I want you to move there with us," he added as if it was an afterthought.

"Oh, no, I can find someplace to stay. Don't worry about me," Remy had said quickly. She couldn't believe he was taking the boys to the Plaza and telling them they were on vacation.

"Remy, they need you. And I need you, too. You have to come with us."

"To the hotel?" She didn't get it. How could she move to a hotel with them? It wouldn't look good. But she saw that determined expression of his and hesitated. He didn't seem to understand the significance of her being there with them.

"Of course, to the hotel. The boys can't stay alone."

"It won't look good," she almost whispered. She

was afraid of thwarting him, and she held back on the heavy-duty protest.

They'd been standing inside the front door of the house, where the stairway went up to the second floor and the echo from the marble floors was loudest. They had only a few minutes together. The police were watching. Wayne's Louis Vuitton suit bag hung by its strap over one shoulder, his duffel slung over the other. He shook his head, his face set in its *Don't go there* expression.

"I'm sorry," she mumbled, hardly knowing what, of all the horrible things that had happened, she was sorry for the most.

Then she cringed as his hand struck the air, brushing the awkward condolence away in a clear gesture that he didn't want to talk about it. He didn't mention Maddy at all. If he was sad or upset about what had happened to her, it didn't show. All she could see was anger at his situation. He'd packed his things and was leaving the house. Clearly, he expected her to be the one to lock up and set the alarm when the police were done. She wasn't sure when she'd see him again. She was dying to ask, but didn't want to sound like his dead wife—always asking where he was going and when he was coming back. Maddy's questions had irritated him so much that sometimes he'd just walk out to go to the bathroom or have a cigarette in the garden, and disappear until he felt like coming back. When he did return hours or even days later, he acted as if nothing had happened. It had made poor Maddy frantic.

And now he was doing it to her. As she waited

for some word as to when he would join his children, he just walked out. She'd seen him do it to Maddy over and over, but he'd never done it quite like that to her. She felt rebellion rise in her as she had so often before in that household. *I'm not a maid,* she told herself for about the ten thousandth time since she'd begun working there. She moved away from the door cursing Jo Ellen Anderson, who'd placed her here.

When CI graduates left cooking school, occasionally they worked for a short time as a chef in a private house, usually for the summer in a resort area. These were the kind of houses where more than one staff member was on hand to take care of the children, do the laundry, and clean the house. That was what Jo Ellen had promised her— a cushy cooking job with a restaurant owner who was opening a new restaurant and would soon give her a place there. That was two restaurants ago. CI students weren't maids. They weren't housekeepers. She'd never intended to work in someone's home.

Now she was at the center of a murder. It was horrible! Her sweatshirt and jeans, even her skin, felt dirty. She hadn't changed since she'd done the unthinkable and stuck her hand in the shower to turn off the water that was pounding down on Maddy. The second she did it she actually felt death reach out and fill her pores. It was the most amazing thing. As soon as she turned off the water, the odor of death seemed to fill up the space. Maddy, who in life had smelled so amazingly lovely, always layered with perfume, was already beginning to decay. Maybe Remy had imagined it, but that was what she'd thought. It made her skin crawl even now. This was different from any other death in her experience. So many creatures had died in her hands—lobsters, shrimp, clams, and oysters, all kinds of fish. Chickens, when she was young. She'd even hacked off the head of a squirming eel once. She was used to carving up the carcasses of cows, calves, lambs, pigs. She knew what was under the scales and feathers and hides—what innards and eyes and brains looked like outside their hosts. Meat and organs had held no fear for her. Fresh meat was sweet. There was nothing sweet about death's alteration of Maddy Wilson.

Remy's whole body pulsed with anxiety as she went to the boys' rooms to collect their things. The rooms had been decorated by a designer. Everything colorful and custom, even the windows and window treatments were fanciful. NASCAR racing and baseball. Ever since the day she'd arrived, she'd thought there was something wrong with all the spending—the lavish lifestyle. Her thoughts returned to her task. The family had gone on vacation so many times in the last six months that she could now pack up the boys quickly. They had their little duffels and their special toys. Then she raced downstairs and showered for twenty minutes, washed her hair, then dressed and packed a bag of her own. Jeans, jeans, sweatshirt, sweatshirt. She told herself not to think about the detectives who were watching her—where she went, what she touched. They followed her around and waited while she went to the bathroom to collect the toothbrushes.

Just before two, Wayne sent the driver to take

their luggage to the hotel. She dropped the bags off, then picked up the kids and listened to their chatter in the car. Angus especially was full of the day's activities. He'd gone swimming and smelled of chlorine.

"I can do the backstroke," he said. "Want to see?"

"Me, too," Bertie said.

He mimed the stroke in the backseat of the Mercedes, Bertie copying him. They had the open faces of children who'd never been hurt. Remy could not tell them they were on vacation.

"Very good," she said about the swimming.

"Going to the Plaza, yea," Angus said.

They'd been to the Palm Court many times. They'd heard the history.

"Will Eloise be there?" Bertie asked.

"Eloise is on vacation." Remy could tell them that lie but not the other one.

They looked for her among the palm trees anyway, then became absorbed with the tantalizing prospect of room service. Their order arrived after a forty-five-minute wait. But they were happy with their tepid hamburgers and soggy fries and finally settled in at a rolling table in front of the TV.

Remy was semi-alone for the first time all day and she immediately called Lynn.

"Remy, why didn't you call me?" Lynn cried. She sounded just like her mistress.

"Why do you think? I didn't have a chance," Remy said, now sounding like hers.

"They said on TV you found her."

Remy didn't say anything.

"I've never seen a dead person. What did she look like?"

"I'm not allowed to talk about it."

"Come on."

"I don't want to talk about it," Remy said. "They can listen in."

"Do they think it's a break-in?"

"Probably not. Look, I forgot about Leah. She must be very upset with all this. Tell her I couldn't talk to her this morning. They were fighting."

"She thought you were snubbing her."

"Well, I wasn't, Lynn. Maddy wanted to fire me. I had other things on my mind. Anybody could see that. Is she okay?"

"Oh, yeah. She was here all day."

"Poor you."

"Oh, she's all right. I don't mind her. Sometimes she helps."

"I'm at the Plaza," Remy said, changing the subject. "We have a suite."

"Do you have your own room?" she asked.

"What do you think?" Remy replied.

"I think you don't," she said.

In fact, Wayne's suite had two bedrooms and a living room, but Remy didn't want to discuss it. "How's Alison doing?"

"She's freaking out. I've never seen anybody so freaked. She wants to fire me, but if I go, she'll have to take care of the kids. And that's not a possibility, now, is it?"

"Lynn, you have to leave there."

"I will. But what about you?"

"Wayne promised me a job at Soleil. I don't have

any doubt that he'll give it to me now. Maybe you could get a server job. Or you could work the front. I know he likes you."

"Maybe," Lynn said slowly.

"You're pretty enough."

"Look, Remy, you're in trouble. Alison's telling everyone you killed Maddy. I'll bet she told the police. I know she told Jo Ellen. Leah said Jo Ellen told her to stay away from you."

Remy's heart did that skiddy thing it had been doing all day. "But I didn't do it," she whispered. Other things, yes. That, no.

"Then you shouldn't stay there," Lynn said. "You shouldn't do everything Jo Ellen tells you to."

"Jo Ellen has always been good to me," Remy said firmly.

"I don't know about that, but I'm scared."

Remy tried to think of something reassuring to say. Since she was the one who looked like a killer because she'd slept with her boss, she thought she was the one who could use some comfort. None, however, was forthcoming. Lynn wasn't going to be any help. "I have to go," Remy said suddenly. One of the boys had spilled his drink. "I'll call you later."

Nineteen

There was no private women's room for high-ranking female officers at Midtown North, or at any other Manhattan precinct for that matter. Police stations were all built long before there were female sergeants, lieutenants, captains, and chiefs, before female officers went out on patrol. There were bathrooms for the public and for female uniformed officers, but ranking officers did not like to use them. In the days when April had worked very unpleasant crime scenes, chased bad guys, and routinely got her clothes ripped up and smelly, she'd kept a change of clothes in her locker and made do with the facilities. Now she dressed at home in Westchester and didn't worry much about how she looked at work.

Mike, however, had his own bathroom and everything he needed to keep himself in tip-top sartorial condition. She remembered that at the end of the day as she headed to the East Side in her own car. She would check in with Fish and then reapply her makeup in Mike's bathroom. She looked forward to the private moments. Dealing with Fish, on the other hand, would be a delicate balancing act.

Mike's precinct building was smaller than Mid-

town North's. April had worked on cases in the
building in the past but had made a point of staying
away from it ever since Mike had taken command
there. She knew the CO's office was on the first
floor around the corner from the front desk, but
she didn't go there right away. Instead she clipped
on her ID as she entered the building, then climbed
the stairs to the detective unit to face the music
with Fish. About twenty-five people were gathered
in the room already crowded with desks. She was
not surprised to find her husband, no longer in uniform, sitting in on the briefing. He gestured to her
as she came in.

"You all know Lieutenant Woo," he said, leaving
off his own name, then—seeing it on her ID—adding
it back on. "Sanchez. Glad you could make it."

She nodded, not letting on that no one had invited her.

Minnow raised his hand in greeting. "Lieutenant," he said.

She recognized most of the faces. "Hi."

"Ted, go on," Minnow said.

Ted Bell was a skinny guy with a freckled face
and a shock of red hair. He returned to referencing
the time charts—reviewing what they knew and had
mapped out the victim's last twenty-four hours. He
finished and turned to April.

"Lieutenant, do you have anything to add?"

She hadn't expected to address the whole team
and cleared her throat, wishing for a cup of tea.
She started with the time line. "Seven forty-five
a.m. Remy Banks and Wayne Wilson left to take
the kids to play school. Mrs. Wilson called her
friend Alison and Jo Ellen Anderson, her employ-

ment agency contact. Alison didn't take her call. Mrs. Wilson did speak with Jo Ellen, though. Have you contacted her yet?"

Minnow shook his head and made a note.

"Okay. Eight a.m. Derek Meke, her trainer, arrived. Derek said she'd been upset about something that had occurred at breakfast, and had fired Remy. According to him, they had a normal session and he left her at nine. He stopped for a Snapple on the corner at nine-oh-five. His partner at his gym places him in the studio on Fifty-sixth Street at nine twenty. I spoke with Remy Banks several times this morning. She said she got the boys dressed and fed them their breakfast. Mrs. Wilson came in as they were finishing. There was an argument. Then Remy accompanied their father as he drove the boys to play school, while Madeleine Wilson stayed home to have a gym session with her trainer."

April paused, looked over at Fish, who nodded for her to continue.

"After dropping the kids off, Remy visited Soleil with Mr. Wilson to see a new oven and walked home from there. When she returned to the house, she heard the shower running and went immediately into the gym, looking for Mrs. Wilson. No one answered, and after a few minutes she looked in and saw the body. The faucets are just inside the door. She didn't have to go in to turn them off. She did not go into the shower, just dialed 911. The call came in at nine forty-five. We think she didn't enter the shower itself because the floor outside it was dry. It was dry when I saw it, too. Apparently no one went in until CSI arrived. You let her off the hook—where is Remy now?"

"She's at the Plaza with the two little boys," Ted said.

April raised her eyebrows. "And Wayne?"

"He's with them."

"Hmmm. What about Derek?"

Ed Minnow smiled, acknowledging that April had gotten to the trainer first. "He gave us the same story he gave you. Mrs. Wilson fired Remy and told her to get out by noon. He seemed pretty shaken up by the death. He cried. We've been monitoring him. He went home, and hasn't moved since. What's your take on him?"

April had been standing outside the crush of people with their hips parked on the corners of desks. Minnow jabbed a big guy out of a chair and pushed it over for her. She sat down.

"They had a close relationship. He was her guru. Gave her vitamins and massages." She ducked her head, lifting her shoulder at the same time to indicate her suspicions about the nature of the massage. A few laughs echoed around the room. Who got massages? Not them. April went on.

"He has a little club of women he caters to in this way. One of his clients was Mrs. Wilson's best friend. Oh, by the way, everyone called her Maddy. Her friend, Alison Perkins, lives at the same address two blocks away from the Wilson house. I talked to her at length this afternoon."

"Alison . . . ?" Pens poised above pads.

"Perkins. Spelled the usual way," April said.

Ted added the name to the chart.

"You'll add your reports to the file," Minnow said officiously.

"Of course," April said. "Now, getting back to

Derek for a moment. He would be the obvious one, given the time frame. Mike, you pointed out earlier that if he and Maddy had a falling-out at the beginning of the session, he would have plenty of time to kill her and clean up before Remy got back. Remy had orders never to disturb Maddy until Derek was gone, and she didn't knock on the door until around nine forty-five."

"What about the murder weapon?" Minnow interjected. It was clear he didn't like this scenario.

"Nothing on that yet," April said.

"Exactly. He didn't go in with a plan to kill her," Minnow agreed.

"It was a rage thing. Maybe he lost it," Ted said.

"No way." The Fish seemed to want to eliminate Derek.

April changed the subject. "Who's on the bank records?"

A pretty Jamaican with a head of plump braids raised her hand. "Mrs. Wilson took out eight hundred dollars from one ATM yesterday at eleven fourteen, and eight hundred from another a block away at eleven forty-five," she said in a lilting island accent. "Looks like she averages about five thousand a week in cash."

"That's a lot of walk-around money. Someone should ask her friend about that," Minnow said.

"I'll do it," April said.

"Drugs?" Mike said.

"Maybe. The ME will have to determine that." April kept her suspicions to herself.

"What about sex? Was Derek her boyfriend?" Fish asked.

"Not her boyfriend, but they had something

going." Suddenly April noticed that the DA on the case was in the room. "Hi, Ben, how ya doin'?"

"Not too bad." He smiled.

He was the old guy, an associate who'd never graduated and moved on. Most DAs stayed for a few years, then moved into private practice as defense lawyers. Ben Hurd, however, had vowed to stay on as an assistant DA until he was kicked out. He was a legend, a short, nerdy, bald man, completely forgettable in the looks department, who knew every important case all the way back to New York City's dark ages. He was the historian of the office. Every new DA was treated to his long discourses on prosecuting the bad guys. When he came to the cops—which wasn't often because usually the cops came to him—he didn't say a lot. He just listened to the conversation with his head swaying from side to side, a little like a snake's. And as soon as the investigation got to a place where he was ready to go, he struck. He was a man with a reputation.

"I want to throw two more things into the pot here," April said. "First, Remy told the responding officers the shower was on when she found Maddy, and that she turned it off. This is important because of the effect the running water would have on the body and how it would affect the time frame. We need to take a careful look at that. And second, we need to know where Remy was during the hour and forty-five minutes after she left the house with Wayne and whether she could have come back forty-five minutes earlier." That was it. April didn't have anything more to add at the moment. They moved on to other reports.

Twenty

All afternoon and evening the news was filled with the Wilson murder. Photos of Maddy Wilson at Fashion Week, at Restaurant Week, at social events that were immortalized in *W* and *Town & Country,* and all the foodie magazines, were shown everywhere. She'd been a skier and a fashion plate, a popular figure. Speculation was rife about what had gone wrong in the Camelot where she'd lived. Intermixed with the story of the murder on Beekman Place were clips of Wayne Wilson, when he'd been a celebrity chef during the first half of his career. He was the former husband of ballerina Jenny Hope, and the owner of four French bistros—an important person in the food world.

It was the story of the day, bigger on national news than strife in any war-torn country and more important—on the TV scale of importance—than suicide bombings in the Middle East, hostage situations in Africa, stock market misconduct, and the prostitution of young girls in the Far East all put together. The brick house, the roped-off street, the police vehicles clogging up the entire area. The body bag being carried out to an ambulance, CSI with their bagged and boxed evidence in hand as they hurried out to their vehicles. Images the public had come to know as well as the parade of movie stars in revealing dresses on award nights. Crime and celebrity were the candy the country craved. And here it was, if not with nationally recognizable faces, at least with people who were well-known and prominent in their city. It was a feeding frenzy and there was a lot of material to disseminate.

Mike and April got another taste of it when they left the station for dinner at eight. They were besieged by a half-dozen reporters the second they stepped outside.

"Is Mr. Wilson a suspect?"

"Was he having an affair with the nanny?"

"Is it true she was mutilated?"

"Were her nipples cut off?"

The questions flew at them, but April didn't look to see who was asking. Mike shook his head.

"Nothing more for tonight," he said, taking her arm. Several reporters followed them down the street with the questions still blasting them like enemy fire. Then suddenly, they got to the end of the block, turned the corner, and became just two people walking to dinner. Mike gave April a quick hug and she clung to him, wishing they were already home in Westchester.

"What was that shower thing all about?" he asked.

Sighing, she let the embrace slip away. Overhead the sky was still NYPD blue, the deep, deep color that set off the stars in the early evening before the light was completely gone from the earth and night closed in on the city. "Starlight, star bright," she murmured. "First star I see tonight." She didn't make her wish out loud. The whole setup bothered her. Wayne and his affairs. Maddy and hers. The babysitter who claimed she wasn't a babysitter and was probably fired that morning by the murdered woman. What was it all about? What was under the surface? Who was trying to cast the blame on whom? She didn't have her usual clarity of vision. The fog all around her was lifeless. No whispers emerged from it to tantalize her. She didn't think the killer was Remy or Derek, but she didn't know exactly why. Wayne was a big question mark.

"What are you driving at?" Mike asked.

"I don't know. Wayne is a chronic womanizer. He kept his last wife about six years. Maybe Maddy's number was up, and he didn't want to pay alimony again." She shrugged. "It wouldn't be the first time something like this happened."

"Is that what her friend suggested?"

"No, no. Alison is treading carefully with Wayne. What's your take?"

"I didn't question him, *querida*. I'm staying out of it."

She laughed softly. "Sure you are."

Mike took her hand and squeezed it. Neither of them mentioned the honeymoon four days away. *"Te quiero, mi amor,"* he said after a moment.

"That's nice." April smiled. "But if you have an affair on me, *chico*, I'll cut your nuts off."

"Thanks for the warning," he laughed. They walked the rest of the way to the restaurant in silence.

Soleil was crowded at eight. With its wide windows, bright south-of-France decor, and famous competition—Lutèce—closed down for lack of business, it was the new hot spot in the neighborhood. On that crisp June evening there was no sign that the wife of the owner had been murdered that morning. The long bar was jammed with people waiting for tables. The food aromas were enticing and votive candles flickered everywhere.

The girl standing at the podium with the reservation book was wearing a slinky black dress that showed off everything she didn't have. No ass, no tits, hardly any flesh at all. What an advertisement for a restaurant, April thought. The girl's hair was short and black and curly all over. Mike smiled at her.

"The name is Sanchez. We have a reservation," he said.

"Oh, Captain Sanchez. I have a table in the corner for you. He's here. He wants to see you."

"He?" Mike raised his eyebrows.

"Mr. Wilson. He's cooking tonight," she added.

Mike looked surprised. "Does he do that often?"

"On Danny's day off, or when he wants to escape. No one ever looks for him in the kitchen." She picked up two menus and led the way to the only empty table in the place. It was in the back where the view of the action was good. "He said you'd want to be in a quiet spot."

"Thanks," Mike said.

"How about a glass of wine on the house?" the skinny girl said expectantly. "Anything you want."

April shook her head. "Hot tea," she said.

"I'll have a Diet Coke," Mike added.

The girl went away to pass along the order and April asked, "Did you know he was here?"

"Nope. I thought he was at the Plaza."

So much for surveillance. She spread her napkin across her lap, hiding the gun at her waist and her skepticism about Minnow's competence. "It will be interesting to find out what the specials are," she remarked.

Then she gazed at him with all her toughness gone because even though she might be unlucky in vacations, she was lucky in love. Mike studied the menu. He looked good in his silver tie and black shirt, his white, black, and gray nubby blend jacket and black trousers. This was the outfit he kept in his closet at work for occasions like this. Very West Coast. She couldn't help admiring what a fastidious dresser and extremely handsome man he was. At least she thought so. For a second she forgot about the Wilsons and glowed with love. Then the mood was broken.

"*Bonsoir*. I'm José." A good-looking Hispanic placed a basket of warm minibaguettes on the table with such reverence they could have been newborn babies. With another flourish he added a plate of pink butter curls decorated with whole red peppercorns. "I'll be your server tonight. Would you care for a glass of wine?" he asked.

"We've already placed our order," Mike told him. They weren't drinking wine on the house or otherwise.

"The chef recommends the shrimp wonton and tea-smoked quail with ginger-mango glaze, baby vegetables, and Singapore noodles for the lady and the taquitos and pork loin chipotle for the gentleman."

April arched a delicate eyebrow at the fusion menu that was not listed on the printed one, but Mike put his menu down and said, "Why not?"

José melted away to the kitchen.

Forty minutes later, after they'd eaten the tiny spicy taquitos, the shrimp wontons as light as any April had eaten, the exquisite boneless quail, and the tender smoky pork, she had to admit she was impressed, the nontraditional presentation notwithstanding. Mike insisted on paying the bill and they followed the server into the kitchen.

They found Wayne in a narrow stainless steel alley as hot as any God-fearing sinner's reckoning of Hell. He had a bottle of wine in one hand, and perspiration dripped down the side of his face as he watched an equally drenched grill chef juggle steaks, chops, and thick fish fillets on a spitting gas grill. Wayne was wearing a short-sleeved white chef's jacket, printed chef's baggies with an ocean of fish swimming on them, a baseball hat with the same fish on it, and clogs on his bare feet.

"How did you like the quail?" he asked, backing out of the cramped space to talk to them.

"Delicious," April said. "Marinated and tea-smoked first, then seared on the grill, right?"

He nodded. "You know your stuff."

"Tea-smoked is my favorite," she said. "Is that a regular special?"

"Of course not. I heard you were coming."

They followed him into a small office, where he closed the door and plugged a fat cigar in his mouth. Then, remembering his manners, he passed the box over and offered Mike one. "Ever had a really good cigar?"

Mike took the box, studied the illegal Havanas. He even lowered his head to sniff at them. "I quit a while back," he said as he closed the box and returned it without taking one.

"*Qué lástima,*" Wayne said with a strong American accent.

"You speak Spanish," Mike remarked.

"A little French, German, Italian. You have to be able to converse with the gorillas working the pits."

Nice, first he fed the Mexican policeman a Mexican-style dinner; then he called his people gorillas. Mike smiled without any warmth.

"So what can I do for you? I know you didn't come for the food."

"Oh, you never know. We might want to do a party here sometime," Mike said genially.

"Anytime. I'll cook myself. How's that for a promise?" Wayne lit the cigar and blew smoke into the air, remarkably poised for a guy who'd lost his wife that morning.

April wondered about his having kept the restaurant open. What kind of message was that? A stack of industry magazines covered the seat of the chair nearest to her. She placed it on the floor and took a seat. Mike remained standing.

"Thank you for cooking for us. A very subtle menu," April said. "We're here because we need your help to find the person who killed your wife," she said.

He nodded. "Of course. Anything I can do. I told you that this morning."

"One thing you told me is that you have girlfriends," April said slowly.

Irritation ticked over his face. "Oh, don't make

too much of that. Maddy and I had an open marriage. It didn't affect our feelings for each other." He brushed the infidelity off.

"Somebody took exception," April remarked.

"Well, don't look at me. I wasn't the last one with her." He sounded like a little boy.

"What do you mean?" Mike joined the conversation.

"Let's just say she had an arrangement with her trainer. I'm sure you know that by now."

"Did it bother you?" he asked.

"Why should it?" Wayne said impatiently. "I paid the bills, didn't I?"

April's sinuses began to object to the cigar smoke. She sniffed to hold back a sneeze. "Let's go over the events of the morning one more time."

He blew more smoke and picked up a wineglass that was sitting on his desk, half filled with a red. "It's all very clear in my mind. Maddy slept late. I always get up early to be with the boys."

"How early?" Mike interjected as Wayne sipped from his glass, swirled the wine in his mouth, then swallowed.

"Five thirty."

"Is that the time they get up?"

"No. I pick up my e-mails, answer my mail. We have breakfast at seven," he said easily.

"Who cooks, you?"

"Remy does the cooking there."

"What did she make this morning?"

"She wanted to give the boys a treat." He smiled. "She's not a bad little cook. She made fresh sausages, crepes, raspberry jam. Hot chocolate."

"Very nice. The three of you ate it—"

"No, four of us."

"Your wife joined you, then."

"Well, she did when we were finished. She came in at seven forty and had a little temper fit because the baby got jam on his napkin. I told her it wasn't a big deal, and she erupted. She just got so mad. I'm sorry about it now."

"Then what happened?"

"Oh, Remy got the boys cleaned up and we took them to school."

"Your wife didn't come with you?"

"You know she didn't. If she'd come with us, she'd still be alive."

"What about her relationship with Remy?"

"She was jealous. Maddy didn't cook, so she felt having a home chef was unnecessary. But food is an important part of my life. I want to teach the boys the pleasure of eating. Meals at home in the kitchen. The family together." He lifted the palms of his hands to emphasize the point. The gesture said it all.

"What time did you drop the boys off?"

"A few minutes before eight."

"Then what did you do?"

"We went to the restaurant. It was a delivery day. I don't miss that."

"Who delivers on Mondays?"

"Dairy, produce, meat. I look at the stuff to make sure it's top-of-the-line. I count the boxes. It takes hours, but anybody who doesn't do it gets ripped off. When I get an alcohol delivery, believe me, I count every bottle."

"Great. That helps a lot. We'll need your lists—who delivered, what you got," Mike said.

"To show that I was here when she died."

Mike nodded. "We also need the names of your girlfriends, and all the people who knew the code to the garage door. And everybody who saw Remy at the restaurant, and what time she left."

"Yeah, sure. Anything else?"

"I'd like to talk to your executive chef before we go," Mike said. He was the one who gave Wayne his alibi.

Twenty-one

At nine o'clock Alison's two girls were in bed. Lynn was behind the closed door of her room doing whatever nannies did when their charges didn't need them, and Andrew wasn't home yet. She had no idea where he was. When she'd called him on his cell two hours ago, he'd told her he was on the way and promised to take her out, so Alison had dressed for dinner. Floyd and Roxie were with her in the family room, where the big TV was. The three of them were sitting on the sofa. She'd taken her expensive jacket off, and Roxie was using it for a pillow, but Alison didn't mind. She was too busy watching Nancy Grace speculate about the identity of Maddy's killer on *Larry King Live* to worry about Roxie sleeping on her jacket. Alison talked back to the TV as she patted the dogs, furious because her husband was late, Derek wouldn't return her calls, and Larry King had yet to call her. She picked up the phone to give Derek one last chance to show some caring, and this time he answered.

"What do you want, Alison?" His voice was weary and sad.

"I'm all alone here, Derek. This is the worst day

of my life. Why didn't you call me?" she demanded.

"This is the worst day of my life, too," he replied.

"Why? She wasn't *your* best friend. *I'm* your best friend."

"Alison, I can't go into this with you tonight. I lost a friend, too, okay? Let's leave it at that."

"Oh, my God, it's true. You *were* fucking her!" she erupted.

There was a long pause. "Please don't hurt me with accusations like that now," he said finally.

"Derek. You told me I was the only one," she cried.

He didn't say anything.

"You told me I was the only one! Answer me!"

"I heard you. It doesn't matter anymore."

"What do you mean it doesn't matter? I told the police you couldn't even put out poison or mousetraps in your studio. You couldn't kill a cockroach. I told them that's the kind of guy you are. When they asked where I got the coke, I told them you don't deal drugs, okay? I stood up for you, so it matters." Then, "Are you a supplier, or what? I'm really upset."

"Oh, give it a rest, Alison," he groaned.

"I thought it was for me, just for me." Her voice rose. "For Christ's sake, tell me the truth. Are you a drug dealer, a murderer?"

He made a choking sound. "Well, thanks, Alison. You're a brick. All your blabbing to the police just ruined my life for nothing. You got me in trouble."

"Well, it *looks* like you're a big, fat, lying jerk. You never loved me, did you?" As soon as the words were out of Alison's mouth, she wanted to bite her tongue or rip her face off. That was self-destructive. She knew it was crazy to say it. He was a trainer, a two-timing bodybuilder.

"Of course I love you. You're a very important person to me," he said slowly. "And I would never hurt a precious child of God. Why would I hurt Maddy?" he whined.

"Well, you fucked my best friend, and now she's dead. I hate you." She turned her head and caught her reflection in a decorative mirror across the room. Despite everything she'd gone through that day, she still looked good enough for TV. "Why didn't Larry King call me?" she whimpered.

"I can't talk to you anymore," Derek said.

"Why not?"

"I'm disgusted. You've been drinking. You're all strung out. You're mixing, and you know what that does to you. You've put me at risk."

"Don't be angry. I'm not drinking to excess," Alison protested. "You know I don't do anything to excess." She took a sip of wine.

"Let's not argue about it," he said softly.

"I'm not arguing. Not to excess! I had a glass or two. Nothing else. She was my best friend, and you were fucking her!" Alison started screaming again. "Doesn't anybody care about what's happening to me?"

"Of course, everybody cares about you," Derek said softly.

"Then come over. I need a massage. I need some relief from all this pain."

"You know I can't come over."

"My husband isn't here. Please!"

"No, Alison. I'm not coming over. I don't want to see you."

"Don't say that. I don't do too much," she whimpered, certain that she was totally sober.

"You're out of control. Get a grip."

"But I'm so unhappy. Andrew never comes home. He's such a prick. And you won't take care of me like you promised. Today was supposed to be my day, Derek," she said accusingly.

"I'm very sorry, Alison, and very sad. Maddy was a gentle soul. Heaven is lucky to have her."

"That does it." Alison bolted up from the sofa. "I'm going to kill you. I'm going to have you killed."

"Oh, Jesus." The phone clicked.

"Wait a minute. Derek, don't go. There's a murderer in the neighborhood," Alison yelled, but he had already hung up.

"Shit." She threw the phone on the floor. It jumped off the area rug and skittered across the travertine, bouncing twice before it hit the wall.

On TV Nancy Grace was still talking. The woman always had a lot to say. Alison bent to retrieve the phone and dialed Derek. She hung up before it could ring, then hit redial. She couldn't make up her mind what to say. Again she hung up before it started ringing. She hit redial a second time and waited impatiently for seven rings until his voice mail came on, then hung up.

"I don't fucking believe this." Infuriated at the insult, she dialed her husband on his cell, but he didn't pick up, either.

Just then Lynn came into the room with Leah tagging along behind her. Alison narrowed her eyes at them. Lynn was another one of those sweet-looking blondes. With her sweatshirt and jeans, she almost looked like a clone of Remy, the girl who might have murdered Alison's best friend. The resemblance used to amuse the two mothers—now it was horrifying.

"What do you want?" Alison demanded.

"Leah and I were just going to get a couple of sodas—we're all out. Do you want something?"

"No, I don't want anything. And I don't want you to leave the house," she said angrily.

"Why not?"

"Andrew is on his way. We're going out for dinner."

"We'll only be a minute," Lynn said pleasantly.

"What if Andrew comes while you're gone?"

"It's just around the corner."

"You never come back when you say you're going to. You'll be an hour, and Andrew will be sitting here twiddling his thumbs." Alison did not want her to go. Whenever she sent the girl on one tiny errand, Lynn wouldn't be back three hours later, and half the time she'd return with that girl Leah in tow. She frowned at Leah, another blue-jeaned creature who worked in the neighborhood.

"What's she doing here at this hour?"

"She was just helping me put the kids to bed. Look, we'll walk the dogs for you, okay?" Lynn offered.

"Wait a minute. I want to talk." Alison wobbled to the sofa and fell on it, disturbing the poodle.

"Are you okay? How about some coffee?" Lynn asked.

"I don't want any coffee. I want to know what

Remy told you about Maddy. Was she sleeping with Derek?"

"I don't know," Lynn said uneasily.

"What about you? Did she tell you?" Alison leveled her gaze on her new target.

"Me?" Leah said.

"You're always together. Didn't she say *anything*? Is Remy fucking Wayne? Come on, you know you know."

The two girls looked at each other, then slowly shook their heads. "She doesn't talk," Lynn said.

"Well, what do you know about her?" Alison poured herself some more wine.

"Just what you do—her father's an alcoholic, her mother is some kind of hippie artist."

Alison patted the sofa. "Come on, girls. Sit down. What else?"

"She wants to be Wayne's executive chef," Lynn said, sitting on the far edge. Leah curled up on the floor. Roxie jumped off the sofa and sat on her lap.

Alison made a face. "I'm sure she killed her. I'm absolutely sure of it."

Neither girl said anything. There was an awkward moment. Then the phone rang. Alison reached over to answer it. It was a reporter asking for an interview.

"Well, I don't really know anything," she said, and began to elaborate.

The two girls got up and went into the kitchen.

Twenty-two

April and Mike lived in the brick Tudor house that had once belonged to April's rabbi in the Department, Lieutenant Alfredo Bernardino. For years after she'd left the Fifth Precinct, where Bernardino had promoted and trained her, she rarely gave him a thought. Maybe a fleeting reminder of those long-ago days came to her from time to time, but nothing lasting. Now her history was permanently tied to his. Bernardino had been there at her inception as a detective, and ten years later she was there when he was murdered. Now she owned his house, and he was always in her thoughts.

The relationship had been a lucky one at the beginning. When April decided to join the Department, she'd disappointed everybody who had high hopes for her. She became a beat cop, something no Chinese wanted for their precious children. She'd been one of two Chinese officers in the precinct, the only woman. A female with no respect from anyone, she'd walked the streets of Chinatown helping people who couldn't negotiate the system. She'd been a translator, a social worker with a gun. But things changed after an unheard-of occurrence in an Asian community: a little girl

from Mott Street was kidnapped and murdered.
April had been the searcher who found the child's
body in some garbage behind the building where
she'd lived with her family. April had also been the
only person to whom the girl's parents and the
other residents in the building would talk. Impressed, Bernardino rewarded her when an opening
came up in his unit. He said it was stupid not to
have Chinese-speaking detectives in Chinatown.

Stoopid had been one of his words. He used it
so often it almost lost its meaning. But one thing
was certain; he'd died a stupid death. His wife hit
the lottery jackpot in the last weeks of her life and
died of cancer a multimillionaire. That fatal stroke
of good luck also ended Bernie's life. He retired,
April organized his going-away party, and an evil
person broke his neck as he was walking back to
his car after the festivities were over.

April thought about that stupid end to his life
every day. Good luck, prosperity, long life, were
the things every Chinese prayed for. But nobody
ever thought there was danger in answered prayers.
The bad luck of losing Bernie, however, led to the
good luck of April's getting his house. She thought
about those circumstances every day, too. Bernie's
daughter Kathy had sold her and Mike the three-
bedroom house with study for practically nothing
because she never wanted to move back there. She
was an FBI agent in Seattle. April called her from
time to time. Bernie was the closest thing she ever
had to a mentor—before she met Mike anyway.
He'd been closer to her than her own dad. Now
that he was gone forever instead of just to Florida

as everyone had expected, she found that she missed him.

The drive home from Soleil was uneventful. April left her car on the East Side and drove with Mike in his new Buick. By eleven o'clock the rush to get home was over, and cars were humming along on the highways. April was happy to let her husband drive. It meant she finally had a moment to call Sergeant Gelo on her cell to find out what was going on at Midtown North. Gelo was working a second tour.

"It's quiet, boss," Eloise told her. "I spoke with the senator earlier. He called to thank you for helping his son. He's putting you on his Christmas card list."

"That's nice." April said, figuring there had to be more to it than that. "What else?"

"He doesn't want to pursue any arrests."

"Unfortunately, the chief has other ideas. When are you going out?" April asked.

"Soon."

"Who's going with you?" she asked.

"Charlie," Eloise said.

"He doesn't do undercover," April replied quickly.

"He went out with me earlier. I thought we'd try him out," Gelo said, her voice careful.

"Why?"

"We're shorthanded, and he wants to go."

"Why?" April said again.

"I guess he likes the idea of naked girls."

"Well, this is your call. I guess you can take care of him."

"Yes, boss. I can take care of him," Eloise laughed.

Hagedorn was a techie, a skim-milk kind of person whose white skin looked like it had never been touched by the sun. For years, whenever April needed deep background checks, she'd had to beg him for help. Now he was part of her team and would do anything for her. But he was backward. Twelve-year-olds not yet in middle school were getting sex, but not Hagedorn. She had a soft spot for the poor schlub and hoped Eloise knew what she was doing. "Are you using Petey?"

"Yeah."

April told Gelo to put someone who looked like a kid on it. Petey Steele was twenty-eight, but he had a baby face. "Good. I'll talk to you in the morning, see how things went," April said, then punched off her cell.

Peret had been found alone on the sidewalk. Before they could arrest anybody or shut a club down, they had to prove where he'd been, and from whom he'd gotten what made him sick. If the senator didn't want his son to be involved, they had to catch somebody in the act of dealing drugs, or selling alcohol to minors, without him. She didn't know if her second whip could handle a sting and had to remind herself that all of her bosses once had exactly the same concerns about her. Nervous, she leaned her head against the window and felt the cold pane against her cheek.

"You okay, *querida*?" Mike murmured.

"Oh yeah, fine. The senator doesn't want to pursue it," she replied.

"You'd expect that. What did Gelo say?"

"She's taking Petey and Hagedorn. They've got a plan."

"What a fun bunch." Then he added, "Don't worry. They'll be fine."

"I hope so," she said, then paused before continuing. "What's your take on Wayne?"

"You mean, do I like him, or did he do it?"

"I know you like him," she said.

Mike smiled. "*Querida,* he may not have been a very attentive husband, and you may not like the way he's acting right now, but he doesn't strike me as a killer. And Danny said he was there all morning."

Danny was the sous-chef. April snorted. "Did you see that guy?"

"He had some interesting tattoos. Dirty hair," Mike said. "Seemed nice enough."

"He was missing a finger," April said.

"Only one. He told us Wayne was there for the deliveries. Easy enough to check that out."

"He and Remy could have run home in between," April mused.

"Between nine-oh-five and nine forty-five, when Remy called 911, maybe."

"We should listen to that tape, too, hear how she sounded. I don't know. All that stabbing—it doesn't play. If there were two of them, why so many blows?" She shook her head and fell silent.

"How are we doing, *querida*?" Mike asked after a long pause.

"Personally? We're doing great," she murmured. In fact, she was very worried about her honeymoon.

Monday was over. Now there were only three days to go. She didn't know why she'd gotten so devoted to that cruise. They'd canceled trips before.

But this time, even though she had no real idea what a cruise would be like, she had her heart set on it. She'd been in a rowboat a few times. She'd been on the Staten Island Ferry. Mike had gone deep-sea fishing on the West Coast. That was pretty much it in the boat department for both of them. Mike had some reservations about being on a moving vehicle he couldn't get off. April was the one who'd wanted to go. All the pictures, the commercials on TV, made it seem a hotel on the move, headed from one beach to another.

They were flying to Puerto Rico Friday morning, then sailing for the Caribbean from there. She had her clothes all lined up. The worst thing was they'd decided not to spend the extra money for travel insurance. She'd wanted to save five hundred dollars. Now she felt badly about that choice. Her thoughts returned to Maddy, Wayne, Derek, Remy, and Alison. And the two little boys, one of whom seemed to be named for a cow. She wondered what had happened that morning in the Wilson household and let her eyes close, hoping that some answers would come to her.

It seemed only seconds later when the car made a sharp left turn, and she twitched awake as Mike drove into their driveway. She stared at the house for a second and thought she was hallucinating. All the lights were on.

"Mike," she cried, alarmed because they were always careful to turn the lights off when they left in the morning.

"You tell me, *querida*," he said in that voice that meant he thought her parents were involved.

"Oh, no, it can't be," she said. Her parents had no way to get there.

The house was perfect in every way except one. The garage was not attached to the house. In the rain it was a small annoyance. They had to park the car behind the house, close the garage door, then walk a few short steps to the back door. Or they could walk around to the front and go through a gate. There were a few obstacles to getting into their house. Tonight there was no sign of any vehicle, but as Mike killed the engine and they emerged from the car, the sound of a barking dog tipped them off. The dog sounded like Dim Sum, the pricey poodle that was April's surrogate in the Woo family.

"Jesus," Mike muttered.

April held up her hands in defense as they came out of the garage. "I don't know anything about this. I didn't have anything to do with it. I swear."

He gave her a look. *How did they get here? How did they get in?*

"I have no idea. Really." She touched his arm, annoyed that neither of them had changed the lightbulb that was burned out at the back door. "I hope everything's all right," she said anxiously.

"Stay behind me."

He took the lead and they circled the house cautiously. It was a little scary at midnight to think that someone, even a loved relative, was in the house and not know the reason why.

Wa wa wa wa wa. The dog had its own signature bark.

"That's definitely Dim," April said.

The toy poodle was making a racket. They went through the front gate, but no one responded to the barking dog or came to the door to greet them. If April and Mike had been ordinary people, they might have put the key in the lock and gone in without any real concern about what they might find in there. But April and Mike had too much experience with random acts of violence to be relaxed in such a situation. Once before, two killers had been waiting for April in her parents' house when she went home to visit them. Her father, who was at least sixty, had killed one of the intruders with his meat cleaver. Now she had a sick feeling in the dark, remembering that bloody day.

Then she saw it all. The picture window in the front room framed Dim Sum, sitting up on the back of the sofa, barking her poodle head off. The TV was on, set to Skinny Dragon's favorite channel, where a surgery was in progress. Skinny was paying no attention to the dog. Her head was bent over in concentration, her fingers moving needles and yarn.

"They're here," Mike said, as if the enemy had landed. He opened the door.

Dim jumped off the back of the sofa in a great flying leap and ran to the front door. April caught her up and hugged her. Skinny Dragon, however, was so busy knitting and watching a two-headed baby being born that she didn't register that her daughter and son-in-law had returned. Beside her, Ja Fa Woo, April's father, had made himself comfortable. He had his shoes off and had imbibed the last of Mike's only bottle of brandy. The empty bottle was beside him, and he was snoring loudly, a hot-blooded killer out cold.

"Ma, what are you doing here?" April cried.

"Ayeeiiiie," Skinny shrieked with delight, and held up her knitting, which looked like it was going to be a tiny yellow sweater. "Babysitting. Making crose for baby. *Hao?*" [Good?] she demanded.

Not good at all, Ma, April thought, since she wasn't even pregnant.

Twenty-three

At six thirty, Andrew threw back the quilt, exposing Alison to the cold morning air. "Hey," she mumbled. She felt like a land mine had gone off in her head.

She'd taken too much coke the day before. First because she was upset about Maddy—and Derek—and then because she wanted to delay the inevitable crash as long as possible. By early evening she hadn't been able to avoid it any longer. She'd started drinking and taking painkillers. She'd finally slept, but now the war was on in her body again. And pain always made her focus on everybody else's faults. What she saw at the moment was her naked husband yawning widely and scratching his hairy belly. It never failed to provoke her.

Unlike her, a perfectionist, Andrew didn't care that he was a mess and getting fatter every day. The rolls started in his jowls and moved down to his neck. His shoulders were padded and soft, and his belly was so big he said he couldn't see his dick anymore. Although he was very critical of her, he didn't think his own weight was a problem. In fact, he thought it was funny. His belly shifted as he planted his feet on the floor and stood up.

Alison turned away and felt for the comfort of her dogs, but they weren't there. No wonder she was cold. Plus Andrew had opened the window. Even though it was June, it was still cold at night. He'd turned off the furnace for the summer, and it was just freezing in the room. She reached for the quilt. Her arm was so heavy she could hardly lift it. She struggled to remember what happened last night. In the haze of an alcohol and Vicodin hangover everything was fuzzy. Then she remembered the important things. Maddy was dead, and Derek had been her lover. She groaned.

"You're drinking again. I hate that," Andrew said coldly.

"No, it's Maddy. I'm so sad for Maddy." She started crying.

"Get up. We have to talk," Andrew said sharply.

Yes, they did, Alison thought, but not right now. Painfully, she pulled herself to a sitting position. "Can't we do it later?"

"No, we can't. Why didn't you wait up for me last night?"

Now she remembered. "I did, but you never came."

"Alison, you were out cold by nine thirty. Sacked out on the fucking sofa. I don't like you drinking like that. It's terrible for the girls." His voice rose angrily.

"It was not nine thirty. I was watching the eleven o'clock news when my eyes closed. I couldn't stay up any longer. It was a terrible day. And you left me alone," she said in a little-girl voice. Alison was sure he hadn't come home at nine thirty. She'd been talking with Lynn and Leah then. He was trying to confuse her, the way he always did to get the upper hand.

"I had to find Wayne a criminal lawyer." Still naked, Andrew moved to a chair by the bed so he could face her.

"Why?" Alison was confused.

"He's acting like a complete idiot. He was cooking for the detectives last night at Soleil. I told him to close the restaurants for a few days, but all he could think of was the food spoiling. It doesn't spoil in a day, does it?"

"He didn't close the restaurants?" Alison was shocked. Then she said, "If Soleil was open, why didn't we go?"

"Don't you ever listen? I told you Wayne was playing chef to the cops. His wife gets herself murdered, and food is all he can ever think about."

Look who's talking, Alison would have said if she hadn't felt so rotten.

Andrew ruffled his bushy hair. "The fool didn't even think of calling me until after they were gone—can you believe that?"

Alison tried to absorb what he was saying. Why would Wayne keep the restaurant open after Maddy was killed? Why would he cook for the cops? She shook her head. "I feel so sick, Andrew. I think I have the flu."

He made a disgusted face. "You do not have the flu. You have a hangover."

She didn't answer. It didn't matter what she said to him. He never believed her anyway. "Why does Wayne need a lawyer?"

"In a murder case no one should talk to the police without a lawyer present. Haven't I told you that before?"

No, he'd never told her that before. No one they knew had ever been murdered. Without a dog, she had to resort to hugging a pillow. She happened to have talked with a policewoman for hours, and he knew that. "What's the big deal?" she asked meekly.

"You can make incriminating statements. You can hurt yourself or other people." He said this angrily, as if he were the one she could hurt.

She couldn't remember what she'd told the Chinese detective, but she didn't think she'd said anything that could hurt anybody. Just that one tiny thing about the coke. And she never actually said anything about it. "I didn't talk to all the police, just one person. And she was very nice," she said slowly, referring to April Woo, the woman whose card she had put in her purse to call if she had any other thoughts. She had a lot of thoughts, and she didn't want to be alone with them.

"What are you, a half-wit?" Andrew said harshly.

Alison didn't grimace at this assessment of her. She'd heard him say it all before. She sighed because it was so difficult to talk to a person who'd been to law school and always thought he was right.

"What do you want me to do?" she asked, trying to focus and be good so he wouldn't be angry with her.

"I want you to stop drinking, okay?" he said more gently.

"Okay," she promised. That was not a problem. She could do without alcohol whenever she wanted to.

"And I want Lynn out of the house today." He ticked number two off his list.

"What?!" This order caused Alison to bolt right out of bed, even though she was shaking all over. She stood in front of him, swaying with a head rush.

"You heard me. I want you to fire her this morning."

"But why, Andrew? I thought you liked her." Alison was completely stunned. She almost forgot she was talking to a naked man. She too busy holding on to the bed.

"You're always telling me she's lazy. You had reservations about her capabilities all along. And you told me you think her friend is a murderer," Andrew said. "That's good enough for me."

"But what does that have to do with it?" she said numbly. She had no memory of saying those things.

"I don't want our household dragged through the press. I don't want to be involved. This is an order, Al. I mean it. Get her out of here."

"I can't fire her," Alison whined, finally letting herself collapse back on the bed.

Andrew got up and turned his back on her. "I have to get going, and you have to do it."

"But I *can't,* Andrew. The girls like her." She couldn't think of anything else to say. She was sick. She couldn't take the girls to play school. Damn! She had the flu, and he was walking away from her. She didn't like his naked back any more than his burgeoning belly. Shit! He went into the bathroom and closed the door.

Alison lay back against the pillows. Her head ached terribly. She'd forgotten all the times she'd said she wanted to get rid of Lynn. And yesterday she particularly hadn't wanted someone who looked like a killer taking care of her children. But that was yesterday. Since talking with Lynn and Leah last night, she didn't really feel that way anymore. She thought Lynn was a caring person, always there when she was needed. But Andrew meant what he said. Sometimes she could get around him, but not about something like this. She wanted him to be happy. She wanted to do the right thing. She closed her eyes.

She didn't know how much time passed before he came out of his dressing room, wearing a dark suit and tie, ready for the office. She opened her eyes and he still looked angry. "I mean it about Lynn. Do you want me to take care of it?" he said, raising the subject again.

"No, no. I'll do it." Alison thought she could be nice about it. Andrew could never be nice about anything.

"And nothing to drink today, okay?"

"It's no problem, honey." She had no doubt she could do without alcohol. Piece of cake. She would pull herself together, and never do coke again. She hated the stuff and needed some time off of it anyway. She'd call Derek. He'd give her his great vitamin drink that helped her recover, and she'd get well fast. Just a few minutes in bed, and then she'd get going. She made her plan and closed her eyes.

Andrew left without saying anything else to her. At seven o'clock the girls tumbled into her bed and woke her up. "Orange juice, Mommy," Jill said. Jill was the younger one. She had pretty dark curls and big blue eyes. She was going to be a knockout.

"Hi, babies," Alison said through an aching head.

"Where's Daddy?"

"He went to the office."

"Where's Lynn?"

"Isn't she in her room?" Alison stretched, patting for the dogs. Dogs still weren't there. She wondered why they hadn't come into the room when Andrew opened the door.

"Uh-uh," Jill said.

"She must be out with the dogs. Can you make our breakfast?" Jessica asked.

"Of course, I can," Alison replied pleasantly. *But do I want to?* she asked herself. "Oh, shit," she muttered, and hauled herself into a sitting position where she could see her children better. Jill was jumping on the bed. Up and down, up and down. Jumping was a new thing for her. It made Alison want to scream. She extricated herself from the sheets and went to the bathroom.

Water from Andrew's shower was splashed everywhere. She didn't know how anyone could make such a mess. She opened her makeup drawer and found her container of Vicodin tucked away with the lipsticks and colored pencils. She took two and stuffed the little zip bag in the back. Then she staggered downstairs to make the girls their scrambled eggs. While they were eating, she called Derek for the vitamin drink she needed. It was only seven ten, and he didn't pick up. She called Jo Ellen Anderson at the employment agency, and left a message to call her right away about finding a new girl. Lynn had to go. She had several cups of coffee and started feeling a little better.

Twenty-four

Remy felt like a thief as she slipped out of the
Fifty-ninth Street entrance of the Plaza Hotel
at six thirty a.m. She didn't know whether Wayne
was up or not and didn't care. The boys were still
sleeping, and after last night she just had to get out
of there. She took no special notice of the jogger
that paused in front of the movie theater across the
street. She hurried down to the corner, grabbed a
taxi on Fifth, and didn't talk to the driver as he
cruised downtown, then turned east on Fifty-second
Street. Lynn was waiting for her on the corner of
First Avenue as she'd promised, and had the two
dogs with her.

"What's the matter? What happened?" she
asked as Remy paid and got out of the cab.

As usual, they were dressed alike, in sweatshirts
and jeans. They carried the same shoulder bags and
wore similar Nikes. Floyd, the standard poodle,
jumped up and Remy patted him. Roxie jumped as
high as she could, and Remy leaned over to pat
her, too. "I had a terrible night," she said after
a moment.

"Did you have to sleep with him?" Lynn said.
Remy knew that Lynn had once been fired from a

job after a wife found out about her husband's advances to her. Lynn was particularly sensitive to the hazards of being a live-in.

Remy made a face. It wasn't that. She'd slept with Wayne Wilson many times before. She'd given him blow jobs, whatever he wanted, and didn't think it was a big deal. She didn't dwell on it too much.

"Well, did you?" Lynn couldn't stop asking that question.

Remy brushed it away. "Why did you bring the dogs? Now we can't go in anywhere. I need something to eat."

"Andrew locked them up last night, and they were crying. They wanted to go out, and I needed the excuse. What was yours?"

"Oh, I just left. All right, I'll have a bagel. Wait for me."

The deli on First Avenue had a bench out front. At the moment no one was on it, so Lynn sat down while Remy went in for coffee and bagels. She came out in less than five minutes with two paper bags, and handed one over.

"Latte and cinnamon raisin bagel for you, pumpernickel for me," Remy said. She sat down and pulled out her coffee first. She took a sip and grimaced. "Too hot. Okay, how are things with you?"

"Same old, same old. Alison got really crocked last night. She thinks I don't know what she gets up to—the three Ds. Derek wouldn't come over last night, and Andrew didn't show, either. So she was left with drugs and drink. I feel sorry for her."

"Yeah, well. Feel sorry for yourself. Things are very weird, Lynnie."

Lynn chewed on her bagel. "I still feel sorry for her. I can always do something else, get a new job. She's stuck there."

"You better start planning now. You're getting canned today."

"What? How do you know?"

"I heard Wayne talking to Andrew last night."

"Jesus, Remy. What did he say?"

"Well, I couldn't hear everything because I was in the other room, but I think Andrew was chewing him out for having me stay there." Remy tossed her hair back and started eating.

"Yeah, well, what did you expect? I wouldn't stay there with them for anything in the world, and I don't even want to ask how it is." She raised her eyebrows, asking nonetheless.

"He said Alison had to get rid of you because of the publicity."

"What publicity? Who cares about Alison?" Lynn laughed uneasily. "Why would Wayne tell Andrew to fire me? It's ridiculous."

"Andrew doesn't want any publicity. He wants us both out of the way, some antinanny thing. He doesn't understand that I'm in a special situation, that I'm not a nanny," Remy said.

"Yes, you are." Lynn had one dog on her lap and one at her feet. She occupied herself with them for a moment, then got serious. "Thanks for the warning, Rem, but I'm not the one in trouble. You are, too. You were there yesterday, and you're still there with him. I don't know what you're thinking, but other people are not seeing this as a good thing. Alison thinks you're in on it for sure. You need to get a lawyer, and you need to move out now."

"I didn't do anything wrong."

Lynn made a disparaging noise. "You're not listening! You're staying with him and his two children. You should think about that."

Remy tossed her hair again, then frowned. The jogger who'd been in front of the Plaza was now across the street by the newsstand. She hadn't studied him carefully, but she was sure it was the same guy. "See that guy over there?"

Lynn turned to look where she pointed.

"He followed me."

"Good Lord, Remy, are you sure?"

Remy nodded. "I saw him at the Plaza a little while ago. Wayne says he's being followed, too. The police came to his restaurant last night and talked to the chef, the sous-chef, everybody. He was on the phone with his friends all night."

Lynn stared at the jogger, who was busy reading the newspaper he'd just purchased. "They can tap the phones, you know," she murmured.

Remy took Lynn's hand off the poodle's collar and squeezed it. "Listen to me. It was horrible what happened to Maddy, but I was with Wayne in his restaurant. He was accepting deliveries, counting the boxes, when it happened. A lot of people saw us there. No one can pin anything on us, and I guarantee that he won't let anything happen to me. I can guarantee it."

Lynn's face was full of doubt. "You're *sleeping* with him, Rem, and you found her. It doesn't look good," she muttered, staring at the cop.

Remy had never admitted that. Now she shrugged. "So what? Derek was sleeping with *her*."

Lynn shook her head at this answer. "Did you stay in his room last night? The maids will know."

Remy shook her head no, and that was the truth. She never talked about this, but Wayne had his little habits, and losing his wife hadn't changed any of them. He liked to have someone hold his penis at night, massage and have sex with him—sometimes quite athletic sex—but he was never romantic in any way. Afterward, he always wanted to be alone so he could talk on the phone, or be on the Internet all night. Sometimes late at night, or very early in the morning, they used to cook little meals for each other and drink more wine, but that was it. If she'd held out any hope for his being more tender now that Maddy was out of the picture, she would have been seriously disappointed. She played with her hair, acting cooler than she felt about the whole thing.

"Are you really okay?" Lynn said as if she didn't buy the act.

"Everybody asks me if I'm okay. How can I be okay? I found a corpse." She was watching the jogger across the street, and didn't feel good about it. "And a cop is following me." She paused. "And I really liked him." She picked up her bagel and stared at it.

"Wayne?" Lynn pursed her lips. "Don't you like him anymore?"

"Let's just say the way he was talking last night opened my eyes. He doesn't care about anybody but Wayne, that's for sure. We're both kind of screwed," she said sadly.

"What do you mean?" Lynn said cautiously.

"Oh, I'm not getting any restaurant job now, and you better find someplace else to live."

The poodle tugged on its leash and Lynn looked anxiously at her watch. "I have to go back now."

"Why?" Remy finally started eating her bagel.

"Because they'll be worried," Lynn said seriously.

"They're going to fire you, idiot," Remy said angrily.

Lynn shook her head. "You don't understand. The girls love me, and Alison has already gone through too many people. She talks about firing me all the time. It's a form of entertainment for her. But she won't ever fire me."

Remy shrugged. "All right, go back, then, but don't blame me if something happens. She lifted her hand and waved at the jogger. He turned away, pretending not to see her.

Twenty-five

Leah was waiting on the street in front of the Perkins house when Lynn headed back from First Avenue. Sitting on the curb between parked cars, she was wearing slippers and a fringed shawl. Lynn tilted her head, uneasy at seeing her there looking like some weird hippie without a home. The dogs raced toward her, but Lynn held back on their leashes. "What's going on? What are you doing here?" she said anxiously when she got close enough to speak.

"I couldn't sleep. I thought I'd come over, but you weren't there," Leah accused.

Lynn tilted her head. "Get up. Don't you know the dogs do their business down there?"

"Where were you?" Leah stood up and brushed off her jeans.

"Walking the dogs. Roxie had to go out." Lynn glanced toward the kitchen door. "You didn't go in there, did you?"

Leah chewed on her bottom lip. "She really freaked out when she saw me. She started yelling at me."

"Well, I'm not surprised. First of all, you can't just walk into someone else's house totally unannounced. Also, have you taken a look at yourself this morning?" Lynn shook her head. "What's with the bracelets?"

Leah pulled her sweatshirt down over her wrist to hide them.

"Let me see them."

Leah backed away. "Don't crowd me. I didn't do anything. I was just looking for you."

"You're not my shadow. You're not supposed to go in there when I'm not there. That's a big one, Leah. You could get me fired!"

"Well, it's not my fault you weren't there. I could punch you for that." She took a boxer's stance.

"Oh, great. Act loony tunes. That will really help." Lynn stepped away. Sometimes she just didn't get Leah. "Check yourself. You can't act crazy."

"She was going to hit me in front of the girls. She was scary."

"Look who's talking about scary. Go home," Lynn said, disgusted. "I'll take care of this."

"Don't tell Jo Ellen. You know how she is."

Lynn turned her back on the girl. "You always get me in trouble," she muttered. She twisted the leash around her wrist. "I'm pissed off. I really am. Don't come back today. I have things to do. Just beat it. You're too much trouble."

"Please, Lynn, I'm sorry. I won't do it again. I'm not trouble."

"I'm not talking to you." Lynn didn't care if Leah cried all day. She'd had it with hysterics. Then she girded herself for an attack from Alison— another nutcase. Her life wasn't easy. She didn't look back at her shadow as she entered the house through the street-level entrance.

As soon as she got into the kitchen, where the two little girls were still at the breakfast table, playing with their food and watching TV, Alison let loose. "Where were you?" she snapped angrily.

"The dogs were crying. I took them out," Lynn told her.

"For an hour? You took them out for an hour?" Alison's voice was shrill but a little slow.

"I'm sorry. I guess I lost track of the time." Lynn unhooked the leashes and let the dogs rush their mistress. "Girls, are you ready to go?" She wanted to act normal for them.

Alison patted the dogs as the children bolted from the table to get their things. No matter what the season, they had a routine. They went to a little day school not far away, and they liked it. If it wasn't raining, Lynn would walk them over. She started to follow them up the stairs to their rooms to get their backpacks. Alison didn't look good, so she didn't want to talk to her, but Alison had other ideas.

"You left the door open. Leah came into the house. That's not acceptable."

"I'm sorry."

"She came into this house. You're done."

"I'm sorry. It won't happen again," Lynn said.

"You're damn right it won't happen again. This is the end. This is it. You girls are a menace. I've had it with all of you. I don't want any of you in the house again. Take the babies to school and get out of here." She ranted on until she ran out of speed, then lurched out of the kitchen. Lynn wasn't expected to defend herself, and she certainly wasn't going to plead for her job under these circumstances. The Wilsons needed her more than she needed them. She'd been called a menace before, but it didn't mean a lot. She went up to the fourth floor to get the girls dressed in their little pink jackets.

"Want to say good-bye to Mommy?" she asked.

"Yea, yea," Jessica said.

"Yea, yea," repeated her little sister.

"Okay, let's go find her."

No one had any doubts about where she was. They went down one flight of stairs to Alison's bedroom. The girls rushed into the room, while Lynn stayed outside the door. They did their good-bye thing for a few moments. Then the girls ran out, and Alison called to her. "Come in here, Lynn."

Lynn went into the room and was not surprised to find the usual mess. Alison's clothes and shoes from the night before were scattered about. Andrew's boxer shorts and socks were discarded on the floor beside the bed. There was a empty wineglass on the bedside table, and the pillows and bedding were in disarray.

"Are you okay?" she asked softly.

Alison had the dogs on the bed with her. "I feel terrible. I have the flu," she said.

"You want me to get you something at the store?"

"It's too bad, but you've left me no choice in the matter. There's nothing I can do about it."

"Let's not talk about it now," Lynn said softly.

"You can't stay here any longer. I put up with

it as long as I could. You'll have to go." Alison's eyes closed, then opened halfway. She was having trouble staying awake.

"Okay," Lynn said. She could tell her boss was already into it. Alison must have come upstairs to take a pill. Remy had warned Lynn that this was coming, and Leah's walking in this morning gave Alison the excuse she needed. But the Perkins family had gone through so many nannies they had a reputation. Lynn knew that she'd put up with the yelling longer than anyone else, and she'd provided stability for Jessica and Jill. Still, she couldn't help worrying about what Jo Ellen would say.

Alison's hand flopped on her wrist. "That's it. That's all she wrote."

"Okay," Lynn said automatically. She wasn't going to argue with Alison when she was like this. Half the time she didn't know what she was doing anyway. Even if she meant to fire Lynn now, there was a good chance that she wouldn't remember it later. In any case, Lynn was afraid to take her at her word. She hesitated. "The girls are waiting. Are you going to take them?" she asked.

Alison's eyelids drooped. "You take them. I'm just going to nap for a few minutes. You can pack up when you get back."

"Are you sure?" This wasn't right. The last time she'd been fired, the mother had said, "Get out now." Rational people didn't fire nannies, then tell them to take their kids to school so they could sleep off their hangover.

Alison didn't answer, though, so Lynn had no choice. She had to take the children to a place where they would be safe. She muttered to herself as she left with them. *Alison's an alcoholic. Remy's acting stupid. Everybody's crazy. They all push me around. I have no power to fix things.* Damn, she was stuck in a mess again. Her chest felt too tight, the way it did whenever she was treated unfairly.

Soon she was hurrying down the street, pushing the stroller because Jill still refused to walk. For once, Jessica didn't complain about going too fast. Both girls seemed to sense that something was up and were unusually quiet. Lynn dropped them off with the other kids and didn't stay a second longer than she had to. She knew that she would not be seeing Remy there today. Remy had told her that the boys' grandmother was flying in to be with them. She folded the stroller and left it for the return trip. Then, as she always did after taking the kids to school, she walked up to Barnes & Noble in the Citicorp building and sat in the Starbucks, sipping a latte and turning the pages of her favorite tabloids.

Twenty-six

That morning Alison was in a rage at her husband for leaving her, at Leah for walking in on her, at Lynn for disobeying her. At Maddy for stealing her lover and stupidly getting herself killed. Everything unbearable was happening at the same time. After firing Lynn, though, the tension left her body and she drifted off to her favorite place. Oblivion. She slept with one hand on each dog, snoring gently, and the Chihuahua, with all four paws in the air, snored with her.

For a short while the house was quiet, and peace prevailed. Then from down the stairs came a soft whistle. The poodle lifted its large head, knocking Alison's hand to the sheet. Roxie rolled over and barked, escaping from under the other hand. The contact with their mistress was broken, but Alison slept on.

After a minute, the whistle came again, this time in three short bursts. Fully alert, the dogs turned their eyes and ears toward the door as they waited for the command to come again. Seconds passed and nothing more happened. The deep silence of the house was broken only by Alison's breathing.

Then it came. Three short whistles. The tense

dogs remained where they were until the chain rattled on Floyd's leash. At that moment they knew for sure what was up, and they heard the word that put it all together. "Walkies!"

As usual, the call came from downstairs, soft and far away—always a welcome summons. They jumped off the bed to obey and ran down the stairs to the door. It didn't matter to them who took them out. Minutes later a maid came into Alison's room carrying a bucket filled with spray disinfectants on one arm, pushing a vacuum cleaner with her other hand. She was wearing a formal uniform, a gray dress with white collar and cuffs and a white apron over it, and thin rubber gloves. Her hair was hidden under a paisley turban. She didn't look at the sleeping woman on the bed as she went about her business.

She moved quickly, as if this was only one of many rooms she had to do that morning. She gathered up the clothes on the floor and threw them into the hamper in the bathroom, humming as she worked. When the bedroom was all picked up and tidy, she moved to the bathroom, washing out the shower, drying the floor. She put the cosmetics away and lingered over Alison's diamond engagement and wedding rings. After a few seconds, she took off one of the rubber gloves and put them on. She studied the way they looked on her hand, pulled the glove back over them, and went into the bedroom, where she turned on the vacuum cleaner. It roared into life.

Alison's body was still relaxed, but her eyes slowly opened and rolled around at the ceiling above her as if trying to locate the source of the offending noise. She turned her head to the side and her eyes connected with the hose of the vacuum cleaner as it entered her field of vision. Then she was awake and seething. She wanted that noise to stop.

"Fuck!" She raised herself up on an elbow. "Cut that out."

The maid paid no attention to her. She went on vacuuming vigorously, moving back and forth across the carpet and around the bed as if Alison weren't there.

Alison pulled herself into a sitting position. "Get the fuck out of here," she screamed.

The maid reached onto the bed for a pillow and smacked it so hard a few delicate feathers escaped from the pillowcase and flew into the air. She took another and smacked that one, too. The vacuum cleaner ran on as she busied herself at the bed, plumping pillows as if no one were yelling at her to stop it.

A pillow hit Alison in the face as the maid tossed it down on the bed. Alison pushed it away, and the maid grabbed it from her. She couldn't see much without her contacts, certainly not a clear view of the features of her tormentor. But she did catch a glimpse of sparkling diamonds on the wrist of the woman's hand as she pelted her almost playfully with the pillows.

Alison couldn't figure out what was happening. She made an effort to get up and force the devil out of her house but not very effectively. The vacuum was roaring, and the pillows became a shell game with her face lost in the middle. She had that wild, panicked feeling that none of this was real

and she was hallucinating, making nightmares out
of common events, as had happened several times
before. Each foot felt like it weighed a thousand
pounds and her hands were helpless to fight off her
own covers. Then diamonds sparkled in front of
her eyes one last time and she had an odd thought,
That's my bracelet, before her pillows silenced her
screams.

Twenty-seven

Lynn wished Remy would show up at Starbucks. She didn't want to go back to the Perkins house and have to deal with Alison. But her wish didn't come true. She had another latte and finished reading *Us*. Then she returned to the house as usual. When she ducked under the stairs, she saw that the kitchen door wasn't shut all the way. She knew she hadn't left it open.

Her first thought was to call Alison on her cell to make sure everything was all right upstairs. Her second thought was to run away, but she had nowhere to go. Her third thought was to go in and fix whatever was wrong. Fixing things had been her role all her life. She was a helper, programmed to clean up the messes the impaired people in her life always seemed to make. Pushing away a strong feeling of martyrdom at one more unfair burden, she went into the unguarded house.

The very instant she was inside, she knew she'd made a big mistake. The dogs were barking, locked up somewhere. Alison never locked the dogs up. Every instinct told Lynn to get out of the house and call for help. But whom could she call? Maddy was gone. Remy was no longer two blocks away.

She didn't think of Andrew. He never helped. She could think only of Jo Ellen, and Jo Ellen would not be her friend in a situation like this. There was no one to call, and the dogs were in a frenzy trying to get out.

With her heart pounding almost painfully, Lynn went into the front hall and called upstairs. "Alison?" For once she would have given anything to hear the familiar angry voice shouting at her to shut up.

"Alison, are you okay?" No answer.

"Shit," she muttered. The house just didn't feel right. She hoped Leah hadn't done anything loony. "Shit," she said again. She blew air out of her mouth and started climbing the stairs, making as much noise as possible. "Alison, it's me."

No answer. Lynn walked slowly down the hall to the master bedroom. The door was open, so why were the dogs locked up? She didn't like it, and then she stopped short when she saw Alison's distorted face. "Oh, no."

She didn't have to go in to know that her boss was dead. She started screaming and couldn't stop as she ran down two flights of stairs, out the kitchen door, and into the street. Her hands were shaking so badly that it was several minutes before she could hit the numbers 911 on her cell phone. By then a crowd had gathered.

Twenty-eight

Ohne small thing April missed in Westchester was the wide-open sky and the view looking west to the Manhattan skyline from Mike's twenty-second-floor apartment in Forest Hills, Queens, where they used to live. On the rare occasions when they were around to see it, she and Mike used to watch the sun go down over the city. Both felt a deep connection to it.

The loss of city view in Hastings-on-Hudson, however, was more than compensated for by the mighty oak tree that stood guard outside their bedroom window. The tree brought them closer to nature than they'd ever been. Before she'd had the tree to watch, April had followed the weather only because of the impact it had on the city's infrastructure—the subways and trains, the streets and highways. And on crime. Rain, fog, snow, and hail were bad for traffic, but had the silver lining of keeping criminals indoors.

The tree, however, gave April a reason to pay attention to the seasons. It was an ever-changing art show. In winter, snow piled up on its bare branches, beautiful and white. The snow melted and froze again, forming long spiky icicles. In

spring the tree took the abuse of the rain that
lashed it and the wind that whisked the new leaves
into dance. Every day the tree was a little different.
Something was always going on, and it had a way
of telling her when to get up.

The day after Maddy Wilson's murder April was
deep in a dream when the birds started stirring in
the tree. It was an old nightmare she didn't have
much anymore. Her teeth were being extracted
from her mouth by a great wad of caramel. It was
a scary dream because her father had a story of
torture long ago in China to account for the two
solid gold teeth placed in the front of his mouth
where no one could fail to see them. As the sun
announced morning, she rolled into a fetal position
to protect herself against his ancient injury.

Mike was already awake, nestling closer. "Everything is okay. You're okay." It was his job as a
husband to say these things and her job as a wife
to believe him. Today she had trouble.

From deep inside the dream, she heard the
scraping of one branch against another. She heard
the birds chatter, felt Mike's reassuring touch, and
willed herself awake. She wanted to go on her honeymoon, and instantly she smelled something
funny. "What's going on?"

He made a small laugh and whispered, "Your
mother's cooking. Don't worry about it."

Then his hands began to travel the curves of her
body with the light touch that always aroused her.
Mike had his own plan. His fingers skimmed her bottom and the hollow between her buttocks, then re-
versed direction. He nuzzled her neck, kissing her
softly as he always did in the morning—their one

quiet time together. After a few moments, he began to explore more intimate places. April sighed. Today, she was torn between pleasure and duty. Should she get up and find out what her mother was up to? Should she call Sergeant Gelo and find out what last night's little foray into the Spirit world had accomplished? Should she forget them for just a little while? Outside, birds carried on in their different voices. A finch warbled; doves and morning called. She pulled away, listening.

"What?" Mike murmured. He was ready for love, nudging her with a fine erection.

She debated for all of two seconds and decided not to waste a good thing. "Nothing," she murmured.

Some time later, feeling sated and drowsy again, April suddenly realized much was wrong in her house. For one thing, the TV was blaring. World news in Chinese was trying to blast through the closed door of the bedroom. Furthermore, the house no longer smelled like vanilla candles and potpourri. The odor that emanated from downstairs was highly reminiscent of the Chinatown tenement apartment of her childhood. Mike was definitely right. Her mother had commandeered the kitchen.

April quickly ducked into the shower. When she came out, the first thing she saw was the black luggage and brightly colored summer clothes she'd bought for her cruise. It was Tuesday. Only three days of work left. The clothes were piled on a chair and hanging from a hook on the closet door. She put them out of her mind, dressed, and hurried downstairs with her hair still wet. There was no sign of her father, but Skinny was busy at the stove.

"Hi, Ma. How are you?" April wanted her mother gone, but she had to step carefully because she didn't want any dire repercussions from hurt feelings complicating her life right now.

"Didn't sleep at all," Skinny replied. She turned around to peer at April through dime-store reading glasses she claimed she didn't need. Then she approached her daughter, not to kiss her, but to smell her like Chinese doctors did to diagnose their patients.

It was her way of saying "Hello, how are you?" She sniffed April to see if she'd been near a dead person, or had sex, or otherwise been doing something Skinny Dragon didn't want her doing. April dodged the encounter, even though she was married and now had a state-sanctioned right to sex anytime she wanted it. "You didn't sleep because you're happier in your own bed," April murmured.

"Worm daughter's health more important than happiness."

April had never enjoyed being called a worm, and right then the reference to her health was ominous. "My health is great," she countered.

Skinny grunted. She was a small woman with a shrewd expression, no excess flesh anywhere on her body. Her short hair was dyed jet-black and permed into a curly frizz that looked as fake as it was. It was impossible to tell how old she was. This morning she was dressed in loose black Chinese pants and a multicolored knockoff blouse probably made in Taiwan that was supposed to look like an expensive designer silk but didn't come close. Over the blouse was a buttoned-up knitted vest of multicolored yarn that didn't match a single color in the blouse. She could look pretty good when she wanted to, but clearly this wasn't one of those occasions.

"Your happiness is number one to me, Ma," April said soothingly.

Skinny shook her head. "Worm's health more important than my comfort." That was the theme of the day.

Oh, God, don't rise to the dig, April told herself. Her mother was an uninvited guest. She'd wheedled a ride from their tenant, Gao Wan, all the way up here to Hastings, and then he'd left her parents there. They had no way of getting home, so that must have been part of her plan. Now she was insulting the lovely guest room that had two windows, its own bathroom, good feng shui, and brand-new twin beds that didn't sag or squeak like Skinny's terrible old ones at home. But the accommodation wasn't the point. The point was Skinny was meddling again, and April had to put a stop to it.

"What's all this?" she asked, wrinkling her nose at the unusual breakfast. Her mother certainly had been busy. On the counter were bowls of steamed sweet potatoes, golden-fried bean curd, and some kind of hot cereal that looked as gluey as sludge. There was also a steaming mug of some milky potion.

"Yin food," Skinny said proudly.

"Yin food?" April was alarmed. If she got any more yin, she wouldn't be able to get out of bed.

"Good for fluid in womb."

April was horrified. It made her weak and queasy just hearing the words, and after all her admonitions to herself to keep calm, she erupted. "You have to stop this. I can take care of myself. I told you that last night. When I'm pregnant, I'll let you know."

"Let me see your tongue," Skinny demanded.

"No, you can't see my tongue. You have to go home."

Skinny ticked off on her fingers the number of months April and Mike had been married, then moved closer to punch her daughter in the arm.

"Ow." April particularly hated it when she did that.

"No go home. You have too much yang, *ni*. Too much bossy. Too much get-up-and-go. Never get pregnant like that."

Since April had just not gotten up and gone, and now was late because of it, she vibrated with fury. She couldn't believe her mother had come over to help her get pregnant. "I can't take this," she said in Chinese. She wanted her privacy.

She and Mike weren't exactly *working* on having a baby, but they weren't trying to avoid it, either. They just didn't want to make a big thing about it, have everyone get in their faces. No wonder she had nightmares. She heard her husband's happy, post-sex feet skip down the stairs.

"*Mamita,* how did you sleep?" Mike, too, had the good sense not to try to kiss her.

"*Bu hao.* Here—" She slapped the mug with the milky potion in his hand. "Drink this."

He looked at it blankly. "This isn't coffee."

"Good for you," she said. In Chinese she added, "No more premature ejaculation."

"Ma!" April's eyes popped in horror. She'd

never heard her mother talk sex like this. Womb fluid! Premature ejaculation! Was she nuts?

Skinny Dragon ignored her. She shook her finger at Mike. "Just soy milk, good for strength. You need it for honeymoon."

Dutifully, Mike took a sip. *"No me gusta,"* he murmured to April. He didn't like it.

"He loves it, Ma," April translated.

Skinny nodded triumphantly and explained that slow sticky sweet potato and sludgy unpolished wheat-bran cereal would lubricate April, while the bean curd and soy milk would energize Mike. Yin and yang foods necessary to fix their problem. Mike got a funny look on his face. He was Spanish, after all, *mucho* macho in his own gentle way.

"Gotta go, Ma," April said quickly.

"Murder?" Skinny asked cheerfully.

"Big murder. A young mother was killed. Gao will come and get you. Thank you for the wonderful visit. I'm sure it will help."

"Not going home. Have work to do." Skinny put her hands on her hips.

"Ma, you have to go." April copied her. "If Dad were up, I'd take you home myself."

"We're not going, *ni*. He retired so we could take care of you and the baby," she said. "We're staying."

"Oh, jeez," Mike muttered. His phone rang and he walked away to answer it.

April took a deep breath, then exhaled slowly. "Tell me Dad did not retire."

"It's true," Skinny insisted.

"Are you sure?" It didn't sound like him.

"Well, maybe retire in a week or so." Skinny

paused, and April could see her forming another sentence. Suddenly the food on the counter didn't look *that* terrible. So what if it was an unbalanced diet? She was ravenous from all that sex. She took a bite of the sweet potato. It didn't taste like bacon and two fried eggs on toast, but . . . it wasn't too bad, either. She tried the bean curd while her mother watched her eat.

Mike returned to the kitchen. Now his heavy footsteps didn't sound so sex-happy. "Get your purse, *querida*. Alison Perkins is dead."

April forgot her mother and started moving.

·

Twenty-nine

The fortresslike white stucco facade of the modern house where Alison Perkins had lived looked out of place on a block where redbrick apartment buildings dominated, and so did all the police vehicles. April was still reeling from the shock of a second death as Lily Eng caught sight of the car and hurried over before Mike shut down the engine.

"What took you so long?" she complained.

"Hey, Lily." April shook her head. They'd gotten a late start this morning, and the traffic had been heavy coming in. There was no need to say any of that. Besides, she was already working the case and didn't feel like chitchat.

They'd both been on the phone all the way into the city. Mike had talked with Sergeant Minnow, who hoped that Alison's death had been natural—a fluke of some kind like a heart attack. She was in bed. No one had touched her. April had called Sergeant Gelo from her cell, and Eloise started her report as soon as she heard her boss's voice.

"We went to Spirit, Ice, and Ramp last night," she said.

"What did you find out?" April asked.

"No one in the clubs remembers who was with Peret two nights ago. The owners all say they check IDs, and Peret couldn't have gotten in. They say he must have bought whatever he took somewhere else. Yada yada. Three of the girls were off yesterday, though, and I have their names."

"Well, talk to all the girls. With the right incentive someone will spill."

"We can do better than that. We have the kid's cell phone. We know where he went because he called some friends to join him. So we have him inside a club. Looks like Spirit."

"That's great news. Was the phone on him?"

"No, and the responding officer thought that was suspicious. Every kid has a cell, right? So he searched the scene after Peret was taken to the hospital, found it, and brought it in."

"Good going. Remember his name."

"Charlie checked out the kid's last calls and his incoming calls. Two of the girls who work at Spirit are in his phone list. One of them actually called him and left a message yesterday. So we're talking to her later. Have you heard about Mrs. Perkins?" Eloise changed the subject.

"Yes. I'm on my way over there now. I want you to do a few things for me, okay?" April asked. Eloise had worked yesterday and last night, but she was on the job again today.

"No problem."

"Look, I know you're not familiar with the Wilson case, but I need you on this. I made a tape of my conversation with Alison Perkins yesterday. Get your hands on it, and make a copy. We'll have to give the original to the task force on the case right away. We've got two nanny suspects, now. Alison's nanny was the one who found her body. I want you and Hagedorn to check her out. Do a deep background on both of the girls, Remy Banks and Lynn Papel. *Papel* is spelled *Peter, Apple, Peter, Egg, Lester.* I have a freaky feeling about this. Really freaky. You can start with the employment agency. It's Anderson."

"Yes, boss." Eloise was silent for a moment. "What are you looking for?"

"I'm not sure yet. We're still working on the Wayne Wilson angle. He could have persuaded Remy to kill Maddy. Alison's death could just be an attempt to confuse us on Maddy's, or to shut Alison's mouth. She talked a lot yesterday. One of the husbands could have done this. The two men are friends—maybe they had a plan. But we also need to check for other connecting points. Find out if the nannies knew each other before they went to work for Wilson and Perkins, what's in their job files. Were they ever in trouble? Hagedorn knows how to do it."

"So do I," Gelo muttered.

"Yes. That was good work you did last night. Good thinking on the phone. Call me with whatever you get."

April ended the conversation and stared out the window at the traffic. Immediately she started brooding on the time of Maddy's, and now Alison's, death. Early morning was a highly unusual time for murder. Night was the dangerous time because that's when people came home from work, had cocktails, got ready for dinner, ate their dinner, and let loose their pent-up emotions and frustrations from the day. They quarreled about lovers, work, children—being too close, or too far away. Night was when people drank, tempers flared, and violence occurred most often.

Morning was usually the aftermath. It was the cooldown time when the law responded with arrests. When the sun came up, aggressors and victims had heavy heads; they had jobs to go to. Often they were remorseful and vowed not to hurt each other again. Victims felt guilty for inciting rage in their partners and, later, for drawing attention to their plight with their injuries. After a fight, if an arrest was forthcoming, officers tried to go in the morning. Normally, people did not kill or get killed over coffee and toast. But suddenly there were two cases in which, within twenty-four hours, two close friends, each with two little children, had died during this usually safe time. For these two women, morning was their window of vulnerability, and the killer knew that. To April, it had become a very personal case. But she made sure she showed none of this when she faced the news shark Lily Eng, who was waiting to be fed her pound of human flesh.

"Why didn't you call me back last night?" she demanded as April got out of the car.

"I worked late, and I can't talk now. Sorry, Lily," April told her. "Maybe later."

"Wait a minute—you weren't working late. I saw you on the news having dinner with Wayne Wilson. Come on, give me a little something. Has he been cleared as a suspect, or what?"

Mike came around to the passenger side. "Hi,

Lily. You know we weren't having dinner with anyone," he said, gently scolding her.

She gave him an innocent smile. "Okay, so you weren't eating with him. But you were there. I could make something of it if I wanted to."

"What's the matter with you?" April said sharply. They didn't have time for this. She started across the street, but Lily followed her.

"I happen to know you spent the afternoon with Alison Perkins yesterday. And today she's dead. There may be a connection. What do you have to say about *that*?"

April's breath caught on the lump in her throat. That was the other question she'd been asking herself all the way into the city. She knew she should never respond angrily to anything Lily said, but the persistent reporter's little jabs always seemed to hit home. Lily had a way of knowing where April had been and what she was doing. Too bad she wasn't a spy for the home team. She looked as if she badly needed to cut down on her caffeine intake, and she was right on target about Alison. Whenever detectives investigated an unnatural death, the first question they asked was, what was the precipitating event? For all April knew, her own close questioning of the young woman might well have triggered the murder. Mike put a calming hand on her arm.

"Oh, come on, I know where you are all the time, so give me a break. I could be helpful." Lily trotted alongside them.

April shook her head. She didn't need a helpful journalist.

"Okay, just tell me one thing. Is it a serial killer, two different killers? What?"

Mike was the one to throw Lily a tidbit. "Why don't you hold your horses, Lily? This may not be what you think at all. We don't know what caused her death yet. It could be a natural." He shrugged.

"No way!"

April's breakfast wasn't sitting well with her. "We'll let you know when we do, okay?"

"I guess I can't ask for more than that." Lily backed off as they got to the police tape. Mike and April went under it and up the stairs into the house.

Thirty

Entering the Perkins house was an eerie repeat of the day before. A lot of people had piled into the starkly modern house to look around, but most of them were gone by now. In the foyer, April was immediately struck by the mournful sound of howling dogs and the lack of homey possessions—umbrellas, toys, mess of any kind. Abstract paintings in black and white hung on the walls of the hall and the living room beyond. Chief Avise must have heard the door slam, because he appeared at the top of the steep stairway that led to the third floor, then charged down holding on to the banister the second he saw her. April thought grimly that his fingerprints would be everywhere. He got to the last step and nodded curtly at Mike. April was clearly the person he wanted. He didn't say hello as he drew her aside.

"I hear you had this woman in your office all afternoon yesterday. What did you think you were doing?" he said softly into her ear so that Mike couldn't hear as he passed them on his way up.

"She didn't want to be mobbed by the press. I took her to a quiet place, my office," she replied calmly. She knew what was coming.

He made a face and waved his hand. "Go on."

"We talked there for several hours. I have a tape of our conversation for the task force."

"Why didn't you pass along that tape last night?"

April lifted her palms. She didn't know there would be a briefing. There were other answers . . . Down the road she could see IA taking her apart, but she had to admit to the tape. "I'm sorry, sir." Sorrier than he could ever guess.

"Why did you take her to the West Side?"

"I met her in Meke's gym. It's on Fifty-sixth Street, so Midtown North was closer and, as I said, quieter."

He sighed. "This is not a good thing, April. What did she tell you?"

"It was a rambling interview, sir. I have it on tape. She was convinced that Remy was the killer. She and Maddy both had a thing going with the trainer. He was probably supplying them with cocaine." She said the last thing slowly.

"Was she high?" he asked suddenly.

"Possibly—" she began.

He interrupted angrily. "You didn't check it out?"

If April had it to do over, she would have done pretty much everything differently. Starting with her downtown meeting in the morning with the chief and ending with the dinner at Soleil. But yesterday had been chaotic. She'd been under pressure from Mike, and she hadn't done anything by the book. She hadn't taken the time to get organized with the rest of the team, just gone out on her own, with her own agenda. She should have turned over the tape yesterday. She definitely shouldn't have jumped around from one suspect to another, letting them wander off before clearing them. She'd hopped from Wayne to Remy, to Derek, to Alison, to Wayne again, because she'd wanted to form a picture quickly, and they'd all just resumed their lives. Not good.

"Maddy's death was a stabbing. I didn't want to put Alison on the defensive about drugs if it wasn't relevant to the case." It wasn't a good answer, but it was the truth.

Avise stepped back so she could see the furious expression on his face. "Well, it's relevant to *this* case," he spat at her.

That stunned her into silence.

"Go take a look at her," he snapped, and walked away.

April stood there paralyzed, watching him go. Why couldn't he just tell her what was going on? Why did she always have to guess? Yesterday it was the whole club thing. For a second she was sorry that she hadn't told him about the progress on the Peret case. Now it was too late. Why did he have to be so cryptic about Alison's cause of death? April was always anxious about making mistakes in investigations that could have a tragic consequence—like a killer's getting away, or someone else's dying. When she'd been working yesterday, she had a lot of thoughts about that, particularly in regard to Derek, but she never in a million years could have guessed that Alison would be dead today. The chief had spoken to her as if it were her fault, but murder never worked like this. It just didn't happen.

She looked at the stairs, dreading what she had

to do next. Here, the stairs didn't do anything fancy like form a bridge over the entry to the living room the way they did in the Wilson house. They just hugged the wall all the way up to the third floor, then turned the corner into a hall. She didn't want to go to Alison's room and see the sad evidence of an overdose—or something else—that could have been avoided. Finally she forced herself to move and started up.

At the top, she heard voices coming from the back and went that way. Mike was nowhere to be seen, but the doorway into the bedroom was blocked by tape. Inside, the Crime Scene Unit was already at work taking photos of Alison and the room where she had died. The body was covered, only Alison's head was visible, and one thing was clear: she hadn't died in her sleep. Her eyes were open, and her face was anything but peaceful. Mike came down the hall behind April, and touched her arm.

"What did the chief want?" he asked softly, as if he didn't already know.

"He wanted to know about my conversation with Alison yesterday," April said, feeling guilty because she hadn't told Mike that Alison was afraid the killer would go after her next. She stared at the small form hidden under a heavy quilt.

The bed had a white upholstered headboard and a white quilted bedspread. Placed at an angle under it was a black-and-white area rug. A white slipper chair was set on each side of the window. On the wall opposite the bed the doors of a black lacquered entertainment center were shut. Nothing was out of place. In fact, nothing much was there at all. It looked as though someone had made the bed over the dead woman, leaving only her head exposed, then had tidied up the rest of the room just the way someone had cleaned up the Wilson gym yesterday. The two death scenes were very different, but gave the same message. Two lives had been cleaned up in death. It was neat, neat, neat.

April was reminded of one awful suicide in which the deceased had taken a great many sedatives, drunk vodka, lain down on his bed, arranged himself just so, and then put a plastic bag over his head. His death had been ugly. The pills had scattered, the vodka bottle had fallen over, and some of it had spilled. People couldn't clean up as they were dying, and the evidence was always in plain sight. The leftover powder and straws from a cocaine binge—something. Furthermore, drunk or drugged or sober, no one *started* a day with a completely tidy bedroom. April frowned. "*Chico,* what does this look like to you?"

She and Mike stood at the door side by side studying the scene as if it were a wax exhibit in Madame Tussaud's.

"She made breakfast for her girls, got them off for the day, and lay down for a nap," Mike said. "That's what the nanny said."

No, April thought. There was a lot more to it. "Was she alone at the time?"

"The nanny took the girls to their play school. They're there now. She said that Alison was like that when she came back."

"She has a name. It's Lynn." April was aware of her breakfast again—that gluey cereal was a rock in her stomach. The end of Alison's dark ponytail poked out from underneath the sheet. Seeing it, she felt ill. "Did anybody touch anything?" she asked.

"Lynn says she didn't."

"What about the chief?"

Mike shook his head.

"Where is Lynn now?" April leaned against the wall. She was going to throw up.

"Downstairs. Alison's husband is downstairs, too."

April closed her eyes against the nausea. She wished she could take herself off this case.

"*Querida,* are you all right?" Mike took her elbow.

"I messed up. I really messed up this time, Mike. I didn't think she was in danger." Her words came quickly. She felt like a suspect breaking down, crumbling under the pressure.

"Hey." Mike's voice, usually soft and supportive, sharpened. "Calm down." He led her down the hall away from the ears of the Crime Scene detectives. "You need a bathroom?"

"No." She voiced the negative, but knew she was going to throw up anyway.

"There's a powder room in here." He led the way down the hall to the front of the house.

April glanced at the room quickly. Where Wayne had his octagonal library, the Perkins couple had a cute little living room. Mike punched a wall with faux bookshelves and books painted on it. A narrow door popped open to reveal a tiny corner powder room.

April was surprised. "How did you know that was there?"

"I took a look around while you were talking to the chief."

I can't use this—it's too close to the scene, April thought. Then a powerful wave of nausea changed her mind. She ducked inside the small space, closed the door, and stood in the dark struggling for control. She didn't believe in hormone myths. Where she came from, no one talked about things like PMS. Moody was moody, weepy was weepy, and none of it was tolerated. You did what you had to do and never mind the plumbing. "Don't tell anyone when you don't feel good" was the credo. And sometimes people took their modesty too far. Recently, Skinny's close friend Ma Ma Choi died of uterine cancer because she didn't want to lose face by telling anyone the embarrassing truth about the tumor she knew was growing inside.

April had a weak stomach. Nausea and other unpleasant symptoms caught her all the time. She heard that a lot of people had the syndrome now, and there was even a name for it: irritable bowel. Stress made it worse, and so did her mother. She swallowed and switched on the light. Then she sat on the toilet, ducked her head between her knees, and did some yoga breathing. The powder room was wallpapered in a tight black-and-white geometrical pattern. The tiny sink was black porcelain. The floor was translucent white marble. She tilted her head from side to side, trying to ease the frozen muscles in her neck.

She wasn't sick after all. Finally the nausea began to recede, and she opened her eyes to her surroundings. Instantly her attention was captured by an item that shouldn't be there. A gray feather was on the floor, like the kind of feather from the underbelly of a duck or goose that was used to stuff pillows. April had a sudden horrific vision of someone pushing a pillow into Alison's dozing face. Her eyes and mouth opening as she struggled for air and freezing that way.

She shook it off and reached into her purse for the plastic gloves, tweezers, and envelopes she kept in there along with her off-duty gun, address book, gold shield, and other vital paraphernalia. She slipped on two of the gloves and used the tweezers to pick up the feather. With it closer to her face, she saw the particular kind of fuzz on the feather that confirmed it as goose down. April had seen it when she was pricing her own bedding. The fuzzy feathers were far and away the most expensive kind, but soft and lighter than air. As April studied the feather, she realized something was caught in it. About three inches long and very shiny, it looked like a human hair, and was definitely not a dog hair. The hair was not black, not dark brown. It was a light color, possibly with a reddish tone, or a honey blond, and it was coarser than baby hair.

Hairs were notoriously difficult to see when one was looking for them. On white sheets or a white sweater or a black suit—whenever it was embarrassing—hairs showed up. But in a room with many pieces of upholstered furniture and rugs on the floor, they blended. April got down on her knees and searched the floor for more hairs. She found another one at the base of the toilet, put the two together, and studied them. Maybe her eyes were playing tricks, but it almost looked as if there was a stripe in them from different dye jobs. Elated, she separated them, sealed one in an envelope with the feather, wrote on the outside where the sample came from, and took the other hair and put it in an envelope in her purse. She saw the splashes of water in the basin. She made some notes. *Match w feathers from Perkins bedding. Check for hair in drain of Wilson shower.* Seconds later, she emerged from the bathroom to hand the envelope over and have a chat with Igor from Crime Scene, who never liked her getting in the middle of his work. Before she headed back to the bedroom, she checked the pillows in the den to see if the fuzzy feather in question could have come from one of them. She punched and felt them. All were stuffed with foam. She was back on the job.

Thirty-one

Lynn was hysterical. April saw right away that she was genuinely terrified. She was huddled on her bed in her room, hugging her pillow, and crying so hard she couldn't answer any of the questions Sergeant Minnow put to her.

"Sergeant, could I talk with her for a moment?" April stood in the doorway with the cups of hot water and coffee she'd asked a uniform to get for her.

"All yours." Sergeant Minnow rose from the small chair he'd been uncomfortably occupying and looked relieved to be offered an excuse for a break. April moved away so he could escape the claustrophobic space.

Unlike the rest of the rooms in the house that April had seen, Lynn's was just big enough for a single bed, a small armoire, and a tiny table and chair. The only light came from a fixture in the middle of the ceiling. There was a sink in one corner and a bathroom with a toilet and narrow shower across the hall. The kitchen was next door on one side and the laundry room was on the other side.

After Minnow was gone, April put the coffee on

the table. "I got you coffee with milk. Is that all right?" she asked.

Lynn hiccuped and swiped at her tears with the sheet.

"Or you could have my tea." April sat in the chair, close to the bed. "Your choice."

"I'll have the coffee," Lynn said after a moment.

April handed it to her, along with a stirring stick and some sugar packets. "I'm Lieutenant April Woo Sanchez," April said.

"I know who you are. You talked to Alison yesterday. She told me about it last night."

April nodded and took a long look at the girl's hair. It was blond. Not as fair as Remy's, but blond nonetheless. And it was too long to make a match with the hair on the floor of the bathroom. April thought she'd try to take one from her hairbrush just in case. "What was her mood then? Was she depressed by the death of her friend?" she asked after a pause.

"Sure, but she didn't kill herself. Don't think that," Lynn said quickly. "I know she didn't."

"How do you know?"

Lynn started crying again. "I just do."

"Drink some coffee. Caffeine helps." To illustrate the point, April removed the lid from her cup of water and stuck in a tea bag that she'd pulled from a zippered pouch in her purse. The water quickly turned brown and she sipped, still thinking about hair and feathers.

After a few moments, Lynn followed her example and began to revive. April smiled at her. "Better?"

"A little," she said tremulously.

"Are you hungry?" April asked.

"No, I had breakfast."

"Good, but let me know when you need something. We can send somebody out." Giving her time, April slowly drank her tea and looked around at her collection of stuffed animals, shoes, magazines, T-shirts, and jeans spread out in no particular order on all available surfaces, including the floor. Lynn was no neat freak, and April was surprised that Sergeant Minnow had chosen this spot for their initial interview. Maybe he wanted to intimidate her. She also looked at Lynn's pillow. They'd have to check that, too.

After a while, Lynn said, "It feels too big, if that makes any sense. I don't know if I can talk about it."

"It's okay, I know what you mean. Take a few deep breaths. We have all the time in the world. We'll get there."

Following her advice, Lynn breathed loudly, almost gasping. It reminded April of what Alison might have gone through trying to get air into her lungs during her last moments. "That will do—you can stop now."

Lynn hiccuped again and put the cup down.

"Okay, what happened?" April said.

"I knew something was wrong when I came back from taking the girls to play school," Lynn said, her voice still a little shaky.

"How did you know something was wrong?" April took out her notebook.

"The door was open."

"Which door?"

"The kitchen door."

"You mean, it was unlocked or hanging open?"

"No, it locks automatically if it's closed right. But the door sticks, and you have to pull it hard. It wasn't shut all the way."

"Did you close it when you left?" April asked.

"Yes."

"Okay, what else was wrong?" She made a note.

"The dogs were locked up. They were barking. You can hear them now."

"They're not usually locked up?"

"No, they're always with her." Tears squeezed out of Lynn's eyes as she tried to hold them back. "She loved those dogs."

"What did you do then?" April asked.

"I was afraid to go inside because of Remy."

"What about her?"

"She called me this morning. She wanted to meet for coffee. I know I shouldn't have gone, but she sounded so upset . . ."

"You left the house?" April looked up.

"Yes."

"At what time?"

"I don't know, sometime around six, six thirty. I didn't think it would be a problem going that early."

"Why was Remy upset?"

Lynn shook her head. "She shouldn't have stayed with Mr. Wilson at the hotel, but she never listens to anybody. She told me someone followed her."

"Did someone?" April asked, writing it all down.

"I don't know. Some guy was reading a paper across the street. I don't know if he followed her or not. She said it was a cop."

April didn't comment on that. "What was on her mind?" she asked again.

"She said she wanted to warn me that I was getting fired today."

"How did she know?"

"She heard Wayne and Andrew talking on the phone."

"Did you get fired today, Lynn?" There was the big question. April watched her face as she answered.

"Yes. Alison said I wasn't reliable. But then she told me to take the kids to play school. That was off, too," Lynn replied, calmer now.

"What was the problem with that?" April asked.

"If you're going to fire someone, you don't send them out with your children." She said it as if anybody should know that.

April nodded again. "Why didn't she take the kids herself?"

"She had to go back to bed." Lynn wiped her runny nose with the back of her hand. April handed her a tissue from a package in her purse.

"Why did she have to go to bed?"

"Oh . . . she probably took a couple of Vicodin. She was pretty much out of it when we left."

"Could she have taken too many?" she asked.

"Enough to kill her? No, no. She wouldn't have hurt herself. She loved her children, her dogs. She would not have left them. She liked to take the edge off, that's all. She might take two, and then two and then two throughout the day whenever she started coming off it, but she wouldn't do more than that," she said with authority. "I know her."

•

"Are you sure?" April asked.

"I know all about this. She wouldn't make that kind of mistake. I know what they do. My mother was just like her." Lynn ducked her head as if in pain. "They drink; they tell their doctors they have back pain and get pills for it. They go from doctor to doctor. They'll take cocaine whenever they can get it; it's a party all day long. They want to take the pain away; they don't want to die."

"Maddy, too?"

Lynn's soft features hardened as she nodded. "Not as bad. She was an athlete. With her it was an occasional thing."

April finished what she was writing and looked up. "What was Alison wearing when she told you to take the girls to play school?"

"Oh, jeans, a T-shirt."

"Where was she when you left?"

"I told you. She had to go back upstairs to bed."

"Did you see her before you left?"

"Yes, I always take the girls upstairs to say good-bye. Most of the time she doesn't have breakfast with them, but she always says good-bye. It's their thing." Lynn closed her eyes again. "The dogs were on the bed with her. She was still wearing jeans. The room was a mess. Her clothes were all over the place."

"Like yours," April murmured.

Lynn smiled. "Worse."

"Any sign of drugs or alcohol in her room when you left?"

"A wineglass by her bed. I know she keeps the Vicodin in her makeup bag."

"Okay, let's return to when you got back. What

did you do when you found the door open and the dogs barking?"

"I don't know. I kept thinking about what happened to Remy—you know, finding Maddy dead like that. I just had the strangest feeling—I don't know what it was. Even with the dogs barking, the place just felt dead. I don't know what it was."

"Lynn, if you were so certain something had happened, why did you go to her room?"

She shook her head. "My mother was a drunk. You take care of them. You go to make sure . . . my feet went there. I wanted to find her asleep. I really did."

"So you went upstairs."

Lynn nodded.

"What did you find?"

She closed her eyes, and more tears squeezed out. "I could tell right away she was gone."

"Did you go into the room?"

"No. No way I was going in there."

"How did you know that she was dead?"

"Her eyes were open, and the room was clean." The words came out a whisper. "Alison never did that."

Bingo. April had been right about Maddy's killer being a cleaner. Already she was thinking homicide. She nodded because unlike yesterday when she'd had a lot of questions about Remy's version of events, she believed every word this nanny said. It all played. Lynn admitted that her boss fired her this morning, and she was experienced enough to know addict behavior when she saw it. She didn't believe it when her boss fired her because she'd taken a pill. "Would the dogs let someone hurt their master?" she asked after a pause.

"Not if they were in the room, but they're food-driven. If Alison was out cold, and someone offered them dog biscuits, they'd go for it. Is it okay if I take them out when we're done? I feel bad for them."

April noted another thing. Lynn was very responsible; she was still thinking of her chores. "Yeah, you can take them out, but you'll have to go out upstairs. But one more thing before you go. Did you like Alison?"

Lynn chewed on her lip. "Loved her and hated her, just like my mom," she said.

"Is your mother living?" April asked.

"If you call it that," she replied.

"Okay, you can take a break. We have an officer at the front door who will go with you. When you come back, we're going over the whole house together. Are you up to doing that with me?"

"Do I have to?"

"Yes. I want you to tell me if anything is missing."

"Will I have to look at her?" Lynn shuddered.

"The room, the bathroom. The closet . . ." And Alison's remains would still be there, she didn't add. Yes, she'd have to look at her.

A few minutes later, April found an unusual trio in the formal living room on the second floor. Sergeant Minnow, dressed in a sports jacket, slacks, and a ratty-looking tie, and Mike, in his sharp blue captain's uniform, sat in two of the armchairs. Andrew Perkins, wearing an expensive-looking business suit, a yellow shirt, and a blue-and-yellow tie, looked like a bull beside them. He was a beefy man with thick black hair that stood straight up on his big head. His bulk dwarfed his own sofa as he leaned forward, talking earnestly to Mike.

He stopped talking when April came into the room and was even more startled when Lynn went out the front door with the two dogs and a uniformed officer. Mike nodded for April to join them and quickly introduced her. "This is Lieutenant Woo Sanchez. She spoke with your wife for some time yesterday."

Perkins's expression showed that he, too, knew who she was. He resumed talking. "I was afraid this would happen someday. I warned her about taking too many pills," he said angrily. "I can't believe she did this, today of all days."

April sat in the chair farthest away from them and prepared to listen. People often behaved strangely immediately upon learning that a loved one was gone. One mother of a hit and run victim had been furious with her dead son for having crossed the street on a green light. It was revealing that Andrew Perkins immediately assumed that his wife was responsible for her own death.

"What was her mood this morning?" Mike asked.

"Her mood was never chipper in the morning," Perkins said sarcastically. "If I said, 'Have a good day,' she'd reply, 'That isn't in my plans.' Can you imagine?" It was clear that her death was not in *his* plan for the day.

"Was she depressed?" Mike asked. He was taking the lead, and April could see that Minnow was making an effort to pretend not to mind.

"Oh, she had her usual hangover. That's all I thought about it," he said defensively. "She . . . had a tendency to drink too much, but a lot of people drink. I talked to her about it and she promised she'd stop." His tone changed as he defended her. "She's had problems in the past, but as long as she stayed away from the heavy stuff, I tried not to make too much of a few glasses of wine. Everybody needs something, right?" Suddenly he seemed not to want to be mad at his wife. He glanced quickly at April, then down at his watch. After he registered the time, he caught the three of them staring at him.

"I have trouble sitting still," he explained. "Why are there so many people here?" He indicated the voices upstairs, the number of detectives searching his house. They were all over the place. They wouldn't let him go into his own room. Crime Scene was still working it.

"It's normal procedure for an unnatural death," Mike said.

"But didn't you just tell me this was an accident, that she died in her sleep?" He looked alternately angry and dazed by it all.

"I said she was found in bed. But we're not certain of anything yet."

"Oh God." Perkins turned away for a moment as if the idea occurred to him for the first time that someone else might have caused his wife's death. "Not . . . ?" He didn't finish the question. His expression was one of complete horror, as if murder was the last thing he could have imagined happening to *his* wife.

"Can you think of anyone who might want to kill your wife?" Mike asked.

At that moment, Lynn returned through the front door, and Perkins's face paled. "Only her," he said slowly.

Thirty-two

After Eloise Gelo hung up with Lieutenant Woo, she called the unit meeting. Five people were on duty that day, including Hagedorn and a forlorn-looking Woody Baum.

"Where's the boss?" Woody asked.

"Still on the Wilson case," she lied.

"I wrote up my canvass. What does she want me to do with it?" he asked.

"I'm sure she'll want it," Eloise replied crisply.

"Can I take over it to her? I could continue the house-to-house."

"She may want you to do that. I'll let you know, Woody."

She didn't want to inform them just yet that there was another death and investigation in progress. Instead, she assigned the sixty-ones (the complaints) that had come in during the night, reviewed the progress of ongoing cases, and looked over the written reports. A couple of them were incomprehensible as to what action had occurred, so she returned them to their authors for a rewrite. Everybody had to write in complete sentences, whether they wanted to or not, and she guessed the poor reports were a test to see what she'd do about it.

She told them to fix the problems and ignored the grumbling that followed.

Finally, when everybody was busy or had gone out, she went into the lieutenant's office to locate the tapes of Woo's interview with Alison Perkins. They were in her desk, carefully labeled, exactly where Woo had told her they'd be. Eloise knew that the existence of a record of the interview could be a bad thing, depending on what the dead woman had said; therefore she was a little disappointed to find them. If the tapes had been lost, they couldn't be delivered to the principal investigators, and no one could be held responsible for anything. The prospect of blame possibly accrued to her boss or herself down the road weighed heavily on Eloise's mind. A little edgy and not wanting to tell anyone else what was going on, she found the equipment she needed and set up the machine to copy the tapes in her own office. There wasn't time to listen to the interview now, but she thought she might sit down with it later. The boss hadn't told her not to.

The second job Woo had given her was to do the background checks on the nannies who'd found the bodies of their two employers. This caused Eloise another twinge of anxiety. She left the reels spinning in her office and headed to the computer where Charlie spent his time staring at a screen. Her opinion of him had undergone something of a sea change since he'd come through for her on the Peret case, and she actually smiled at him.

"What's up?" He seemed surprised by both the smile and the visit.

"You know that woman the boss brought in here yesterday? Alison Perkins?"

"How could anyone forget that knockout?" he said.

"She just turned up dead," Gelo replied sharply. She hated it when men referred to women as dogs or knockouts.

Charlie's pale face sobered quickly. "No shit? When?"

"Just now, a little while ago," she amended.

"Wow. I didn't hear that." He seemed as shocked as she was. "Where is she?"

"In her home."

"I meant the boss," Charlie said.

"She was on her way to the scene when she called in. It's like yesterday—the nanny found her."

Charlie thought about it for a moment. "Looks like a little window of opportunity there," he said slowly.

"What do you mean?"

"In the morning the two husbands are gone; the nannies are out. You see the pattern. They're vulnerable then."

"Yeah, she wants us to check out the nannies. Anderson Agency," Eloise told him.

He nodded. "Okay, that's not a problem."

"But won't there be a task force working on this?"

"So?" Hagedorn raked a hand through his thinning hair and punched some keys on his keyboard.

"We'd be doubling up on a key part of the investigation." As a newcomer in the precinct and a boss for the first time, Eloise needed some clarification. The lieutenant hadn't instructed her to coordinate with the task force, and they were supposed to work together on cases like this. Every interview had to be written up and handed in to the officer in charge. Lieutenant Woo might be the officer in charge of them at Midtown North, but was she in charge of the task force putting together the file? Eloise had always been a team player and didn't like the idea of working out of the loop.

"Don't make it a problem," Charlie advised her.

"But how does this work?" Where Eloise came from, they didn't do things like this. There was one file in one place and everybody contributed to it.

He shrugged. "She helps them out when they ask her to. We help her out. Everybody's happy."

Eloise frowned. "But couldn't it bite us later?"

"Well, sure, anything can bite back later, but I've worked all the big cases with her. They pull in people from other units to do stuff all the time. It may not be kosher, but the boss has a hundred percent solution record." He shrugged. "And she's very well connected."

Gelo wasn't ready to let it go so easily. She put a hand on her hip. "Do you guys work this way often?"

"Don't worry about it. They have hundreds of people working a case like this."

But all in one location, not all over the place, Gelo wanted to say. When people worked independently, things got passed over that shouldn't be, or not included at all. Other agencies around the country made these kinds of mistakes, not them. She didn't say anything for a moment, wondering again what was on the tapes being copied in her office. Well, Woo was turning them over, wasn't she? Charlie interrupted her internal debate.

"Here we go. Look at this."

Eloise was amazed by how quickly he'd jumped from one case to the other. They'd been out until late. She'd had to sack out on a cot in the female uniformed officers' room because there was no special place for ranking female officers. A lot of other things were vying for her attention, including the stripper they were interviewing at two p.m. for the Peret case. Charlie, however, had moved on. He was already working the East Side homicides.

"Anderson is the premier employment agency for domestic positions in the U.S.," he said. He clicked on PRINT, and the pages started spewing out. "Okay, what we have here are domestic positions for the very rich—cooks, laundresses, butlers, chauffeurs, nannies, bodyguards, nurse-companions, caretakers, baby nurses."

Eloise leaned over his shoulder to see the screen.

"Mmm, you smell good," he said.

"Fuck off," she shot back, but not as angrily as she might have last week. She looked at the application page. "Wow." Salaries ranged from 32,000 to 120,000 dollars a year for bodyguards and cooks. "Call them and find out what you can. I have a tape to review."

Thirty-three

Lynn studied the disturbing scene in the bed-room where Alison was still swaddled in her quilt. Two men completely covered in white, right down to their shoes, were measuring and going over the room as if the body weren't there.

"What do you want me to do?" she asked Lieu-tenant Woo Sanchez.

"You said earlier that the room didn't look like this when you left to take the girls to play school. Tell me how it looked then."

Lynn sniffed back her tears. "It's always a mess in here in the morning. Andrew's underwear and socks are on the floor on his side of the bed." She pointed to where that was. "He never picks up in the morning. Alison dropped her clothes on the floor, too—whatever she was wearing. I think she just threw the decorative pillows off the bed. They never landed on the bench."

The bench at the bottom of the bed had nothing on it now.

"And there's almost always an empty wineglass on the bedside table. She prefers white wine," Lynn added.

"What else?" The Chinese detective followed her gaze as it traveled around the room.

"That's about it in here, except for her magazines. She read them in bed. I don't see them now."

Woo consulted her notes. "Earlier you said that when the children came up to say good-bye in the morning, she was often in bed."

Lynn made a face. "They have sex in the morning."

"How do you know?"

"The spots are still wet when I make the bed at noon," she said simply.

"They had an active sex life. Okay. What else?"

Lynn looked past the bed toward the bathroom. "There's always water on the floor in the bathroom. Maybe they showered together. I don't know." She closed her eyes. "Two wet towels on the floor, her jewelry on the vanity. He's meticulous about his toiletries. She's messy with hers. They have two sinks. She leaves her rings on the side of the sink, and never wears them to sleep. She doesn't like them to get oily from body lotion or soap."

"Do you know all her jewelry?" the Chinese detective asked.

"Only what she's worn. There may be some pieces I haven't seen. She keeps the box locked."

"Do you know where it is?"

"Yes, it's on a shelf in her closet."

"What are your duties? Do you do the cleaning?" The detective moved away from the bedroom door, down the hall to the front of the house.

"I do light housekeeping." Lynn followed her

into the sitting-room side of the master suite that took up the whole third floor.

"What would that consist of?"

"I pick up, and make things look neat. I have to put the towels and the kids' clothes in the washing machine and dryer, but I don't iron or do the sheets. A cleaning lady comes in twice a week to do the heavy work."

"What days does she come in?"

"Monday and Thursday."

"That would be yesterday."

"Yes."

"What about this room?" April asked.

Lynn noticed that the coffee table in front of the love seat was piled with Alison's fashion magazines and recent issues of *People*. Two armchairs with a reading light between them. Plasma TV on the wall near the fake wall with the powder room behind it.

"Looks the same, except her magazines are in here."

"They weren't in here this morning?"

Lynn shook her head.

"Was this room cleaned yesterday as usual?"

"Yes."

"What about the bathroom?"

She nodded. "Top to bottom, everything's cleaned. No exceptions. That's the rule."

"Who uses the bathroom?"

"Nobody."

"Are you sure?" the detective asked.

"People have their habits. I use my own. The girl use theirs. Andrew and Alison each have their own toilets. They don't use this one. It's really small," she added.

"Just look at it for me."

Lynn shrugged and punched the wall so that it popped open.

"Anything different about this?"

"Well, the sink's wet . . . and somebody's used the hand towel."

"Anything else? Look carefully."

"No."

"Thank you." April said, shutting the door.

They moved into the dressing room, where all the clothes were in careful order except for Andrew's and Alison's clothes from the night before, which looked as if they'd been hurriedly dumped in a heap. Lynn commented on that, then pointed out the jewelry box. In the bathroom a diamond watch was on the vanity right where she'd said it would be, but no rings.

"Anything missing here?" the detective asked.

A lump rose in Lynn's throat. "Her rings. She had three—a big diamond engagement ring, and two diamond bands that she wore on either side of it. Maybe she forgot to take them off last night," she said uneasily.

"Maybe."

They came back into the hall, where a number of people had gathered.

"We're ready for you now," someone said, and Lynn knew that it was Andrew's turn to look at the body.

"Lynn, could you wait downstairs? I'll be back with you later." The detective gave her a reassuring smile. "Thanks."

Lynn didn't want to see Andrew again, so she ducked through the door to the narrow back stairs and ran down to hide in her room two floors down.

Thirty-four

April reached Woody at Midtown North at eleven fifteen. "Where are you?" he asked.

"Alison Perkins is dead. Didn't anybody tell you?"

"Yeah, Sergeant Gelo just told me a little while ago. How can I help, boss?" he asked.

"Did you take photos of the people present in the crowd yesterday at the Wilson house?"

"Yes, ma'am, I did."

"Have you had them developed yet?"

"Yup, I've got them here. Are we looking for anybody in particular?" he asked.

"Not yet. You have notes from everyone you talked to yesterday?"

"Yes, you want me to come over?"

"Please, and bring your camera. I want you to take more pictures at the Perkins house. Let's see if there are any overlaps on the people hanging around today. Also, make copies of your report and bring it."

"Address?" he asked.

She gave him the address and dialed the medical examiner's office. It took a long time to get Dr.

Gloss on the line. She refused to talk to anybody else.

"I guess I have to call you April Sanchez now. How's the bride doing?" he said when he finally answered the call.

"Great until yesterday," April said. "How about you?"

"Same." He sighed. "What's going on up there? I was working on the Wilson woman's brain and somebody comes in and tells me her friend is dead."

"It's a sad thing. Another young mother. About the same age as the Wilson woman. Also killed in her home—different COD here, but there are some similarities in the MO. We have to nail this one quickly."

"Well, naturally. Is that why no one's here?" he asked.

"Yeah, that's the reason," April said, even though *she* would have avoided the autopsy anyway. She was the opposite of her mother, who liked nothing more than watching surgery all day long. "What do you have to tell me about it?" She didn't want to fuss, but she was in kind of a hurry.

"Mrs. Wilson was a generally healthy, well-nourished woman . . ." he said slowly. "But it's taking time. There are a lot of things to consider here. I'm not nearly finished with everything yet. It's going to take a week or ten days for a full report."

"How about a few generalities, like your gross impression of the case—the COD, the weapon or weapons we should be looking for?"

"There are a few things that stand out. . . ." he said slowly. Then, after his initial reluctance, he went into great length about bones and ligaments—healed traverse fractures on Maddy's left radio-ulnar, something about the long external lateral ligaments of the right knee, and the something-something tendon of the popliteus muscle as well as calcareous material that was apparently forming on synovial fringes.

"What are they?" April interrupted finally. It was always difficult to contain a pathologist once he got going.

"I gather she was a skier," he said obliquely.

"Yes, she was a skier," April confirmed. It had been in all the news stories.

"Right. She had healed fractures in her left arm. Torn ligaments in both knees, as well as the beginnings of osteoarthritis in her knees and elbows. She would have been a candidate for knee replacements sometime down the line." He went on to comment on Maddy's teeth, which had been capped; her eyes, which had the benefit of fairly recent plastic surgery; and her nasal passages, which showed signs of disintegration, probably from frequent cocaine use.

"She must have been getting fairly regular nose-bleeds," he finished.

"You're doing toxicology tests to determine alcohol and possible drug levels." It wasn't a question.

"Of course," he replied.

"Would any of the above bear any relation to her cause of death?" That wasn't really a question, either.

"No, not the cause of death. The presence of

cocaine could have heightened her excitability, raised her blood pressure, done a lot of things that might have helped—or hindered—her defense against her attacker."

"What about COD?"

"She sustained multiple stab wounds to the chest, neck, eye. Deep gashes in her palms and the under-surface of her fingers indicate that she tried to grab a knife, and it was pulled away from her. She also has cuts on her right foot and leg, indicating she also attempted to kick a knife out of the attack-er's hand."

"You said a knife. Can you tell what kind of knife was used, or if there was more than one?"

"April," he said sternly. "You know how difficult incised wounds are to analyze. A lot of things come into play—whether the cutting is done parallel to the lines of cleavage or across the lines of cleavage."

She was an experienced detective, but she did not know what cleavage he meant. "It looked like some of the cuts were made postmortem."

He snickered. "See, that's the mistake a lot of people make. I guess you don't know much about incised wounds."

"No, not like this, where there's no blood spat-ter. I've read some articles, but I'm not an expert," April said.

"Exactly right. I think you're referring to gaping wounds as opposed to wounds where the edges re-main closed. That's what I was just telling you—whether the edge is jagged or smooth, open or closed, depends on where on the body the cutting is done, as well as the instrument that's used. It's not a pre- or postmortem issue at all. You'll have to leave the question of postmortem stabbing to me. It's not that easy to ascertain. You need to go inside for that. And all cuts do not produce the same degree of bleeding. I'd say two knives, probably a boning-type knife with a slender blade and then maybe a thicker one. By the way, the body was exposed to water for no more than twenty minutes."

April exhaled. "The girl who found her said the shower was on. She was the one who turned it off just before calling 911. Can you confirm the time?"

"We'll do some tests, of course. Prepare to get into the shower for us," he joked.

"Ha-ha."

"But I'd say no more than twenty minutes," he said more seriously.

"That would pretty much let our three primary suspects off the hook," April told him.

"Then, you'd better start looking for someone else, because when I tell you skin has been underwater for twenty minutes or less, it's not going to mean thirty-eight. But don't pin me down on this right now. We'll test it out."

"Okay. What else can you tell me?"

"Well, I haven't seen the crime scene yet, have I? At this point I can just make a few guesses. Does that shower have a bench in it? Does it have steam or dry heat?"

"I believe steam," April confirmed.

"Okay, a slash on the triceps of the victim's right upper arm indicates she might have been lying down, possibly steaming at the time of the attack. The front of her right arm resting on her forehead may have covered her eyes. She was in repose."

"It's possible. If she didn't see the attack coming, steam would explain a lot of things." April made a note to test how long it took to make steam, and how dense it got. Every minute counted. Also, the sound made by the steam coming out of the pipe could have dulled her hearing. Sometimes it was a loud hiss.

"It looks to me like the killer may have entered the shower with the intention of stabbing her in the chest, and had not expected a fight."

"What makes you think that?"

"The killer didn't know anything about anatomy and wasn't very powerful. There were a lot of hesitation strikes," he said after a pause.

"Tell me more." That would let Remy off the hook. From butchering lessons, she knew anatomy very well. And as a trainer, Derek probably did, too. And Wayne was a chef.

"For now let's assume the first blow was deflected by the sudden movement of her arm. Maybe she heard something and started to get up. The kind of wounds she had suggests that she started fighting back right away, and the killer didn't know how to end the game. Just like not being able to make the point in tennis, he just struck again and again, without getting anywhere. Six blows hit bone or cartilage and didn't penetrate deep enough to do mortal injury. Furthermore the weapons did not twist inside the wounds, indicating the killer couldn't find soft tissue to penetrate and wasn't strong enough to muscle through cartilage and bone, especially with the victim in pretty good physical condition and fighting back."

"What about the eye?"

"Again, not that deep an incision. It looked horrible, but it didn't kill her. She might have been pushing the attacker away when that blow occurred, or she may have fallen. There would have been a good deal of bleeding at the time. Both the attacker and the victim would have been covered with it. The pattern of wounds suggests that the victim moved from side to side. The attacker may have had a weapon in each hand and stabbed with both hands."

"So the cause of death was . . . ?" April asked again.

"The fatal blow is situated between the fifth and sixth rib three-quarters of an inch from the inner side, three and a half inches from the middle line of the sternum. In other words, it missed the lung and penetrated the thoracic wall, and pericardium. He finally got lucky and penetrated her heart. Death at this point would have been instantaneous. I'm still working. I have to go now. No quotes, okay? This was entirely off the record."

"If he wasn't strong and didn't know how to do it, how did he end the game?"

"I'd say she fell, and was lying on her back at the time. The blade went in from above, and the killing cut was not the widest one. As I said, it was so perfect, it must have been a lucky shot."

"Right- or left-handed?"

"That's like asking what color the killer's hair is. I'm guessing two weapons, and I don't know which hand was the good one. You guys will have to act it out."

"One more thing."

"I know. How deep is the cut? How long are the

knives? What kind of knives? It's not one more thing—it's a dozen things, and I'm not answering yet." Then he answered. "Lying down, her breast would be flattened. The hilt didn't bruise her, so it didn't go all the way in. So the knife could be any size. Not serrated, though."

"Thanks for taking the call. It helped a lot," April said as she heard her name shouted from upstairs.

Thirty-five

After Wayne left the hotel, Remy was frightened by the police. A man who said he was a detective called and told her to stay where she was. Someone was coming by to pick her up.

"Why? Am I being arrested?" she asked anxiously.

"No, no. Just an interview at this time," he said.

She called the agency immediately. No one was there, so she left a message for Jo Ellen to call her back on her cell phone when she got in. "It's an emergency," she said.

But the police didn't come, and Jo Ellen didn't return the call until almost noon. By then Angus and Bertie's grandmother had arrived and taken them to the park, and Remy had been in the hotel room alone for more than two hours. She had her knapsack packed and ready to go, but she didn't dare leave for either the police station or parts unknown without alerting Jo Ellen.

"I'm sorry I couldn't get back to you, Remy. You wouldn't believe how hectic my day has been," she said sternly when she finally returned the call. "I know all this has been difficult for you, but what's the big emergency?"

Jo Ellen—Miss Anderson to her staffers—never failed to acknowledge that certain aspects of working for her clients *could* be stressful at times. But being at the center of a murder case was more than just stressful. "I can't stay with . . . Mr. Wilson any longer," Remy started slowly. "I did my best for you, but this is too much."

"What's too much? Tell me everything," Jo Ellen said soothingly. "I'm here for you. You know that."

Remy had heard that before. She paced the living room of the suite, back and forth in front of the two windows, which had a good view of Central Park. "The police called me. They want to question me again. And Wayne freaked out this morning. I really thought he was going to hit me. I can't do this anymore. I'm sorry if I'm letting you down, but this isn't working." That was an understatement.

"Remy, have some understanding," Jo Ellen intoned self-righteously. "The poor man lost his wife."

Jo Ellen's knee-jerk reaction to everything was "Have some understanding." It didn't matter what was going on with her clients—an unwarranted temper tantrum, a missing tennis bracelet (perhaps lost in a taxi or on the sidewalk), a broken Ming vase (by a cat), refusal to give a hardworking employee vacation time or a raise for no reason at all—she took their side in every dispute. Usually it was just maddening, but now it was dangerous. And she didn't even mention the police.

"I was understanding. I'm very sorry he lost his wife, but he didn't have to see it. He didn't have to hang around all day. I took the hit for everything. I was the one interviewed by the police practically all day yesterday, and they're not finished. They're focused on *me*. I need help, Miss Anderson. He has a lawyer. Maybe I need a lawyer—"

Jo Ellen cut her off. "You told me all that yesterday. Believe me, I'm sympathetic. But if you leave the Wilson household before this thing is settled, I'm just not sure what I can do for you. You'll have to relocate, anyway, and I do have someone looking for a chef in the Bahamas. . . ."

Remy was appalled by this response. She was fearful that the police had a different kind of relocation in mind. And even if they didn't, the last thing she wanted was to be someone's chef in the Bahamas! She yearned for the glamour of a restaurant. She was quite fed up with Jo Ellen's coaching and considered saying, "I quit for you, too," but she didn't have a chance.

"What did you do to provoke him?" she demanded.

"Nothing. I went out for a walk. That's all," Remy said defensively. Jo Ellen always thought the worst of everybody.

"You left the children, and you know better than that."

"No, no. I didn't leave them. It was six-thirty in the morning. No one was up." Remy was reduced to defending herself to everyone. It was horrible.

"Well, where did you go, then? Haven't you learned anything I taught you? You're supposed to stay put. What happened last night? What did he do?" The questions came fast.

"He talked on the phone with some lawyer. I don't know, somebody Mr. Perkins got for him. He told Mr. Perkins he had to get rid of Lynn."

"Yes, yes. I know all that. I'm completely fed up

with you girls. In a hundred years, we've never had to face anything remotely like this. I'm distraught. You two are not making me look good. Where did you go?" She was back on that again.

"I didn't go anywhere in particular. I was upset. I had to get some fresh air and consider my options." Remy didn't want to tell her where she'd been. It was none of Jo Ellen's business.

"What options are you talking about?" Jo Ellen's voice became angry. It was plain she was just furious about everything.

"I don't know," Remy mumbled.

"That's exactly right—*you don't know.* I feel bitterly betrayed by you, Remy. I did everything you asked. I placed you with the exact person you wanted to meet. You could have gone another route and applied for a restaurant job, but you didn't want to do that. You wanted intimate access to the great Wayne Wilson himself. I gave you that. It turned out that you were very well liked there, but you messed up. You just couldn't be content. You had to push the envelope and go where you shouldn't go. You know that's against my express rules."

Remy gathered that she was talking about her and Wayne. "What did she say to you?" she asked meekly.

"If you're talking about Mrs. Wilson"—Jo Ellen blew air out of her mouth to express her frustration—"I'm just disgusted with you. I trusted you in a good home. But once you start alienating affections, you're done. I've told you that a thousand times. Don't mess with the husbands. Didn't I tell you that?"

"I didn't alienate his affections," Remy insisted.

"It was *her* perception, and *she* paid your salary."

Actually, Wayne paid her salary, but Remy wasn't about to correct her. "I'm sorry," she said meekly. "It wasn't a big deal, and I didn't mean to complicate things."

"Well, it was a big deal to her, and you complicated things. Now you have to stay where you are and behave yourself until I say that you can leave. I could make things very rough for you if you don't," she threatened. And then she said she had important things to do and hung up.

Where were the police? Where was refuge? What were her options? She had no idea. With the horrified feeling that she was trapped in a madhouse, Remy stood looking at the dead receiver. She was a soldier stuck in a war not of her own making, pinned in place, and watched from all sides. She didn't even know how to start planning. Finally she replaced the headset and did what she always did on occasions of deep stalemate—whatever was asked of her. She started tidying up the children's clothes. This time was no different from any other time in her life. No matter what her state of rebellion she always had trouble taking that first step. After a few minutes she turned on the TV. On the news she was shocked to see police outside of the Perkins house. Emergency vehicles. Reporters with video equipment. She stared in disbelief. It had happened again.

Thirty-six

It took all morning for the preliminary work on the Perkins house to be completed. The process of uncovering Alison Perkins's body took over an hour longer. At this point Mike was long gone and Minnow had left the building only to return later. April, however, felt that she owed it to Alison to stay with her body until it was tagged, bagged, and taken away. It seemed that every month that task took longer and longer as crime-scene techniques became more sophisticated. By the time the assistant from the medical examiner's office got to the Perkins house, one corner of the bedroom had a sizable pile of waste from packaged test materials. The room was gritty with powders, and the odor of ammonia lingered in the room.

When Sergeant Minnow entered the room for the first time, he'd wrinkled his nose. "What's that smell, poison?"

"Smells like household cleaner to me," said Igor, the more experienced half of the CSI team.

Minnow frowned at April as if to say, *What are you still doing here?*

She smiled benignly at him as she gathered her thoughts. She had the same sense now that she'd experienced yesterday, that someone was sending a message. The first body had been washed in the shower, the second possibly with household cleanser. What was that about? She shook her head sadly. She needed to see Alison's body, and it was taking forever. Igor and Tam, a new face in the unit, peeled back Alison's bedspread centimeter by centimeter, carefully checking for foreign materials of any kind, stray fibers, hair, a broken nail— anything at all that might have been left behind by someone leaving the scene. They picked off tiny items with tweezers. Dog hairs, people hairs, threads, and feathers—something that looked like a scab, but Igor identified as "probably a booger."

April glanced at her watch for the hundredth time. The minutes ticked away, postponing her long to-do list. She had that hair sample from the powder room in her purse. She had her own plans for it. She'd already raided all the hairbrushes in the house. It was too short and coarse for the little girls' hair. Too short for Lynn's as well. She'd made some notes to herself. Hair from the cleaning lady from yesterday? How long did it take for water drops in a sink to dry out? Could it still have been wet from the day before? Probably not. Maybe the killer's hair. What color?

Whoever it was had definitely been in Alison's closet, had been in the bathroom, had been in the sitting room. Lynn was sure the magazines had not been there earlier in the morning. Igor had tested them for prints, and all of them had been wiped clean. Maybe the exit path had been through the little sitting room, and the killer had stopped there to wash up. Another note to herself. Alison's rings were missing. What else?

Finally Igor and Tam lifted the rolled bedspread off the end of the bed and bagged it. By then there was no longer any doubt about the nature of Alison's death. Her body was clothed in a long white nightgown, carefully tucked around her ankles. Her hands were folded across her chest. The witnesses to the unveiling made a tableau around the bed—Sergeant Minnow, April, the assistant from the medical examiner's office, and Igor and Tam.

"Oh, Jesus," Minnow exclaimed.

The smell of ammonia was strong on the body, and it was clear that whatever mess Alison had made in dying had been washed away with household cleanser. Her body had been swabbed with it. The cameras started again, taking pictures of the dead woman from all angles.

"Some sick puppy, the person who did this," Minnow muttered.

No one else said anything. The assistant ME did a cursory examination of the victim's head, chest, arms, hands, and shoulders. There didn't appear to be any tissue under her fingernails, bruises on her neck, arms, shoulders, head. Just that horrible anguished face and the wide-open eyes. Her hands were paper-bagged anyway.

Minnow turned away. He was done there. "You got anything?" he asked April as they walked down the hall to the stairs.

She told him about her conversation with Lynn. "Was that guy who followed Remy one of your people?"

He laughed. "Uh-uh. Ours was a female. She didn't pick it up," he said with a moment of pride. "Yeah, we knew Remy came over here." Then he sobered quickly and ticked the events off on his fingers. "Let's get this straight. The two nannies meet for coffee at six forty-five. Yesterday's killer tells today's killer she's getting canned, so she offs her boss, too? What is this, the revenge of the nannies?"

April shook her head. "I'm seeing a small window of opportunity when someone close to the two victims knew they would be alone and vulnerable. Maddy Wilson was in her steam room relaxing after her workout. Her husband and her nanny were off together in his restaurant. We've got some witnesses to that. We talked to the chef last night. Wilson was taking inventory. Remy was with him. This morning, Alison had taken a tranquilizer, or possibly two, as was her habit when she'd abused too much. Yesterday was a stressful day for her, and she'd done too much cocaine, I'm guessing. She was popping Vicodin to come down and had gone back to bed for a nap. Again, Lynn was out taking the girls to play school. So in that window, I'm seeing someone else."

"Then you don't think it was either of the nannies?" Minnow said. They started down the stairs to the living-room floor.

"Remy was not truthful in her interviews, but I believe that was because she was having an affair with her boss," April said.

"In my book that's a motive."

April shook her head. "It's a reason to feel guilty."

"Sounds like a motive to me, but okay, have it your own way," he said as if he would never let that happen. "Just for the sake of conversation let's eliminate the nannies. Who then . . . the trainer?" He scratched his head as if he didn't like that idea.

"Well, no. I spoke to Dr. Gloss. He said Maddy Wilson's body was exposed to the hot shower for less than twenty minutes. That would eliminate him."

"No way!" he exclaimed.

"Working backward. Derek was in the deli at nine-oh-five and in his gym at nine fifteen. If Remy found the body and turned off the shower at nine forty-five, the attack would have happened after he left." It wasn't rocket science.

"You spoke to the ME?" Minnow said, sounding surprised.

"Yeah," April said modestly, because it was a coup to reach him. She stopped inside the front door of the house, not wanting to finish the conversation on the sidewalk surrounded by reporters.

Minnow screwed up his face. "So what's your hypothesis?" he asked.

"I don't know. But I was wondering, is there a surveillance camera here?"

"No." He looked as if he wanted to know what she was planning, but was afraid to ask, so she helped him out.

"I'm going to talk to Remy again," she said. "She needs to come clean on everything she knows."

He nodded and didn't query where this interview was going to take place. Apparently he wasn't in the loop about what had happened yesterday. Then he said, "We'll be getting more people on this now. How about you give me your cell phone number so I can reach you if something comes up."

"Oh, yeah, of course," she said. It hadn't occurred to her that nobody had given it to him. She gave him the number. They opened the door, and the barrage of reporters' questions began.

Thirty-seven

At noon, Eloise closed the door of her office, sat down at her desk, and rewound the taped interview of Alison Perkins. Then she took out a pad of paper and started listening to the first cassette. After a few minutes, it was clear to her that April Woo really knew her stuff. She had led Alison through a detailed history of her friendship with the woman everyone had called Maddy. Alison and Maddy had met in a gym long before they had children. They'd planned their pregnancies together, used the same obstetrician and hospital. They'd had babies at the same time, almost to the month, attended natural-childbirth class together, and traveled to health spas out West. They'd shopped together, and used the same employment agency to get their baby nurses and nannies. It was at the point in the narrative when Alison began talking about the nannies that her voice became more agitated.

"These girls. They come from nowheresville, never lived in a good house. For a few weeks they're nice as can be—cheerful, helpful. The kids are happy. It seems like everything's finally going to be peachy. Then they start ganging up." Sound of nervous laughter.

"What happens?"

"They start wanting everything, our houses, our clothes, our jewelry, our husbands. They bring their friends around. . . . What time is it? I have to go."

"In a minute. Tell me more about these nannies."

"Oh, some of them are lazy. They start slacking off, and you have to negotiate what they'll do and won't do. You think they want to please you, but then they start faking it. And then little things go missing—and big things, too. One of them stole my tennis bracelet—seven carats of diamonds. It wasn't as big as Maddy's, but I loved that bracelet. I threw her out fast. It was too bad—that one had been really nice. But Jo Ellen always has a replacement. The better ones cost more, of course, and every time it's a new contract."

"What kind of contract?"

"We pay twenty percent of the salary for a year. If they leave before a year, then I'd get a discount on the next one, but they never leave. I have to fire them. Then we start over. It's a racket."

Eloise made a note. *Anderson placing unacceptable girls?* At the same time she heard Woo's voice asking, "Did you ever try another agency?"

"No. Anderson is the best. Jo Ellen vets the girls. She gives them personality tests, and does background searches. Of course they have to be legal, have driver's licenses and everything. I wouldn't trust anybody else to be that careful."

"How about Remy? Did she come highly recommended?"

"Oh, that was not a good match for Maddy from the get-go. Maddy wanted a first-class nanny, pure and simple. She was not interested in food. Wayne wanted a chef for the boys because Maddy didn't cook. Conflict right there. Remy needed a place to stay while she finished cooking school. They made a deal."

"She's a pretty girl. Was that a problem for Maddy?"

"No, of course not. You wouldn't want unattractive people in your house, would you?"

Not a smart girl, Eloise thought. She fast-forwarded a number of times, listened to the cocaine questions, and turned off the machine. She found Hagedorn in front of his computer. "Want to go for a drive?"

His pale blue eyes came alive as if she'd just offered him a joyride in a Ferrari. Then he said, "I'm the computer guy. Why me?"

"Everybody needs a friend, Charlie," she said.

He nodded slowly, smiling a little at being invited to the party for the first time. He wasn't used to being anyone's partner, even for a day. "Okay, but we have to be back for Lorna Dorne at two," he said.

"We'll be back. I never forget a stripper." She laughed.

They hurried downstairs, and he took the wheel of the unmarked Buick. They crossed town at a snail's pace, and their personal interaction was a replay of the night before. He drove carefully and didn't initiate any conversation.

"You ever do an interview?" Eloise asked him after a while.

"Back when I was on patrol," he replied.

"Where was that?" Eloise asked.

"Staten Island."

"No kidding?" Eloise had been to Staten Island only a handful of times. She lapsed into silence for several blocks. Then she asked him how he liked working for the lieutenant.

"She's very determined," he replied after a pause.

"Is that a good thing?"

He shrugged. "It is what it is."

"Very profound," she said as he parked in a bus zone.

The Anderson Agency was on the second floor of a fine old Lexington Avenue building on Sixty-third Street. The building had a pricey antique shop downstairs and a discreet entrance with a brass plaque that looked as if it belonged on Madison Avenue. The elevator was wood paneled and marble floored. When they got out, without appearing to be aware of doing it, Hagedorn stood up a little straighter. He reached for the office doorknob to open it for the sergeant, but the glass door of the Anderson Agency was locked. He rang the bell for entry, the lock clicked, and they went into a place that looked like an apartment. The reception area was a large waiting room with French chairs and leaded windows with velvet drapes.

A reed-thin middle-aged woman with a bun and no makeup sat at a long table loaded with magazines—*Town & Country, House & Garden,* and *Avenue.* She looked them over. "Do you have an appointment?"

"I'm Sergeant Gelo from the New York City Police Department. This is Detective Hagedorn. Is Miss Anderson available?"

"One moment." Staring at them as if they were wild animals, she got on the phone and pushed a few buttons. "Miss Anderson, some people from the police department are here to see you. Yes, Miss Anderson." She hung up the phone. "She's just finishing something up. Will you follow me?"

The receptionist stood up and led the way through curtained French doors into another room. This one looked like the antique shop downstairs. It had fabric on the walls, an ornate desk, a number of French-looking gilt armchairs with brocade seats and backs, a fireplace, and the kind of small tables and decorative objects that couldn't easily be copied. They gawked for no more than thirty seconds.

"Oh, good, you've found the parlor. I'm Miss Anderson."

A rather frightening woman who looked as if she came from another era entered through a different door. She wore a suit that hadn't been seen out on the street since the 1930s. The tweed was old-fashioned. The jacket was long, the shoulders were padded, and the skirt came down to the middle of Anderson's sturdy calves. Under the jacket was a paisley blouse that matched the paisley turban that made her head look like a small beach ball. Miss Anderson looked like the psychic in a Noël Coward play Eloise had been in a long time ago in high school. No lipstick or rouge softened her stern countenance. Eloise found it difficult to believe this was the woman Maddy Wilson and Alison Perkins relied on for their household help.

Although normally she was not daunted by anyone, she actually deflated a little at the powerful beam of disapproval Anderson sent her way. She was wearing the clothes from her locker—tight blue trousers, a revealing sweater, and a leather jacket that did not even try to hide the Glock at her waist. Her hair was in its usual seductive disarray, and she had to remind herself her makeup was perfect.

"I'm Sergeant Eloise Gelo, and this is Detective Charles Hagedorn. We're from the New York City Police Department," she said.

"Yes, I know. You're the sergeant?" Anderson replied.

"Yes, ma'am," Eloise told her.

"Humph. Well, appearances can be deceiving." She sat in the chair that most resembled a throne, crossed her ankles, and gestured for the two detectives to arrange themselves around her.

"One of your customers was murdered yesterday."

"Clients," Anderson corrected. "Yes, Mrs. Wilson."

"And another one of your clients was murdered this morning."

"Oh, who?" Miss Anderson tilted her head to one side as if this were a rude bit of gossip.

"Alison Perkins."

"My, my! That is a startling coincidence, isn't it?" She looked shocked.

"You placed the nannies in their houses," Eloise told her.

"We've been working with those two clients for years." She frowned and tilted her head the other way. "It's hard to believe. . . ."

"How were they to work for?"

"You know how young mothers are these days."
She smiled with no warmth, as if that covered the
subject.

Eloise took out her notebook and Charlie followed suit. With no further preliminaries, she said,
"We need your files on Remy and Lynn."

"Dear me, I know they have no part in this. I
checked them out myself." Miss Anderson clasped
her hands together.

"It's routine."

"I don't think you understand. The Anderson
Agency has been in business in this very room for
over a hundred years. No employment agency in
the country has a longer or more distinguished history. We've staffed the great homes of America—
the Rockefellers, the Vanderbilts, the Fords, the
Kennedys, the Roosevelts—royal families all over
the world use our services. Queens, princes!"

"We still need the files," Eloise said before Miss
Anderson got too wrapped up in her speech.

"They come because I'm discreet. I understand
their needs. They sit in the chairs where you're
sitting. They tell me the intimate details of their
lives because they know that I will keep their secrets. All these years I have kept the secrets, and
I will not change that for anything." Although she
did not look that old, Miss Anderson gave the impression of being nearly a hundred years old herself, stuck somewhere between World War I and
World War II with her turban and mannish shoulder pads.

Eloise glanced at Hagedorn. He was taking notes

at a furious pace and she wondered what he was writing. "Do you have secrets to keep about Mrs. Wilson and Mrs. Perkins?" she asked.

"I will not desecrate their memories," Anderson said flatly.

"How well did you know them?"

"Well enough to know that they were difficult to staff. Young people are different these days. But I try to be understanding." She shut thin lips and lifted her eyebrows. "This is the exodus, you know."

"The exodus?"

"The time they leave for the summer. Every year it's a problem. The husband in one place, the wife and children in another. And they're never happy, are they?"

"They weren't happy?"

She raised her eyebrows. "These were not the best families," she said after a dramatic pause. "You know how that is."

"Ah," Eloise murmured knowingly, although she had no idea what the woman was talking about.

"I see the whole idea is foreign to you." She tapped a sensible shoe.

"Are you talking about the Social Register?" Eloise said as if she finally got it.

"No, no. Nobody cares about the Social Register anymore. Quality goes deeper than that."

"So Mrs. Wilson and Mrs. Perkins were not high-class people. Is that a major flaw?" Eloise asked.

"Don't misunderstand me. I have all kinds of clients. Some of them are people one wouldn't sit down to dinner with."

Eloise smiled, aware that she would be one of them.

"That's not what I mean in this case, though. These were the new school—ungrateful young women who have everything in the world but are never pleased with what they have or the service they receive from others," she said sternly.

"So they fired everybody."

"Everybody."

"I imagine that would be a good thing for you. You get a commission for each placement."

"I can't comment on that."

"Mrs. Perkins said that you get twenty percent of a year's salary. That can add up if you have several in a year."

"Indeed."

"So maybe you didn't always place the very best girls with them. Did they have previous employment problems?"

"There's no need to be challenging. I will give you the files, if you want them," Anderson said suddenly. "That will be all for now." She stood up and ushered them to the door.

Gelo and Hagedorn were used to every kind of behavior. They cooled their heels with the chilly receptionist until a younger woman brought them a manila envelope. Relieved that they didn't have to get out the big guns, they took it and bolted.

Thirty-eight

Woody tried, unsuccessfully, to get into the Perkins house. He was waiting for April by the car when she finally emerged and pushed through the thicket of reporters. She saw him step forward and wave, but stopped for a moment to talk to Lily, who had her cameraman all set up for an interview.

"It's a homicide, but I can't tell you any more than that at this time," she told the reporter, who'd freshened her lipstick when April emerged.

"Is that the best you can do?" Lily demanded.

"The very best," April said, tilting her head to give a bad angle to the cam.

"Oh, come on. We've been here all morning. What were you doing in there?" she asked.

Talking on the phone, talking to Igor and Tam while they worked the crime scene, talking to Lynn Papel and Andrew Perkins, searching the house for Alison's missing diamond rings. April smiled ruefully. "The usual," she murmured.

"Fuck, April. I thought we were friends."

"We are friends, but you know the rules. I'm not the go-to person on this. Let's have lunch soon, okay?"

"Aren't you sailing on Friday?" Lily waved away her cameraman.

The red light on the video cam went off, but April was startled nonetheless. "How did you know that?" She'd forgotten all about her honeymoon.

"Oh, I have my way." Lily smiled, and at that moment looked exactly like Lucy Liu, playing the stereotypical evil Chinese dragon lady.

April smiled. Despite the facade, she didn't think Lily was so tough. "Okay, what do you know?"

"I have some stuff." Lily checked her watch. "How about lunch? I don't have to be at the studio until five."

"This is homicide, not a game, Lily. If you know anything at all about this, give right now."

"Dinner?" she teased. "It'll be worth it."

"It's a crime to withhold information." April didn't feel like playing. "I have to go."

"All right, breakfast tomorrow, then. I promise you won't be sorry."

"Okay, we'll see." April crossed the street, and Woody stepped forward to meet her with a happy smile.

"Boss, how ya doin'?" he said.

"Not a good day for me." She moved toward the car, pushing the reporter out of her mind.

"I have the photos from yesterday that you asked for." Woody looked around. The street was closed, but pedestrians and their dogs and children were still loitering on the block. "Some of the same people are here."

He opened the passenger door of the car, and she settled in with a sigh. "Did you take any photos today?"

"Of course," he said.

"Good, we'll take a look later."

He held the door open for a second, gazing at her with expectation. "Where to?"

"The lab. I want to talk to Ducci."

"Okey-dokey."

Woody walked around to the driver's side and headed east. As they turned up Sutton Place, he started whistling through his teeth. April didn't hear it at first. She was debating calling home to see what mischief her mother was up to. The wise option would be to call, but she didn't think she could handle someone yelling at her right now. "Take the Fifty-ninth Street entrance to the bridge," she instructed Woody.

"So . . . was it as bad as yesterday?" he asked after a moment.

"Yes." She didn't want to talk about it. On the bridge going to Queens, the traffic slowed to a crawl. "What's going on with Sergeant Gelo?" she asked.

"Looks like she's chosen Hagedorn for her partner," he said, whistling again.

Interesting call. "Cut that out, Woody."

He continued whistling.

"Woody!"

"Sorry, boss." He shut up.

Twenty-five minutes later, they parked in the lab lot, checked in at the desk, went through the metal detector and the cage, and headed to the elevator. As they went down the hall, she heard a familiar voice teaching a class on crime scene techniques. Woody pushed the button, the elevator doors opened, and they went up.

Fernando Ducci was known as the Duke of Dust. He had a large, ultramodern space in the new police lab that he'd managed to clutter with his huge collection of specimens practically the day he moved there. He was an old-time dust and fiber man who'd spent years making samples of dirt and dust, thousands of materials and fabrics, the hair and hide of every conceivable animal and bug— pretty much anything dry that he could think of— just in case he needed them in a case sometime down the road. In his thirty-odd years on the job, he'd seen bits and pieces of everything from every corner of the city—from the largest crime scene in American history, the World Trade Center site, to beaches, airports, car trunks, warehouses, and so on. He knew his materials like no one else. He was white-haired, not tall, and thick from shoulders to knees from a lifetime addiction to Snickers and Mars bars. Every time April visited him, he offered her lunch from his candy drawer.

Today she'd called him from the road, and he was waiting for her at his cluttered desk, thoughtfully chewing on a Snickers. When she came in, he put the uneaten portion down on the edge as if it were the butt of a burning cigar. "Pretty one, let me look at you," he cried.

"Hey, Duke." April prepared for the onslaught of recriminations of neglect, and it came quickly.

"I never see you anymore. I guess you don't love me now that you've married that bum. You only come when you're in trouble."

"Well, of course." She laughed and took his hands.

"Are you pregnant yet? Let's see." He held out his arms.

She laughed. "No, no, not pregnant."

He gave her a hug and held on for a few seconds too long. "Nope, not pregnant yet," he agreed. "What are you waiting for, World War III?"

"I thought we were in it already." She didn't mind the banter or the bear hug. Ducci was an eccentric who'd never married: tiny specks barely visible to the naked eye had been his true love— that and stunning shirts. She guessed that some hole-in-the-wall Chinese laundry was responsible for the excellent ironing of the elegant dress shirts he always wore. Today's was a yellow-and-blue-striped number with a pristine white collar and cuffs, probably Polo without the logo. The tie he wore with it was equally dashing. He turned to Woody.

"Who let *him* in here?" he complained.

"You know Woody, right? You're going to be hearing a lot about him in the future."

Woody grinned like an idiot, and Ducci grimaced.

"I've already heard a lot about him. Tree, tree, what the hell kind of name is that?" Duke's white hair was slicked back. His aging choirboy's face tried to be antagonistic.

April held back a smile. "So, when are you retiring like everyone else?"

"Why would I do that?" He picked up the Snickers and took a bite.

April turned to her driver.

"Woody, would you go and find Mark or Chad and tell them I'll be down in a few minutes."

He nodded and departed.

"Are they the team on the Wilson case?"

"Yes. Unfortunately, we got different people on

Perkins. Now we have to coordinate the two to see what we've got," April told him.

"They're all right." Ducci shrugged.

She didn't know what team he meant. He grabbed a chair from his absent neighbor and dusted it off with a lily-white handkerchief from his pocket. "Have a seat and tell me what you need."

"I'm helping out on the Wilson case."

"Yeah, I heard you were on it. You want a candy bar?"

"No, thanks." April's stomach rumbled, and she put her hand on it protectively.

He looked at her startled, as if inadvertently, she'd revealed a secret.

"What?" she demanded.

He smiled. "You sure about that candy bar?"

"Absolutely certain. Now, what have you got for me?"

"Take a look around. I don't have anything yet. You're too early."

With all his stuff from many cases everywhere, it was hard to tell what he was working on, but it was upsetting that they hadn't started on the high-profile homicide yet. "What are you waiting for?" she demanded.

He shrugged. "What can I say? We're short-handed. What's the story? No one tells me anything."

"A young mother was stabbed multiple times in her shower yesterday morning. She's the wife of a restaurant owner, Wayne Wilson—"

"I know that much. You got the murder weapon?" he asked.

"Maybe you don't know that the shower was on,

the body was artfully arranged, and the scene was squeaky clean."

"Oh." He lifted heavy eyebrows to look at her over skinny reading glasses. "You got a murder weapon?" he repeated.

"There were a lot of knives in the house. Wilson is a collector. And the nanny's in cooking school so she has quite a few herself. You know how tough it is with incised wounds to tell exactly what kind of knife was used."

"Where are these many knives?"

"They're in the building somewhere. We have to get going on this."

"So you're looking for blood on the knives," Ducci said.

"Yes, that and other things."

"What other things?"

April paused for a second. "There was another homicide this morning," she said as coolly as she could. "Alison Perkins lived two blocks away from Maddy Wilson. She was the dead woman's best friend. Four little kids have lost their mothers in two days." She felt badly about this, as if it were her fault.

"It's a shame. Same neighborhood? Same method?"

"We don't have a COD on Alison yet. She was found in her bed, probably smothered. Whoever did it washed her body with cleanser."

Ducci nodded. "So how can I help?"

April reached in her purse for the envelope with the hair she'd found in the Perkins powder room. "The way the house is set up, the third floor consists of two connected closets, a bathroom, and the master suite, which has a bedroom and a TV room with a tiny powder room hidden behind a painted wall."

"Uh-huh." Ducci reached in his drawer for another candy bar.

"When I searched it—"

"Oh-oh. Don't tell me you're taking things from crime scenes now. We don't go for that." He shook his finger at her.

"Duplicates," she said airily. "Crime Scene got everything I have. I just don't have time to wait. Yada yada yada. If they're going to be helpful, I need to know now." She had to resolve this case fast.

"Where's the fire?" he said.

"Please, I'm just trying to rule things out."

He shook his head. "What are you looking for, color?" Duke opened the envelope, poked at the lone hair in there with a thick finger, then got up and moved across the brightly lit space.

"Yeah, and anything else it can tell me."

"Fine, give me an hour."

"Thanks. Other hairs were tangled up with a feather. Looked to me like a goose down feather. You have the pillows from the vic's bed here." April shrugged. "I'm guessing the perp killed her with the pillow, then used the powder room to wash up."

"Okay." He got started and seemed to forget about her. When she got to the door he said, "And thank you for dropping by."

Thirty-nine

Eloise and Charlie stopped for a couple of slices of pizza before heading back across town. She didn't want to take the time to sit at a table, so they put the box between them and ate in the car. "I didn't know you like pizza," he said admiringly as they sat in a no-parking zone on Lex.

"Who doesn't like pizza?" she demanded.

She'd requested extra napkins and spread them out across her chest, hopeful of catching the oily drips—an unrealistic wish. It didn't bother her that much. She was herself, take it or leave it. Charlie watched her wrestle a long string of cheese into her mouth, then cleared his throat.

"The boss doesn't, for starters. She's kind of a dainty eater," he remarked.

"No kidding." Eloise was not surprised. The lieutenant was always pristine in tasteful, clean, well-pressed clothes, and Eloise had never seen her eat anything. Tea seemed to be her CO's only indulgence. She raised the folded slice of extra cheese, extra pepperoni, to her mouth, and two heavy drops of grease hit the thin layer of napkins in her lap. Dainty and tasteful didn't seem to be in her repertoire. "What did you think of Miss Anderson?" she asked.

"That one's not playing with a whole deck," Hagedorn snorted. "What was that outfit?"

"Vintage. Don't you know vintage when you see it?" Suddenly her appetite was gone. She dropped the crust into the pizza box and wiped her hands on a napkin. "I wish I had a Handi Wipe," she said wistfully.

"Here." Charlie reached into his pocket and passed one over.

"Gee . . . thanks," she said, for once restraining the urge to make a stinging remark. Who but a complete nut carried foil-wrapped hand cleansers in his jacket pocket?

"Let me get that box out of your way," he said as he grabbed it and hopped out of the car to dump it in a garbage can. He didn't look like a guy who could hop, and once again, she withheld the smart remark. Being a staunch New Yorker, it wasn't easy.

They got back to the precinct with no further incident. Charlie took one of the files that Jo Ellen Anderson had given them, and left Eloise the other. After she'd returned a bunch of calls and talked to all the people who wanted to talk to her, she opened the file. It was Remy's. It contained the Anderson application form, which showed some basic information about her education and previous jobs, as well as a list of her skills. She'd grown up out West, gone to a local high school and state university. Along the way she'd worked in a bunch of chains—baking, frying, grilling, prepping salads, making desserts. She liked kids and could drive, didn't have a passport. There was nothing out of the ordinary about the résumé except several dozen notes on three-by-five cards in tiny handwriting, presumably Jo Ellen's.

Talked to Remy Banks. Presentation needs work. In a good house, must wear slacks and sweaters, not jeans and sweatshirts, read one. *Talked to Remy. Worried about attitude problem and reminded her that she was to fulfill any command without debate.*

Talked to Remy again today about the children. Does not want to be responsible for the children's playdates.

Talked to Remy today about her relationship with Lynn. The girls are too close and break confidentiality rules.

Talked to Remy this morning. She's rebellious: won't keep to dress code, wilfully flirts with her employer. Danger on that score!!!

Talked to Remy about her jealousy. Constantly looks for attention.

Talked to Remy today about her request for a raise—too soon, not a proven entity yet.

Eloise counted them and found, to her surprise, that the file contained more than forty comments about every aspect of Remy's conduct. Jo Ellen was concerned abut the amount of food Remy consumed at the house, her hours, her demeanor, her personal habits, the amount of money she spent while running errands. Jo Ellen had mounting doubts about Remy's viability as a domestic.

Half an hour after Eloise started, Charlie came into her office. "This is worse than one of our files," he said. "This girl sounds like a nightmare. She was fired from her former job. Jo Ellen was giving her a second chance. At this job she was accused of stealing a diamond bracelet, but nothing could be proved. There were other people in the house at the time. What about yours?" he asked.

"No accusations of theft, but that Anderson woman seems to be something of a nightmare herself."

The phone rang, and Eloise picked up. "Sergeant Gelo."

"Hey, I'm at the lab. What did you find out?"

"Hello, Lieutenant. We paid a visit to the Anderson Agency."

"How did that go?"

"It went well. We got the files. It seems Lynn was fired from her former job. Perkins was her last chance at Anderson. She may have stolen a diamond bracelet from Alison. Remy was too cozy with Wayne Wilson and had an attitude problem. The two girls were closer than Anderson liked. The Anderson woman seems to be unusually intrusive for a placement person."

"Okay, what about the warrant check?"

Eloise smiled at Charlie. "Charlie's working on that now," she said. "Are you coming in?"

"Maybe later, I'll let you know," Woo replied.

"Okay."

"Anything else?" Woo asked.

"Yes, in a few minutes, we're meeting the stripper from Spirit who gave the drugs to Peret."

"I wish I were there," Woo said.

"How do you want us to handle it?"

"You have her number in his cell phone and her message from that night in his voice mail, right? We can put her away for dealing if we need to."

"What if she has no priors?" Eloise asked.

"Hang on to her for a while, and give her a little taste of the law. She'll tattle on her boss and everyone else she knows."

"Will do."

"And keep in touch," were Woo's last words.

Forty

April hung up with Eloise and went downstairs to the Crime Scene unit. She found Woody talking to Chad, who looked as if he had all the time in the world. Although she and Igor went way back, Chad and Mark were pretty new to the unit and she'd never worked with them before. Chad Westerman was a skinny guy with a round shaved head and pale blue eyes—a real white ghost. Mark wasn't around. At the task force headquarters in the Seventeenth Precinct there was an electric atmosphere of urgency. Here, it didn't look as if much was happening.

The lab was where the engineers of crime brought the hundreds of tagged items taken from every crime scene to be analyzed. Here was the nuts-and-bolts world of forensic science. The CSU worked with the specialists and were the ones who stayed on task day and night, making models—of rooms, buildings, sometimes whole areas. They prepared the charts, graphs, and computerized reenactments of homicides, and tested the tools of death for a match. In a multiple-stabbing case like that of Maddy Wilson, they would find or create something that closely resembled human tissue and bone and use a variety of sharp instruments on it to try to find patterns consistent with Maddy's wounds. Ingenuity was the name of the game. The two detectives idly watched her hurry toward them through the maze of desks.

"What's going on?" she asked.

"I filled him in on Perkins," Woody said.

Chad looked pensive. "Maybe this is some kind of mission killer," he said.

That was someone who had a sick purpose for his crimes, who wanted to punish a particular type of person like nurses, prostitutes—or young mothers. Nobody had used the term before, and April swallowed the feeling of panic that had been building in her all morning. Maddy's murder had looked like a single tragic, but isolated, event. Alison's murder was unexpected and raised the serial-killer specter. The FBI would come on the scene and the case would mushroom in the press. But beyond that, the killing itself was a frightening escalation that didn't fit with any serial killer's profile she'd ever seen. At the onset, the need to kill and kill again usually developed over time. The perpetrator had to become confident that he was smarter than everyone else and could get away with murder before he tried attacking again. It was a head game as well as a craving. Usually, this kind of killer would relish a violent act in his fantasies for months, or even years, before striking again. It took a lot of energy to plan and carry out a face-to-face killing.

Even in those violent crimes that occurred in remote places where a killer took advantage of a passerby's vulnerable moment, it was not so easy to design a murder and carry it off. Every step was stressful and required preparation. New York City was a busy place. Even in quiet neighborhoods, people were on the streets, walking their dogs and going to work, and somebody always knew something. April imagined an arrogant individual walking down the street, getting into those two town houses in the early morning hours, surprising Maddy and Alison, and killing them. That person had been comfortable enough to spend time there afterward, arranging the bodies and washing them up. In Alison's case the killer had touched her clothes, tidied her bedroom and possibly taken her rings. It was ghoulish and upsetting, and had ritual elements about it. Then the killer had walked out of that house—or stayed to "discover" the bodies. He (or she) would know that an army of experts would be in there, searching for traces he'd left behind. Every step had to be intensely stressful.

It was not like shooting a gun from across the street. It would be more like running the Kentucky Derby, performing in the Super Bowl—hot and furious and deeply personal. What kind of person could summon that kind of energy, that kind of killing passion, twice in two days? April shook her head over their list of suspects. The trainer, who milked the victims for cash and knew their habits, hadn't left his apartment since last night when he got home from his police interview. He had to be ruled out for both murders. The disgruntled nannies who had just been fired—each acting alone or in concert with two husbands fed up with trophy wives—seemed unlikely murderers. But a mission killer? She'd been over it and over it, and prayed that it wasn't someone off the police radar screen, hiding in the shadows, and waiting until tomorrow to kill again.

"I went upstairs. Ducci doesn't have anything. Rick doesn't have anything. What's holding things up?" April didn't have all year.

"We're going good on it. We're still processing." Chad glanced quickly at Woody.

"When are you getting started? I need a time frame here."

"We are started," he replied coolly. "What do you need?"

"Cooperation. We're looking at the two homicides as connected. There are similarities in the crime scenes. You have to get with Igor."

"No problem."

"How far did you go in the Wilson house?"

"We did the usual."

"What about blood? Did you find any?"

Chad shrugged. "Not much. There were traces in the grout. Marble tiles, you know, are set much closer together than porcelain, but there were traces in the grout in the walls and floor."

"What about the drain?"

"She must have washed her hair in that shower. There was a lot of hair in the drain."

"Blood?"

He nodded. "In the hair."

"Anything else?"

"What are you looking for?"

"I'm not sure. Fibers from the killer's clothes. Hair from the head of the killer, or his body if he was naked in there with her."

"Was she sexually assaulted?" Woody asked.

"Damn." April had forgotten to ask the ME.

"Is that a yes?"

"We don't have a prelim yet," April said. "I don't know."

"So, what's the rush?" Chad scratched the side of his face. He had his own time frame.

April ignored the question. "What about mops, towels, cleaning things?" she asked.

"There was a bucket in the garage. It's filled with cleaning utensils, including a mop that had recently been used."

"Blood?"

"We haven't tested anything yet, but it did have a piece of plastic stuck to it."

April frowned. "What kind of plastic?"

"I'm guessing the kind they use for fold-up travel raincoats, or to cover outdoor furniture. It looks dried out, old. We'll check it out. I'd guess raincoat, though," he added, as if he were a raincoat connoisseur.

"Interesting," April murmured. "What about the knives?"

"We haven't started on that. As I said, we're still processing."

"Okay, thanks. We'll be in touch. Woody, meet me at the car in five minutes."

Deep in thought, April went upstairs to see Duke. He didn't turn around when her heels announced her presence. He was busy with his equipment.

"How are you doing?" she asked.

He pulled away from the hair he was studying and checked his watch for time. "I told you an hour. It hasn't been an hour yet," he complained.

"I can't wait. I have suspects to talk to," she said.

He softened. "Okay, pretty one, anything for you," he said with an indulgent smile.

"Here's what I can tell you now. The hair probably comes from a female. It's been dyed a number of times, probably every month, six weeks. You can see the stripes of color. As you know, hair grows at the rate of about a quarter inch a month and no matter how carefully the roots are done, there's always a color change. Type of hair, coarse, and I'd say it's probably dyed to cover gray. I can't tell you what brand of hair dye was used yet, but I'll work on it. Happily, there's a follicle on this one— enough to do DNA down the road, if you need it. But the provenance on this is not good since you lifted it from the scene." He shook his head.

"I told you CSU had another." April ignored the rebuke and considered the information. If the hair came from a gray-haired female, she had to be over thirty. It might be the cleaning lady or a guest from some time ago. If that was the case, it wouldn't help them.

"Anything else?" he asked.

"Yes, what color is it?"

He took out his color spectrum and showed her. While the single hair in the envelope had appeared to be light, like a blond or strawberry blond, or even ginger, the Duke made the head at unmistakably dark red.

"Are you sure?" she asked, disappointed.

"Yes, I'm sure. Are you okay?"

"Of course. Thanks, you've been a big help," she told him even though she hadn't learned a thing.

"You're welcome, and don't wait so long to come back next time," he said as she left in a hurry.

When April met Woody at the car a few minutes later, she was ready to search his photos for a red-headed woman, but she was not at all hopeful about finding one.

Forty-one

Remy was on the sofa in the living room of Wayne's suite on the tenth floor at the Plaza Hotel when two detectives knocked on the door. Her backpack was beside her, ready to go, and she was watching the news about Alison's murder. The day before when she was questioned for hours by the police, her thoughts had been all over the place. Whenever things had gone badly for her in the past, she'd hit the road and taken off. A pretty girl with some college education and a way with food, she'd always been able to get a job cooking somewhere.

Experience had taught her long ago that most people weren't very good, or at least weren't good for long—like her dad promising to stay off the bottle. So when things soured, she just moved on. She liked to think of herself as an actor in a movie, waiting for her real life to begin. Now the wish for a bus was strong, but she couldn't run away with so many people watching. She jumped at the knock on the door.

"Police, open up."

She pulled herself off the sofa and went to the door. Two overweight men she hadn't seen before were standing outside. They looked bloated from too many french fries and doughnuts and might have a stroke if they had to run after her. The thought that she could beat them in a race didn't comfort her.

"Remy Banks?" one queried.

"Yes. Could I see your identification?" she said with more determination than she felt.

She looked down the long empty hall behind them and considered bolting as they reached for their gold shields. She wondered if they would shoot her in the Plaza. Too late, the shields appeared, and they blocked her escape route as she studied them. "No one's here," she said meekly, as if there were the slightest chance they hadn't come for her.

"That's okay, little lady. We're going for a ride."

That was all they said. They herded her between them, like a criminal, downstairs and through the hotel lobby. She got into the backseat of a black sedan, and they drove away with her as their hostage, not telling her where they were going or anything else. Rage and rebellion coursed through her. She wanted to kill them. At a police station on East Fifty-fourth Street, they marched her upstairs, through a space full of people, to a small room with a mirror that she knew was a viewing window. Her heart thudded as she thought of all the men outside watching her and making the kind of remarks she knew men made when they could get away with it. She didn't feel safe there at all. Since she'd found Maddy's body, time had slowed down. When she was left in the interrogation room, it stopped altogether. It seemed as if a week had passed before an angry guy who looked like a mobster opened the door.

"I'm Detective Tommy Piccaterra," he said.

"I'm Remy Banks. I want a lawyer," she replied. It was the only thing she could think of to say. If Wayne could have one, she should have one, too.

"What do you need a lawyer for?" Tommy Piccaterra was a wiry guy with a broken nose and a sheen to his skin.

Remy glanced at his big-knuckled hands and guessed that he'd done some fighting in his time. She had another scary thought—that he was there to rough her up before the other guys came back in. "So you don't hurt me," she said.

He laughed. "We don't hurt people here," he replied, walked out, and shut the door, leaving her alone again.

After about an hour, she heard a commotion outside, and Piccaterra returned.

"Someone's coming in. We have to move," he said.

He didn't say who was coming. When she reached for her purse and backpack, he said, "Don't worry about it. Someone will bring it to you."

She got up with a sinking feeling that she would never see her things again, suddenly realizing that this was probably how people felt when they went to prison. She was that afraid of these detectives. No one looked at her as she moved through a bunch of them, talking on their cell phones. Out in the hall Piccaterra opened the door to another, smaller room that had no windows or ventilation or two-way mirror. When he put her in there and closed the door, she remembered her mother locking her in a closet as a child for her own protection against her father when he was on a drinking binge. Like then, she couldn't calm down as she listened to the activity in the hallway outside. She could hear people talking, their footsteps going up and down the stairs. Her purse with her cell phone in it was gone. No one brought that or her backpack to her, and no one came to ask her questions.

By late afternoon she was hungry and thirsty and worse than that, she was exhausted but too frightened to close her eyes to sleep. She'd been up late the night before and hadn't had anything to eat or drink since the bagel and coffee at seven. She didn't know what was happening. She wondered if the detectives were too busy with other things and had forgotten her, or if they were getting her the lawyer she'd asked for. She doubted that. More likely they were trying to scare her, and it was working really well. She was terrified.

Finally, just after four thirty, the Chinese lieutenant opened the door and walked into the room. April Woo Sanchez didn't look as good as she had the day before. Her suit was wrinkled, and her face was pale. "How are you doing?" she asked.

Remy exhaled with relief. "I would have called you, but those cops took my phone," she said quickly.

"Is that so? Why would you call me?"

"You said you would help me. This is very scary," she blurted out.

"Not as scary as it was for Maddy and Alison," the detective snapped.

Remy looked at her hands. She'd expected a little more sympathy than this.

"You know Alison was murdered this morning after you met with Lynn?" Woo said.

"Yes. I saw it on TV. At least you can't pin that one on me."

"That's not a smart response. You want to tell me why you had a meeting with Lynn this morning?" she said sharply.

"It wasn't a meeting. Can I go to the bathroom?"

"Of course, you can go to the bathroom. This isn't prison." She opened the door, checking her watch for the time. "The bathroom is right down there, but be quick. I'm running late."

Remy was annoyed by the sharpness of her tone and shocked by the reference to prison. She hadn't expected this from the woman who'd been nice to her yesterday. She moved to the door. The stairs were right in front of her, but the detective was watching her. She couldn't run down the stairs and get away. If this wasn't prison, she thought, it was very close. She went into the bathroom, washed her face, drank some water, and returned to the little room, where the detective quickly ended a conversation on her cell phone.

"Sit down, Remy. You told me a lot of lies yesterday, and now someone else is dead," she said coldly.

"I was scared. I didn't want to get anybody in trouble," Remy said defensively.

"Well, you got yourself in trouble. Mr. Wilson told me about your relationship with him. I know how many times you spoke with Lynn yesterday, and that you visited her this morning, right before Alison was murdered. You're in this very deep so you better start telling the truth."

"I didn't kill anybody." Remy started to cry. After a minute she wiped her eyes on her sleeve. "What do you want me to do?"

"Let's start all over." The detective took out a pen and a black-and-white-speckled pad. "How did you come to be employed at the Wilson house?"

"I already told you this. I got into the institute." Remy looked at the ceiling, then at the door. "It takes a couple of years, and it's expensive. I knew if I worked in a restaurant, the hours would be difficult, plus living expenses in the city would be too much. I was told if I were a live-in chef in someone's house, I could have most days during the week to go to school, and cook in the evening and on weekends."

"Who told you that?"

"The admissions people at the institute suggested I call the Anderson Agency and they would find me a good job."

"Was Mr. Wilson the first interview you did?"

"Yes."

"Did you know Mr. Wilson before you went there?"

"I'd heard of him, of course. He's a legend. I didn't meet him until I interviewed for the job."

"And what happened?"

"I told you this. He promised I could work in his new restaurant." She rolled her eyes.

"What does that mean?"

"I think he only said it so I would take the job. She wanted a nanny for the children, but I never would have done that. He wanted a chef. Turned out, I did both."

"According to him, you did more than that."

"It didn't mean anything," Remy said sullenly. "A good meal is more important to him than anybody. He liked to go out and party; Maddy wanted to go to bed early. I was just his dessert." She said this coolly, as if she were a guy, and it didn't matter.

"How did you feel about that?"

"I liked him until Maddy died." Then she started crying again. "I really did like him, and I never wanted to hurt her."

"Remy, if you or Wayne hurt Maddy, you better tell me now because it's going to come out. You can't keep this thing secret."

"I didn't hurt her that way. Didn't Derek do it?" she asked meekly.

"No, Derek was somewhere else by then. What changed your feeling about Wayne?"

"He was such a creep. He wanted me to tell the kids we were going on vacation to the Plaza. He wouldn't tell them the truth." She shook her head. "I didn't want to stay there. Did you see my picture in all the papers? It was horrible. He made me look bad."

"Uh-huh." The cop didn't seem impressed.

"And then he told Andrew to fire Lynn."

"When did he say that?"

"I heard them talking on the phone last night." She focused on the detective, remembering something. "He cooked dinner for you at the restaurant, and Andrew wanted him to get a lawyer. It was all crazy."

"Is that why you went to see Lynn this morning?"

"I wanted her to know what the plan for her

was. Jo Ellen loves drama. She likes it when people get in trouble."

The lieutenant got up and went out of the room. She came back a few seconds later. "Do you want something to eat?"

"I'd like a tuna sandwich, but they took my purse. I don't have any money."

"Don't worry. We can afford that much," Woo assured her.

Remy looked at the peeling paint on the ceiling. "It doesn't look like it," she remarked.

"You're a smart-ass," the lieutenant said. "You want to know what happens to people like you? They get caught."

Remy didn't like that. A few minutes later a female uniformed officer came to the door. "What do you need?" she asked.

"A tuna sandwich on rye toast and a Diet Coke for me, please," Remy said meekly.

"I'd like hot water, and would you get several Diet Cokes, please. Thanks." The lieutenant handed her some money, then shut the door. "Tell me about your relationship with Lynn and the Anderson Agency," she said.

"I thought you were in a hurry," Remy said.

"Not anymore."

Forty-two

At seven p.m. April returned to Midtown North. Hagedorn and Sergeant Gelo, who'd been due to end their second tour at four, were waiting for her. Three hours into the second shift of the day was a quiet time in the unit. Most of the detectives were out. The secretary was gone. The phones were still, and no one was raving in the holding cell. April collapsed at her desk, took a few minutes to go over the paperwork on her desk, then summoned Eloise. Charlie followed so close on her heels that he could have been her shadow. April stared at him in surprise. The milk white yin of a male for whom she'd had no expectation in the personality department seemed to have acquired an expression overnight. He was smiling.

"Boss," he said with a toothy grin.

"Hey, Charlie, how ya doin'?" she asked.

"Real good," he replied.

The reason for the smile looked like a cocktail waitress in an all-night bar. Wearing tight pants and a clingy sweater, Eloise took a chair and crossed her legs. Woody, the prepster, entered without being invited, passed a mug of hot water over the desk to April, then moved back to hang out by the door as if he were her bodyguard.

"Thanks, Woody." Automatically, April reached into her desk drawer for a tea bag.

In the old days when Lieutenant Iriarte had been the boss, April and Woody had been out; Hagedorn and two monkeys had been in. Now the apes were in counterterror units, and this was the unit's inner circle. April studied her team. If she hadn't been so tired, she would have smiled; they were an odd trio. Hoping for an energy boost, she dumped the tea bag into the hot water. She had seven cups to go for good health. As soon as the tea hit the water the smoky aroma of Lapsang souchong wafted into the air.

"How did it go with Lorna Doone?" she asked.

"Name's Lorna Dorne actually and she goes by the name Cherry Red," Eloise said.

"Because she has red hair," Charlie explained.

"No kidding." April glanced at Woody. "You have a photo of her?"

"It can be arranged. Why, do you need one?" Charlie asked.

"Just a fluky thought." April had looked through Woody's photographs from the Wilson house the day before. There were lots of pictures of kids and strollers, reporters, and dog walkers. Old people. One redheaded woman, young, wearing jeans and a peasant shirt, and she had long hair. Someone was checking it out.

"Lorna's twenty-three, looks like she has a heavy habit herself. Real thin with big boobs and lots of long red hair," Eloise said. "She spilled like a fountain. She was all over that Peret kid—she and two other girls. They didn't know who he was, and made him think they really liked him. It won't be a problem giving the chief what he wants. We can keep Peret's name out of it. Maybe," Eloise added. "And she told me they have a private ambulance."

April was startled out of her musings. "What?"

"She said they have a room downstairs where they put ODs. They collect them, then drive them to the ER in their vehicle and drive off. We can catch them at it, no problem. Peret was the kind of customer they don't like. He got out under his own steam, then crashed outside."

"This is great news. I'm really proud of you." April looked from one to the other. "Good work," she said again. Maybe she could go on vacation after all. "Did you copy the Alison tapes and get them over to the task force?" she asked.

"Yeah, no problem there. Sergeant Minnow has it. He's something of a cold fish, isn't he?" Eloise replied.

"They call him Fish for a good reason. Anyway, what did you find out about the nannies?"

"Here's where we stand on that. Charlie—"

Hagedorn cleared his throat, taking over. "There are no priors on Lynn Papel or Remy Banks. The Anderson file indicates the Wilson house as a first-time placement for Remy. Lynn, however, was fired from her last job."

Eloise took it from there. "We paid a visit to her previous employer this afternoon at five-oh-seven. Anna Currant lives in a town house on Sixty-first Street between Second and Third."

"Another town house," April remarked quietly. She jotted down the owner's name. "Any other similarities?"

"Well, she has a daughter and son, two and six. Lynn worked for her for nine months."

"Nine months is three months less than a year," April murmured.

"What's the significance?" Eloise asked.

"The fee for placing them in based on a year's salary. The client gets credit on the next one only if the girl leaves, not if she's fired. What did Mrs. Currant tell you?" April asked.

"She told us that Lynn was attractive, competent, and reliable, but she suspected that something was going on between the girl and her husband. Mrs. Currant had a good relationship with Miss Anderson, who had placed other household help with her in the past. She considered Miss Anderson a friend because she seemed to take a personal interest in the household and called from time to time to find out how things were going. On one such call, Mrs. Currant confessed that she was concerned about Lynn getting too friendly with her husband. According to Mrs. Currant, Miss Anderson said that kind of behavior was totally unacceptable. She advised her to fire Lynn and take a new girl who had just come in with great recommendations. Which Mrs. Currant immediately did."

"Was there any basis to the woman's concern?" April asked.

"Well, Mrs. Currant is not an attractive woman," Charlie said.

"What about Miss Anderson?"

"I hear she's a dog, too," Woody remarked.

"Stop it with the looks thing." Eloise slapped him playfully.

"I meant priors," April said wearily.

"No priors on Jo Ellen Anderson. She doesn't even have a driver's license."

"Okay, this is very good. We have a new angle to work. Something's not right here. We're going to take the agency apart. You mentioned the excessive probing into the girls' lives. I'm wondering if this Anderson woman isn't manipulating delicate domestic situations, so she can move the nannies around to create more business for herself."

Charlie nodded. "It might be a Better Business issue. We can see if there are any complaints there."

"And I want to see the hiring history of both the murdered women. We need names of every single person who has worked in those houses. We can widen it from there. The victims were close friends and shared many of the same sources. Maybe someone worked for both of them."

"You mentioned before that they were users. What about their dealer?" Gelo said.

April shook her head. "The trainer was dealing and sleeping with both of them. He loses both ways. The time frame isn't right for Derek, and he hasn't been out today. We'll keep on him. If they want to make something of that later. . . ." She shrugged. It wouldn't be their call.

"What about *his* supplier?" Eloise asked.

"We'll let Minnow work on that angle. He needs to do something."

They snickered, and April was sorry she'd said it.

"Remy and Lynn?" Charlie said.

"Lynn is a helpful witness. She told me Alison's wedding rings were missing." She shook her head again, remembering Lynn's very real fear the moment she'd walked into the house after she returned from taking the girls to play school.

"But she took Alison's diamond bracelet," Eloise said.

"Alison gave me a different story on that, so someone's lying. Let's see the file," April asked.

Charlie went to get it. April sipped her tea.

Charlie returned in less than thirty seconds with the file. "Here's the note about the bracelet."

April reached for her own notebook and read the page where she'd written what Alison had told her about a previous nanny's taking her bracelet and how Jo Ellen had convinced her to replace the girl with Lynn. As she spoke, a chill entered the room. She could feel it curl up from the floor and grab hold of the hairs on the back of her neck. For a long moment nobody moved. Then April reached for the phone and called Sergeant Minnow.

"Sergeant," she said when he picked up his cell. "It's April Woo Sanchez."

"Hello, Lieutenant," he said coolly. "We're about to get started over here. Will you be joining us?"

"Yes, and we need to find a place to park Lynn and Remy where they can't be reached for a while."

"We're already working on that. What's up?"

"I'll tell you when I get there." She hung up and smiled apologetically at her team. "You're going to have to give me the files. I'll take them over," she said.

"I already made copies," Charlie replied, and Eloise grimaced at another broken rule.

"Okay, everybody go home and get a good night's sleep and come back in the morning. Looks like you don't get your day off tomorrow."

Nobody seemed the least bit surprised about that.

"And Woody, I want you to pick me up on First and Fifty-sixth Street at eight a.m. Good night, all."

"Wait, you don't have your car. I'll drive you over there," Woody said.

"Thanks." She grabbed her purse and her jacket. She hadn't even been there an hour. On the way back across town, she left a message for the medical examiner. She wanted to know Alison's cause of death as soon as possible.

Forty-three

The task force gave itself an informal name: Town House Killer. The p.m. meeting was jammed. Every chair and desk corner was taken, and the tension was tremendous. April took a low profile in the back by the door, and Mike sat up front, near Sergeant Minnow. As the primary on the case, Minnow led the meeting. He was milking his role to the fullest, allowing the minutes to tick away as he slowly went through the reports. Detectives had begun canvassing people in the neighborhood, especially those with windows that overlooked the town houses below and the neighbors who lived on the two blocks where the murders occurred.

In the days to come, the search for witnesses would widen. Detectives and uniformed officers had been going through the bags of garbage left out on the street for pickup. The Crime Stoppers Unit had been out both days and its hotlines were flooded with hundreds of tips coming in. It would take days to process them. When the operations reports were concluded, Minnow talked about where they were with the suspects. Wayne's life had become a media event for reporters. The cops were assembling the minutiae of his life for detailed examination. His affairs, expenses, and phone records, as well as his comings and goings in the last six months, were being analyzed to see if his habits had changed. His close associates were being questioned. He'd been interviewed again and didn't have anything new to add. His alibi for the time in question was strong, and his statement was being prepared. Andrew Perkins, whom Remy had reported as so cocky and sure advising his friend the day before, was now in such a state of shock from the murder of his wife that he could barely form a sentence. He and his little girls were under a doctor's care at his brother's home in New Jersey. At the time of his wife's murder, he'd been in a meeting at his office. Derek was off the hook for the murders, though he was being questioned in regard to the amount of money he'd received from the victims as well as the illegal substances he may have provided them. Furthermore, the personal phone, bank, and credit card records of Maddy and Alison were being examined for more insight and information about their last days. Everything took time.

The electrifying moments in the meeting came when April spoke about the contents of the Alison tapes, as well as Detective Hagedorn and Sergeant Gelo's visit to Jo Ellen Anderson at the Anderson Agency and the files of Lynn and Remy that had been taken from there. Although the two nannies were being looked at as strong suspects, Minnow hadn't listened to the interview of the second victim, nor had he sent anyone to the agency to get the histories of the suspects. So much for the helpfulness of her attempt at transparency. He was pretty pissed off.

Toward the end of the meeting, the DA was pressed for his opinion of the cases. April was glad that the veteran Ben was in attendance again. He pulled on his shirt collar as he thought about it. "Who has a reason to want us to assume those girls did the unthinkable? That person is your killer. Maybe his goal is to hurt them." He shrugged as a big argument ensued over that view. It wasn't much of a motive. Mike Sanchez listened, but didn't say a thing for over two hours.

At ten thirty, April left her car near the Seventeenth Precinct for the second night in a row and began the drive home with her husband. The meeting had been tough for her to take, as it must have been for Mike. She liked helping people, but had never had much tolerance for the organizational aspect of criminal investigations, especially when she wasn't the primary. No matter how carefully things were done, there were always mistakes. There were mistakes here. Something was being overlooked. She kept wondering, who left the short red hair in Alison's powder room? Not the maid who'd cleaned the house the day before. She'd made a point of asking Lynn about that.

"She's from Equador," Lynn had said. "Her hair is jet black."

April had shown her Woody's photos. "Do you know any of these people?" she asked.

Lynn picked out some faces of people she'd seen on the street many times but didn't really know. She pointed at the redhead and said, "That's Leah. She's around a lot."

"What's Leah's last name?"

Lynn shook her head. "I don't know."

"Where does she live?"

"Across the street somewhere." She didn't add anything else on the subject.

April was working out of two places with two unconnected units, and had too many things roiling around in her head. While she was in the Seventeenth her thoughts were back at Midtown North, where Eloise was turning out to be a very smart detective. And Minnow made it very clear that he wanted her people out of the picture. But everybody needed their own people for comfort, and April was no exception. She had promised to play nice, but she didn't know if she could.

After the meeting had ended, she didn't want to leave the city. The killer was out there somewhere, and it made her nervous to think he (or she) was holed up somewhere, waiting for morning. She reminded herself that serial killers usually targeted people no one cared about, prostitutes and runaways—not high-life mothers who lived in expensive town houses. But everything about this was unusual. Remy and Lynn were being watched.

She sat in Mike's car as they crossed town, wishing it were already tomorrow so she didn't have to feel as if she were letting Maddy and Alison down by running away to get some rest. If only she and Mike had a place to sack out somewhere close, and did not have to travel forty-five minutes for a few hours' sleep. But they didn't have such a place, and her frantic phone calls to Gao Wan had not panned out. He was taking her father's spot at the midtown restaurant where they both worked, and had not been able to go up to Westchester to remove her parents from her house. They were still there, and they had to be dealt with.

"Thanks for getting Lynn and Remy taken care of," she said after a long silence. Mike had found two secure places for them to stay where no one could find them and they couldn't talk to each other or anyone else.

"No problem," he mumbled, also not in a talkative mood.

As they got on the Henry Hudson Parkway and headed north, a spring shower commenced. April watched him flip on the wipers and felt an ache for the old Mike who'd thought only of her. In the months since they'd married, he'd become less watchful of her and dependent on her moods for his happiness. Mostly she liked the change. But occasionally when his boat was rocked by things that were out of his control, he seemed to slip away and forget about her. It made her feel lonely. Right then she knew he was angry at Sergeant Minnow for not following through quickly enough and not widening the net. And she wondered if there were other instances in which the CO of the detectives' unit had let him down.

The spatter of rain on the windshield intensified into a torrent. Mike turned the wipers all the way up, but the downpour impeded his vision. Suddenly they were in a blinding storm. Lightning struck, and the crack of thunder that followed was as loud as anything April had ever heard.

"Ow, that was close," she said.

Mike took his hand off the wheel and grabbed her cold fingers. "It's going to be fine, *querida*," he said, and she was relieved that he was still with her.

"Promise?"

"Absolutely."

"Then do me a favor and slow down."

"Sissy," he muttered, but complied immediately. Then he was ready to talk. "So what's going on?" he asked.

"Fish and Jell-O are two food groups that don't mix," she replied.

"Yeah, well, Minnow's threatened. Gelo's better than he is, looks like a comer."

"She certainly does," she murmured. "What about you? Why were you so quiet?"

He made a face at the highway that was beginning to flood in all the usual places. "Like the old days, huh?"

"Your kind of weather," she agreed. He'd always liked steamy cars at night. She couldn't help reminding him that they were passing a dangerous curve where several fatal wrecks had occurred. "Slow down."

"Yes, ma'am." He slowed for another fifteen seconds with his hand still on hers. It was kind of a nice touch.

Then thunder struck close by again, and April flashed to their race through Central Park one night long ago, chasing a teenage killer on a night just like this one. They went back a long way, and hadn't crashed yet. She tried to relax.

"I talked with both Remy and Lynn for many hours. They're not telling me everything, and that's troubling," she said after a moment.

"You think they're involved somehow?"

"I think they know things they're afraid to tell. Maybe about Jo Ellen, maybe the two husbands. It's not clear. What worries me is that something else will happen."

"Let's hope not. What about our trip?" He knew his customer, changed the subject, and moved on.

"I'd forgotten about it," she said simply.

"Well, maybe we'll get a break tomorrow," he said, and sped up again on a straight stretch of highway that he knew so well.

He kept on through the driving rain, and when they finally reached home and saw that the lights were on, April was almost glad her parents were still there. For once there would be hot food waiting for them. Tonight Skinny Dragon was at the door screaming at them before the engine was off. The sound carried through the storm.

"Ayieee. Why so late? Wait so long for dinner," she yelled as if she wanted the whole neighborhood to know her grievance. "What's long with you? Don't know work supposed to be over? Time to go home?" Skinny shrieked out that she'd worried all day. Nobody came to check on them or bring them food. What kind of bad daughter didn't take care of her sick old mother? "Why no call, *ni*? 'Nother murder?" she demanded at last.

"That's it, Ma."

"Ayiee," Skinny wailed. Another murder meant the ghosts of the dead were too close to her precious daughter again.

April made it through the front door without further assault and was horrified to see that a mirror had been placed in a strategic position by the door, the dreaded colored strings hung from the corners of the living room, and a few things moved around to suit the Dragon's idea of optimum feng shui. It looked as if she was planning an intervention on April's health and intended to stay awhile.

"*Ni hao ma.* What's for dinner?" Mike asked with a faint smile. He had learned the Chinese way. He'd become a man who knew when to pick his battles.

"I hope it's not something weird," April muttered.

Forty-four

On Wednesday morning at seven thirty a.m. Lily Eng was waiting for April at the Sutton Diner on Fifty-sixth Street and First Avenue. Outside it was still pouring. Mike dropped April off and she dashed for the small patch of sidewalk that was protected by an awning outside the restaurant. She charged it, and a wall of rain sleeted off the edge of the awning onto her head. "Shit."

Inside the door, she immediately caught sight of Lily, who was seated at a table in the window looking dry and chic and every bit the TV reporter. She was wearing a distinctive pastel tweed suit that could well have been Chanel. A pink plastic raincoat was folded over the back of the chair next to her. Compared with her splendor and calm, April felt both poor and frantic. She had not had a good night or morning with Skinny Dragon and was irritated that Lily, who came from highly educated college-professor parents and made a great deal more money than she did, didn't have a lot to worry about.

"Thanks for being on time. I ordered a tea for you," Lily said, pointing to a cup and stainless teapot opposite her.

April sank into a wooden chair by the window and dripped all over the floor. "Shit," she said again. Already nothing was going right in her day.

"What's the matter?" Lily asked.

"Nothing." She was just soaked, and she felt sick again. Her mother had appeared in her house like a deadly mold, giving her food that upset her stomach. No doubt the Dragon was going to have to be forcibly removed before she'd ever feel well again. Mike was being nice about it now, but that wouldn't last forever. The case was at a critical point. Today she was hoping for a COD on Alison and some important break in the nannies' stories. She was poised for heavy action, and hardly in the mood for a tête-à-tête with a TV reporter who didn't have anything else to do but get her nails done and look good on the six o'clock news. When she looked at the beautiful clothes Lily was wearing, she really did think she'd chosen the wrong career path.

"I hope the rain will give us a break from these murders," she muttered, trying to keep herself on track.

Lily was taken aback. "Are you expecting another one?"

"No, I didn't expect the first two. But a storm like this can put off the bad guys." If only it had rained all week, she would have gotten her honeymoon, no problem. Then she was ashamed of herself for thinking of better jobs and better parents and a honeymoon on a cruise ship. She made a frustrated gesture. "Sorry, I think I'm getting the flu. What did you have to tell me?"

"I did a little checking on Remy Banks yesterday

and came up with something interesting," Lily said, pulling out a manila envelope.

"Oh, yeah? What?"

"She was placed through the Anderson Agency. I did a feature on the agency a few years back, and I know quite a bit about it."

"Great. What do you know?" April raked her hands through her wet hair, then poured herself some tea, and made a face. It was a generic brand of tea. The water turned the unappetizing color of rust and didn't taste much better. "I'm sorry. I must have missed the program."

Lily laughed. "You miss everything, April. You're always working."

April nodded—the story of her life.

"So how about a trade?" Lily asked.

"No way. I've told you a thousand times I can't say anything," April replied impatiently. "Don't waste my time."

"How about I ask you questions and you give me a yea or nay?"

April shook her head.

"A shake of the head, then." She laughed again. For once she was relaxed, and April was all nerves. "Come on, it's my day off," she wheedled. "Make me happy for once."

"No one makes me happy," April grumbled.

"Bullshit. Didn't I do that great story on you? And you got promoted?" Lily reminded her.

April didn't want to tell her that she'd done the interview under orders from a superior, but another correction was in order. The interview had nothing to do with the promotion. "I took a test for the promotion," she said.

"Still, the story didn't hurt."

April smiled. "All right, I'll let you break the story when we're ready to make an arrest, okay?" That was a big concession. "But you'll have to keep your mouth shut about your source."

"Serious? How soon will that be?" Lily bounced in her chair.

"I have no idea. We're following leads. What was your take on Anderson?"

"Oh, it's the oldest domestic employment agency in the country still run by a family member. I did the piece as a human-interest service story just after 9/11 when thousands of people lost their jobs in the city and were looking for any kind of work, kind of like the Depression," she reminisced.

"I mean the owner," April prompted.

"Well, actually she did the interview with me because she wanted my help to write a book about her service to the rich and famous."

"No kidding." April woke up.

"I didn't have time to use what she gave me because the slant was the high-end field of domestic workers. But what she had was dynamite. She claims to have the inside dope on three generations of high-profile, wealthy clients. You should see her home. It's filled with memorabilia and photos of herself with megastars. She showed me gifts from movie stars and politicos, princes and presidents. Frank Sinatra, mob bosses. You wouldn't believe the people she knew. It's like a museum."

"What about her? What's she like?"

"This is the part that I thought would interest you. She kept files on everybody—the people she worked for, the staff members she placed, their friends. She made a point of knowing everything about everybody. Get this—she called it good business. She bragged to me about having their complete trust. She went into their places to water their plants when they were out of town. I thought it was kind of creepy. It seemed to me that if you had her or one of her people in your house, you were kind of harboring a spy."

April had already been alerted to that possibility. "That's very interesting," she said. "What happened to the book?"

"Oh, I referred her to some agents I know. She needed a writer, of course. And that got her all paranoid. She was afraid someone would steal her material."

"So nothing came of the book?"

"No. What do you want to eat?"

April glanced at the menu, then checked her watch. Five minutes to Woody time. "I'm really sorry. I have a long day, and I have to get cracking."

Lily looked disappointed. "This was my day off," she grumbled.

"We'll do a long lunch soon, okay?"

"Right."

"One more thing. Where is Miss Anderson's home?"

"Beekman Place. She has a town house on Fiftieth."

"Fiftieth Street?" April's head jerked up.

Lily nodded. "I wouldn't forget something like that. It's a real freaky place, been in her family for a long time. Didn't you know?"

"Oh, the home address was on my list for today,"

April said slowly. Jo Ellen had been on her list for the day.

"It's close, right?"

"Yeah." April touched her hair. It was drying off now, absolutely flat on her head. It reminded her of another question she needed to ask. "By the way, what color hair does she have?"

"Jo Ellen? Gray."

"No kidding. She doesn't color it?"

"She didn't when I talked with her."

April started gathering up her things. "You've turned out to be a doll," she said. "I'm really grateful for your time."

"Was I useful?"

"Very useful. Where are you going? Do you want a ride? I'll take you anywhere between here and Midtown North."

Lily laughed. It was almost a straight line west. "No, thanks," she said. "And good luck."

April nodded. She needed it.

Forty-five

Woody was right on time, waiting double-parked outside when April emerged from the restaurant at five past eight. The wind had picked up in the last half hour, and sleeting rain pounded the pavement.

"Morning, Boss. Was that Lily Eng?" Woody said as she scrambled into the car.

"Yes."

He knew better than to ask what they were meeting about. "The shop?"

"Yes. How are you doing, Woody?" She knew he hated to be left out.

"Me? I'm fine. It's quiet," he told her, as if crime was all that really mattered to him. He pulled the car out, angling across First Avenue through the traffic to make the turn west onto Fifty-seventh Street. For once, he did it without hitting the siren, and for that, she was grateful. At the red light on First Avenue they watched pedestrians fight the gusting rain as they crossed the street. The sky had darkened almost to night. As Mike would say. *"Está feo, feo."* It was ugly weather. Woody whistled through his teeth.

"Turn up the box," she said anxiously. If something happened this morning, she didn't want to be the last to know.

For a few minutes only static blew in. Then the dispatcher's voice came on with business as usual. Woody stopped whistling before April told him to, and she was thankful for that, as well. The slightest positive thing helped on a bad day. She was feeling bloated and queasy from another of Skinny Dragon Mother's sticky breakfasts and the diner's rusty-nail tea. She hadn't drunk very much of it, only enough to know it wasn't going to be a health aid. "Anything new?" she asked after a pause.

"Looked like Charlie worked all night, and he's wearing the same clothes from yesterday. Maybe he didn't go home. I didn't see the sergeant," Woody reported.

"Anything else?"

"Barry was hinting around. He wants in."

Barry Queue was their former intelligence officer, the one who was so secretive and didn't try to make friends.

"What did you tell him?" It could be that Queue was someone's spy and she had to watch out for him. Or else he was coming around. She hoped it was the latter. She preferred team players.

"Didn't say nothing, just that I'd let you know."

"Thanks for the heads-up." She had more questions about a few other people but not the energy to pursue them right then. It occurred to her that as Iriarte had done before her and every other boss did, she was always gathering information on the whereabouts, activities, and personal habits of the people who worked for her. Part of it was simply chain of command. To run an efficient unit and avoid surprises, one had to know what was going on. The question was, where did the job stop and controlling begin? And that was her question about the Anderson woman, too.

She'd been deeply troubled by what Lily had told her. It appeared that Jo Ellen Anderson was more than just intrusive with the girls she placed; she also meddled in the lives of her customers. She went into their houses and watered their plants. That was unusual, and particularly troubling because it gave her access to their private spaces. What else did she do there? And who else could have used those keys? April's thoughts raced ahead. Even more interesting was the fact that Jo Ellen lived in a town house on Fiftieth Street, two blocks from Maddy and even closer to Alison. She had gray hair. April's mind wandered back to the photos Woody had taken at the two houses. A gray-haired woman who fit Jo Ellen's description hadn't been in any of them, but she wondered if the woman had been questioned by anybody else during the canvass of neighbors, and the name just hadn't popped up yet.

"Are you okay, boss?" Woody asked.

"Yeah, fine," she said. But she didn't feel fine at all. She'd lost her cookies only once before on account of something her mother had fed her. A few years ago when Lieutenant Bernardino had been in the car, she'd had to get out and barf on the street. The horrible feeling of that lost face still haunted her. She'd vowed never to do *that* again no matter how bad she felt.

"You sure you're all right?" Woody demanded.

"I said I was fine. Why are you bugging me?"

"You're groaning."

"Jesus." She held on for fifteen more agonizing minutes, concentrating on the rain outside and her prayer that no one else would get hurt today. She was out of the car before it stopped in front of the station, and went straight to the public women's room, where no one would see or hear her. In a second she was on her knees, hugging the toilet seat in the stall farthest from the door. The smell of disinfectant was strong, but not strong enough to cover that chipped old toilet's decades of use. She heaved right away, and everything came up.

"Oh, God," she moaned. Most of the time she could overcome the quakes in her stomach. Even seeing Alison's body the day before didn't take her over the edge. But today her lifelong weakness had gotten to her. She felt like a wimp or worse, turning on cheap tea, the smell of human effluvia, and fear. It was Wednesday. She had only today and tomorrow before her scheduled cruise, and she didn't want anyone else to die. Her fear was another humiliation.

Someone came into the bathroom. She was on her feet, flushing the second she heard the door. The unseen individual tinkled in the stall next to hers, flushed, and then left without washing her hands. April exited gingerly, not feeling much better. She washed her face, popped an Altoids into her mouth, and groaned again at the sight of herself in the mirror. Her hair was flat. Her face was pale, and for the first time in her life she looked to herself—distinctly old.

Shocked, she blinked and looked again. Suddenly she could see what she'd be like in ten years, middle-aged and still doing what she was doing now. Time had passed without her realizing it, and now she saw her future. Suddenly she understood why people left the Department, went to the private sector, and moved on. The facilities were the least of it. The truth was, the job was a mill that ground people down. There never was time for anything, not a personal day, not a vacation, not a single luxury. She remembered what Alison had told her on Monday: maintenance was important; men liked younger women. They got restless and drifted away. Right then it was clear that she was not maintaining herself. She didn't look like Lily Eng. She wasn't patient with Woody, or Eloise, or Charlie Hagedorn. Certainly not poor old Skinny Dragon, who'd been neglected for months. She did not have time to be with her mother. Crime never went away, and the victims never stopped talking to her, no matter how long they'd been dead. She remembered what Alison had told her, and like all the other times when victims had come first in her life, she pulled herself together for them.

"Good morning, everyone," she said a few minutes later to the four people she'd assembled in her office. "Charlie, do you have anything to tell us?"

Hagedorn cleared his throat and glanced at Eloise. Eloise was wearing black-and-white-checked pants, a red sweater, and a 9mm Glock. Her head was a mess of blond curls. April was going to have to talk with her. Her smoky eye shadow gave her a sultry look, and her tough-guy's mouth was twisted to one side. She nodded at Charlie, and her message was definitely mixed.

"The Anderson Agency was a private company

until 2000. In 2000 the founder's daughter, Sally George Anderson, Jo Ellen's aunt, sold it to Hunter International, a much larger company. Hunter has a history of acquiring smaller agencies and over time consolidating them into their corporate structure. Their stand-alones include Harris Brown, a recruiter of business executives and support staff for overseas operations; ITEL, a company that specializes in business intelligence; and Crater Corp, which provides security personnel."

"You said it was a quirky place. How does it fit in with Hunter's objectives?"

"There's nothing on the Web site or anywhere else that says it's owned by Hunter. It's not clear what the deal is there. They may have acquired it for the name."

Eloise cut in. "There's a staff of only eight people. It's a small operation, very uncorporate in style. Jo Ellen may have a contract to stay for some period of years."

"Charlie, would you find out who's in charge at Hunter International and what the deal with the Anderson Agency is? What about the aunt?"

He made a note. "She passed away two years ago, left the house to Jo Ellen."

"What was the relationship between them?"

"It must have been pretty close. They lived together in the town house. The number is four twenty-five. It's right across the street from the Perkinses' house." He glanced at Eloise for some sign of approval, but she wasn't looking at him.

"That's good work, Charlie," April said, making a few notes.

"There's more. Since 2002, a bunch of complaints

came in from residences where Anderson placed staff, a couple of thefts. All of them in town houses. No arrests were made."

April wondered how he came up with that information, since complaints that were dropped didn't enter the record, but she didn't want to get into it at the moment. She turned to Queue, whom she invited on a tryout. "Barry, I want you to go downtown and get a search warrant for the Anderson house and agency. She has the keys to her clients' houses and lives across the street from Alison Perkins. I think that's probable cause for going in for a look-see, and the DA on the case agrees with me. Charlie, you're working on Hunter. Find out what the payment was for the company and what the deal with Jo Ellen is. Also, the status of the house, if anything is owed on it. Any personal information on Jo Ellen Anderson would be useful, too."

"You think it's her?" Gelo said.

"She was definitely exploiting both her clients and the nannies who worked for them. Looks like what she did was work on the mothers' concerns about reliability, etc., to get the girls in trouble so that she could replace them. Motive for that— probably greed. She could also have used her access to the houses for theft. You said some jewelry was stolen."

They nodded.

"Okay, that's it. Woody, come with me. Eloise, you're in command here. You can continue on the Spirit case for the moment. Thank you all, we'll be in touch."

No one asked her what she was doing.

Forty-six

Feeling personally humiliated by her boss, Eloise returned to her office to sulk. She didn't know exactly what she'd expected. But after her and Charlie's initiative on the case the day before, she didn't want to be the only member of the team left out today. She and Charlie could well turn out to have been the ones who cracked the case, and there was still a great deal of information-gathering to do on it. Returning to the work of shutting down strip clubs wasn't even a close second in importance, even though the chief of detectives had deemed it a priority on Monday. The clubs would be there tomorrow and the day after that. Time was on their side in nailing any of them. Today, two weeks from now. It didn't matter when they made their move. They'd close them. For a while there would be a flap, and then they'd open again under new names. Big deal.

The homicides were different. Alison Perkins had been in their unit the day before she'd died. She'd sat in the very office where the detectives had just met, and she'd revealed a lot. Eloise had heard her voice lamenting the loss of her friend and the difficulties of having strangers in her house, who took care of her children and took advantage of her. Knowing how people exploited each other whenever they could, Eloise felt sad for Alison and wanted to see where she had lived and died. She wanted to continue with the investigation personally and be there for the resolution. Even Barry Queue was in it now. She wondered how that had happened and felt deeply hurt at what she took as a personal affront, even a punishment, by her boss. It reminded her of Steve, and she was overwhelmed for a moment by a feeling of crushing loss.

Whenever unexpected emotion caught her off guard, this was what happened to her. Ever since 9/11 every stress and personal setback tended to spin her back to the catastrophes. Panicky nightmares came to her even when she was awake. She was lost in a copter inside the black cloud of collapsing buildings. People just out of reach screamed for her to rescue them, and when she couldn't, they jumped from high windows to escape the inferno. She, too, was burning alive, and the man she'd loved more than any other had left her behind for a new life in Florida. That day a dozen people she'd loved were taken from her—some instantly and some later on. Because of it, she'd lost her feeling of security and safety in her job and her city, and now any little thing could put her back there and make her question her reason for living.

Consciously, she was thinking about Jo Ellen Anderson, how much she wanted to be the one to talk to her again, find out everything about her morning habits, instead of backing off and leaving with only half the story as she had yesterday. Charlie had given her the bug. Someone beneath her in rank had taught her that they didn't have to be in a task force to be useful. They didn't have to sit in on endless briefing meetings and listen to idiots trying to connect dots they didn't even have. She could help from the outside. She could get it there on her own and get it done. It was a dangerous thing to be thinking.

She glanced at her watch. It would take the lieutenant all morning and maybe longer to talk with Jo Ellen Anderson and her employees about all the issues that concerned her about the Anderson Agency and its former owner. After listening to the Alison tapes, she knew that April took her time. It would be a long dance before the music stopped. She wondered how long it would take Queue to get the search warrant. If she had it, she could get there first and be the one to search Anderson's town house. That idea grabbed hold of her and restored her mood.

Forty-seven

By nine thirty April and Woody were in the Anderson Agency offices. It had the old-world atmosphere that Eloise had described the day before—gold paint on the moldings, French doors, heavy curtains, a vase of fresh red and yellow tulips on the table in the reception area. But instead of inspiring the confidence of old traditions, it was kind of creepy. A gray-haired woman worked the phone at an antique desk, apparently too busy to acknowledge them.

"Lieutenant Woo Sanchez from the police department to see Miss Anderson," April said as soon as she deigned to look up.

"She's not in yet. Is there anything I can help you with?"

"What time does she get in?"

The woman consulted a chunky gold clock with a cupid sitting on it. "She usually gets here around ten, ten thirty."

"We'd like to see her assistant."

"Certainly, please take a seat and I'll call her."

April did not take a seat. She wandered over to the window and gazed out at pedestrians on Lexington Avenue being battered by the rain. Several

long minutes passed before a prim young woman
with a black headband and black-rimmed glasses
came in. She was dressed in a navy skirt and white
blouse, and wore no jewelry. April thought that
with a radical makeover she could be pretty.

"I've called Miss Anderson. She'll be here in
about five minutes," she announced quickly, and
turned to leave.

"I'd like to have a word with *you*, please," April
told her pleasantly.

"Of course." With a wintry smile, the girl leaned
forward in a half bow. "How can I help you?"

"Let's go into your office where we can talk."

"We're not authorized to take people into the
office. I only have one chair there, and it's not private. I can offer you the parlor."

"Is the office equipped with surveillance cameras?" Woody said suddenly.

She nodded. "How can you tell?"

"In the parlor, too?" he asked.

"Everywhere. We had an incident last year. The
new owners put them in."

"What kind of incident?" April jumped in.

"I don't know. You'll have to ask Miss Anderson," she said apologetically.

"I'd like to see the office, Miss . . . ?" April
waited for a name.

"I'm Josie. Can you wait until Miss Anderson
gets here? I could lose my job if I let you in there,"
she said nervously.

"No, I'm sorry. We don't have much time."

"Oh, God." She exchanged worried looks with
the woman at the desk, then opened a stout
wooden door that led to an old-fashioned bull pen

the way here. She's like the queen. She doesn't like to handle money," the girl said with a sudden sparkle.

April smiled. She didn't like to handle money, either. "You don't note the time when she comes in?"

"Well, if she's really late, I have to make another pot of coffee," Josie said slowly.

"What about Monday? Was she late then?"

"Honestly, I don't know."

"You said you take messages. Was there a message from Mrs. Wilson on Monday?"

"Not that I recall, but Miss Anderson can access the voice mail from outside. She sometimes does that early in the morning so she doesn't miss anything important."

"Did you make a second pot of coffee on Monday?"

"Probably," she admitted. "She's been coming in late recently."

"Josie, did you do a background check on Remy Banks and Lynn Papel?" April asked.

"That I do know. I don't work on the trouble girls."

"What are the trouble girls?"

"Oh, my God." She bit her lip. "I don't know why I said that. I really don't know what I meant. Everybody here is great. We don't have problem people. We don't take them on. That's a rule. Can I go now? I'm really sorry." She rose from the chair.

April's cell phone rang. She picked it up and walked over to the window. "Woo Sanchez," she said.

"You called last night. I'm calling you back. It's not good news about Alison Perkins."

"Dr. Gloss, thank you for getting back to me," April said, then quickly, "What's the bad news?"

"I can't give you a definite COD at this time."

"What do you mean 'at this time'? Is that something that is likely to change?" April said softly.

"Look, don't quote me, but there are no clear indicators like contusions on her neck, or a crushed hyoid, to point to strangling. The cause of death was, she stopped breathing. The exact reason an individual stops breathing is not always readily apparent. There can be contributing factors."

"Like?"

"She was impaired in some way, intoxicated or drugged."

"Is that what happened here?"

"Not exactly. My guess is that she was prevented from breathing. She might have been smothered, but sometimes you can't really tell what happened."

April was speechless. "But it wasn't a natural death—"

"No, not considering the position in which she was found, and the fact that she was washed with something like Mr. Clean. We're doing some tests to see what the cleanser was and if it was in the house. But you know in a court of law, you could have a defendant with a motive and even rubber gloves and disinfectant on his hands who you could prove was in the house at the time of death, and his lawyer could claim she was already dead when he cleaned her up. There's no law against washing a dead body."

"That is bad news. What else did you find?" April stared out of the window.

"Oh, some deterioration in the nasal passages.

We don't have the toxicology reports back yet. Her liver was enlarged. She was heading for trouble on that score later on. The big surprise was she was pregnant. You'll want to check with her doctor on that. She may not have known it."

Once again April was stunned. Alison was pregnant? She wasn't sure about the law in New York State about killing a fetus along with its mother, whether that would be ruled a double homicide. California had changed its statute on that after Laci Peterson's body was found. In any case, Alison's pregnancy raised the stakes for her killer. Three people were gone, not two.

"That's sad," April said. "I'll bet she didn't know it. I think she was high the day before she died. Dr. Gloss, I'm wondering about something that you said. You're guessing that she was smothered. What is your reason for supposing that?"

"Feathers. There was one in her hair and another in her mouth. Check her pillows. And don't ask me about the prelim on either of them. I need a few more days."

"Thanks, I appreciate the call," April told him.

"Well, I always enjoy working with you. Let's have lunch someday."

"As soon as I can keep it down," April murmured.

"What, are you pregnant, too, kid?"

"No way, just a touch of the flu," she said, as she watched a large woman in a plastic raincoat run across Lexington, dodging oncoming cars with a kind of bravado not even seasoned New Yorkers attempted very often.

Forty-eight

At ten, Eloise called Barry Queue on his cell phone to find out what was holding him up with the search warrant.

"I haven't gotten in yet. I'm waiting for a judge. I'll call you when I've got it," he promised.

When he hadn't gotten back to her fifteen minutes later, she tried again. This time there was no answer on his phone. She figured he was in with the judge and couldn't pick up. After a debate with herself that lasted only a few seconds, she decided things were quiet enough for her to do a little investigating on her own and left her office to find Charlie. He wasn't at his computer, and she didn't want to wait for him. She rationalized that she shouldn't become too dependent on anyone so soon in a new job. She could take an hour to look around herself and prove she could fill the lieutenant's shoes. She told the secretary that she was going out and could be reached on her cell phone. "I'll be back in an hour," she promised.

"Where are you going in case the boss asks?"

"It was the rule to tell. Eloise was on her way out the door, hesitated, then continued as if she hadn't heard the question. It was a big mistake, one of many that she would make that day. When she got outside, the rain had stopped, and the traffic was still backed up. She couldn't tell whether the sky was clearing up or not and considered her options. If she took a car, she might get caught in midtown gridlock for an hour. She could walk a couple of miles across town or take the E train across to Fiftieth and Lex. Since she'd been told to stay put, it didn't seem like a good idea to leave a paper trail by signing a car out. Usually she would have a driver. No one went alone. She had a fleeting thought that she should return for Charlie, and let him sign out the car. But she didn't want to take the time.

She started walking and forgot about the subway option. A few minutes later she was crossing Broadway and wondering what she thought she was doing. Most of the corners in the city dipped into little valleys that quickly flooded when it rained. Her boots were water-resistant, not waterproof, and she questioned her choice of transportation. But she couldn't let wet feet abort her mission to catch a killer and show everyone in her life who'd ever thought blondes were dumb. By ten thirty she was on Fiftieth Street and First Avenue within sight of the Perkins house. It was easy to pick out because it still had yellow police tapes around it. Exhilarated from the exercise of a power walk across a soggy city, she congratulated herself on making good time. Then she took a moment to let the architecture of the block speak to her.

The Perkins house had a new facade that screamed modern and filthy rich. In stark contrast, the Anderson brownstone with its original steep stairs leading to a dark second-floor entrance, and spiderweb of cracked muddy-colored exterior, looked ripe for renovation. Eloise walked the block once and tried Barry's cell one more time. He still wasn't picking up. She left a message telling him where she was and to meet her there ASAP. Then she climbed the stairs and rang the bell. She felt woefully unprepared and was sorry about all the things she hadn't asked Jo Ellen Anderson the day before. It had been clear from the look of her, and her manner, that she wasn't married, but did she live alone? Did she have a housekeeper or companion? Eloise breathed a sigh of relief when a woman opened the door almost immediately: young—mid-twenties. Long red hair. She was a very pretty girl.

"Hi, I'm Sergeant Gelo from the police. Is Miss Anderson at home?" she said.

"No. She's at work." The girl had a sulky voice and sounded put out at the intrusion.

"And you're?"

"I'm Leah. I do the cleaning." Then the sullen look vanished when the girl smiled. "You don't look like a cop."

Eloise relaxed a little with the familiar response. "What's a cop supposed to look like?"

"Mean. Do you have a gun?"

Usually Eloise didn't like it when someone asked about her gun. A cop couldn't be too careful about letting someone get close to his weapon. But it didn't alarm her now. She felt very much in control of the situation. "Leah, do you come here every day?" she asked.

"No, I live here."

"Great. I'd like to talk to you a little, and look around."

Leah hung on to the door. "What are you looking for?" she asked.

"There was a homicide here yesterday. Didn't you talk to the police about it?"

"No."

"You didn't?" Eloise was surprised.

"No, Miss Anderson told me not to open the door to strangers."

"You opened the door for me," she pointed out.

Leah smiled. "Well, you're cute. What do you want to know? I'll talk to you."

Eloise was used to flirtation. A lot of people were attracted to her—girls, guys, animals. It didn't mean Leah was a lesbian. Although the thought did cross her mind briefly, she wasn't alarmed by it. The girl looked like a lot of young people she knew—slightly disaffected, eccentrically dressed. She was using a man's tie for a belt on her jeans. On top was a man's vest from an old suit. The vest wasn't buttoned, and a watch chain held the two sides together. Under it, her bra showed. On her wrists a number of sparkly bracelets looked like diamonds. They caught Eloise's eye right away.

"What do you want to know?"

Eloise didn't answer. She looked into the front hall. It was narrow and dark. Stairs hugged the wall on the right. The only daylight filtered in from somewhere way in the back.

"Is anyone one here with you?"

"No," Leah said. "No one ever comes here. Jo Ellen doesn't like visitors."

"Why not?"

Leah shrugged. "She's old," she replied as if that was a reason.

Eloise had a million questions for this girl whom all the other detectives seemed to have overlooked. Maybe she didn't know anything, but maybe she did. Eloise hesitated. She had no way of knowing if the girl was alone, or what she might find in the house. The best idea was to remove her and question her somewhere else. But she didn't have a car to put her in, didn't have backup. She hadn't expected anyone to be here and hadn't thought things through.

"Come on in. I never get visitors," Leah said, suddenly welcoming. "It's so boring here, and I'm not supposed to leave."

"Why not?" Right away Eloise was sucked in.

"Jo Ellen's rules." Leah shrugged again. "We have some cool stuff in here. I bet you'd like to see it."

Eloise sure would. She wondered where the bracelets came from and thought she could find out a whole lot of things. All her years of training prohibited this kind of solo act, but she wasn't thinking about that now. She checked her cell phone. There were no missed calls. No one was looking for her yet. She'd left a message for Barry to meet her here and figured he'd be there within the hour. What could happen before then?

"Okay," she said, and entered the house with full confidence that she could handle anything.

Forty-nine

"You got me out of the bath to come here. What is this about? I already talked to the police." Jo Ellen Anderson stood in the Anderson Agency parlor in wet rubber boots, looking indignantly from one detective to the other.

April figured that she weighed 180, 190, maybe more. She was a large woman with the kind of straight back and ample figure that earlier generations used to admire. She carried her head way back like some older women did to keep their double chins up and others did out of pride. She was wearing a brown tweed suit and a tan fedora. The raincoat that had covered her outside was gone now. Remembering what Chad had said about a piece of plastic caught in the mop in the Wilson garage, April was eager to take a look at it. The hair prickled on the back of her neck. She had the feeling she was in the presence of a killer.

"I'm Lieutenant Sanchez," she said, keeping the name simple.

"Oh, a lieutenant now. We're moving up the ranks," Jo Ellen remarked with a spark of humor. "What can I do for you?"

"And this is Detective Baum."

She didn't bother looking at Woody. "Don't tell me someone else is gone," she said as if she knew that wasn't the case.

"It must be difficult for you to lose two clients in two days," April replied.

"Of course it is." Jo Ellen flung her hands in the air impatiently. "Two lovely young women, and they were both my friends. It wasn't just business. I talked to them frequently, as I'm sure you know. Better be careful—people spy," she added, indicating with her index finger the small camera that Woody had detected earlier in one corner of the ceiling.

"Who spies?" April asked.

"The Hunter people, and I don't like it at all," she scolded as if they were listening at the moment. "They're probably behind all this. I wouldn't be surprised to learn they'd killed my clients just to get me out."

Just a little paranoia, April thought. "Is Hunter the owner of the agency?"

"Yes, and it was a hostile takeover, like the Nazis. My aunt was tricked out of it, and I don't care who knows it."

"How did it happen?" April had learned a long time ago that people had to tell their stories their own way. Tangents were par for the course.

"They wanted it. Anderson is a name that has ensured quality to four generations of New York's finest," Jo Ellen said.

April couldn't help noting the irony. "New York's Finest" was the slogan of the NYPD.

"It was a tragedy. And now this. This is the new

corporate thing." She pointed at the camera again, then regally lowered herself onto the throne chair that showed her back to the camera, while she offered April the seat that faced it. April took out her notebook.

"They can see what people are doing, and hear everything. They say it's for efficiency and training. But I'm wondering, is it legal?" She tilted her head to one side, waiting for an answer.

"Yes, the owners of a company can install surveillance in their own facilities. If there's a camera in the ladies' room, that's a different story."

"Oh, heaven forbid." Jo Ellen covered her eyes with a big hand.

April had a feeling that the hair under her hat was dyed red and she vibrated with excitement.

"Do you think I have any recourse?" Jo Ellen was saying.

"I'm here to talk to you about something far more serious than surveillance in your workplace."

"But I love my work. I've increased the business over a hundred and fifty percent since my aunt passed on. The acquisition was a robbery, a terrible thing. And no one cares."

"Maybe I can help you with it," April suggested.

"Oh, would you? That would be such a blessing. It's so hard to work with people spying down your neck. I can't even set my own salary anymore. They cut my commissions in half—just the opposite of everything they promised. My aunt thought we'd be able to keep the house, but her death taxes took it all. I don't know what I'm going to do." She drummed her fists on the arms of her chairs.

"What is your agreement with Hunter?" April asked. The way the woman looked and acted, it was surprising they'd kept her on for a single day.

"They said I could stay as long as I wanted, but now they're asking me to leave by Labor Day. Do you think I'd have an age discrimination case?"

April shook her head. She didn't know if Jo Ellen Anderson had any case. "I'm here to find the person who killed Maddy Wilson and Alison Perkins."

"Well, I know a lot about them," she acknowledged, "but how would I know who killed them?"

"I think you may know something about it."

She looked wary. "Why would you think that?"

"You live in the neighborhood. You talk to people every day. You may have seen, or possibly even know, the killer."

"Impossible."

"What time did you come into the office?"

"Oh, my, which day? I have a memory deficit about these things. I'm not sure, Monday— sometime between eight thirty and nine. That's my usual time. Does that help?"

"Alison Perkins lived across the street from you—"

"Yes, she came to tea at my house. She was going to help me with my book."

"Your book?"

"Yes, I'm an author. My book is about all the people I've helped in my time. You may not know that Princess Diana was an au pair over here. I placed her with her family, so of course she invited me to her wedding. My book is going to be a big best seller."

"I'm sure it is. But right now we're looking for a

killer. Alison Perkins called you yesterday morning. What did she want?"

Jo Ellen clicked her tongue. "Oh, they were leaving for the Vineyard soon. She needed to change girls."

"Why did she need to change girls?" April watched the brim of the hat tip up to the ceiling.

"Why is the sky blue? Because Alison was never satisfied. She wanted the perfect girl. No girl is the perfect girl. You can try to train them to suit the households, but you can't train the households to keep them. People like Alison change their staff because they can. I've been very successful in this business because I come from quality myself; I know how wealthy people think. I try to pass this knowledge on to my girls, but it doesn't always help them."

"Your notes on Remy and Lynn seem unusually detailed. Were they a problem?"

"I told you, I work with them on their improvement."

"And it sounds like you enjoy moving them around. Don't you get double fees if they have to be replaced?"

"Oh, that doesn't mean anything to my clients. They can afford it. I know what their needs are. I can always fix whatever goes wrong in their houses," she said airily.

"It sounds like you may have had a hand in making things go wrong," April said.

"No, no. Don't try that. I've never had a complaint about my services. I know how to handle things," she retorted angrily. "Are you here to make trouble for me?"

"Your employees were telling you what was going on in the houses, and you exploited that information to encourage turnover," April said straight out.

"They told me a little, here and there, but I never exploited anybody. I have a great sensitivity to my insider position. Knowledge is power, you know, and you have to be careful with power." Jo Ellen adjusted her hat.

"Somebody killed your clients," April said angrily.

"Yes, I could put it in my book." Jo Ellen looked pleased. She didn't seem to get the gravity of the situation.

"Let's start with the hiring history of Mrs. Wilson," April told her, settling in for a long interview.

"You mean everyone who worked for them? That's a lot of people." She made a face.

"Did anyone work for both Mrs. Wilson and Mrs. Perkins—a cleaning lady, somebody who had keys to both houses?" April watched her face.

"Oh, I don't know. They have to return the keys when they leave. That's a rule," Jo Ellen said flatly.

"To you?" April asked.

She put her finger to her lips. "I do have some keys," she admitted.

April glanced at Woody. "Does anybody else have access to them?"

"No, of course not," she said indignantly. "I'm very careful."

April let that pass. "Is it unusual that Remy and Lynn were both fired at the same time?"

"In this business anything can happen. Sometimes there's a stealing issue." Jo Ellen screwed up her puffy face some more. "My high-net-worth clients have so many possessions, they can't keep track of them all. They buy a dozen sweaters and leave six in the bag. They shop at Tiffany and don't remember what they bought. They misplace cash and think it's stolen. I get calls all the time. I have to calm them down, but sometimes the staff gets blamed anyway. It's a vicious cycle. People get hired; people get fired. It's all part of the game."

"But Remy was fired because of her relationship with Mr. Wilson," April reminded her.

"Well, yes. That's another reason. Girls these days." She shook her head and looked sad.

For someone who had been so keenly interested in every intimate detail of Maddy's and Alison's lives, Jo Ellen was remarkably uninterested in their deaths. She was not connecting. April changed the subject.

"What was the incident that caused Hunter to put in surveillance cameras?" she asked finally.

Jo Ellen stared at nothing for a moment. "I have no idea." Then she changed her mind. Her face deflated a little. "I believe someone was assaulted," she said slowly. "But I can explain everything."

April turned the page in her notebook. Now she was getting somewhere. "Who was assaulted?" April asked Jo Ellen.

"One of the women. She was in late. I don't remember the details."

"I'd like to talk to her."

"Well, you can't talk to her. She isn't with us anymore," said airily.

"Do you have a telephone number for her?"

"I really couldn't answer that."

April gestured to Woody. He nodded and left the room to start grilling the employees. Twenty minutes into the interview and already armed with a number of Jo Ellen's conflicting statements about several key questions, April began to zero in on the difference between accepting gifts from clients and stealing from them. And meddling in their lives so she could restaff their houses again and again for the fees. Jo Ellen didn't seem to understand what was wrong about it.

"The Duchess of Windsor was one of my best friends, rest her soul," she said. "She gave me one of her own bracelets as a token of her appreciation for everything I did for her."

"I'd like to see it," April said, and she planned to do that very soon. Her cell phone rang, and she picked it out of her pocket. "Lieutenant Woo Sanchez."

"It's Barry Queue. I have the warrant," he told her.

She glanced at her watch. "I'm on my way. What do you say, twenty minutes?"

"The traffic's bad. Call it thirty. I called Sergeant Gelo. She isn't picking up."

"Well, it doesn't matter. She can stay at the shop for now," April assured him.

"She's not at the shop," he said.

"What? Where is she?" April was surprised and annoyed. She didn't like it when people didn't follow orders.

"She went to the Anderson house."

"What? Why did she do that?"

"I don't know," Barry said.

"Okay, well, keep calling. We'll be there soon."

April hung up and returned to Jo Ellen. She was a big woman, arrogant and seemingly without much feeling for anyone. She didn't understand the seriousness of the situation. Furthermore, she seemed to think that because her family had been tops in the domestic-employment game for so long, she was entitled to use the trust people had in her name to exploit them.

April connected the dots and suspected that the house keys Jo Ellen admitted to having were given to her by the girls she'd placed in those homes. Further, she guessed that Remy and Lynn revealed intimate details about their bosses' lives and knew when they were not at home. That made the girls accomplices to, or even guilty of, thefts that occurred and would explain why they were fearful to talk openly about what they knew. The three of them were guilty of something. But murder? Why would Jo Ellen, or any of her staff, kill her clients? Even if she was disturbed, it made no sense. Why kill the source of the income she desperately needed, and so close to her own home? More importantly, it didn't fit her profile. She was a manipulator and possibly a thief, but that didn't make her a killer. Then April had a new thought. There might be someone else in Jo Ellen's close circle they didn't know about. She started sweating.

Jo Ellen had a tight little smile on her face as if all of this were merely good material for her book.

"Miss Anderson, would you remove your hat?" April asked her quietly.

"Oh, no, I can't," she cried.

"Why not?"

Jo Ellen pointed behind her at the camera.

"Do your roots show?" April leaned forward.

"My roots?" She looked startled.

"You have red hair, right, colored from gray?"

Jo Ellen winced and her eyes squeezed shut in a private agony. "You caught me," she said.

"Why did you kill them?" April was elated. She'd cleared the case.

Jo Ellen opened her eyes. "Kill them? I didn't kill them."

"I think you did. A piece of your raincoat was found at Maddy Wilson's house, and your hair at Alison Perkins's house. It puts you on the scene."

"No," she said wildly. "It's not possible."

"I can help you with this," April offered.

"No, I can explain it."

"Good, explain." April's pen started moving on the page.

Then Jo Ellen shook her head. "I don't believe you. You're making that up."

"Miss Anderson. Take your hat off."

"What if I say no?"

"You can't say no."

Jo Ellen let out a little sob, then reached up and took off the fedora. April sucked in her breath. Underneath the hat, her head was bald as an egg. "I have cancer," she whispered. She pointed to the office and the camera. "I didn't want them to know."

Oh, jeez. April was shocked for a second. But it didn't stop her. "You had short red hair before it fell out?"

"Yes." Jo Ellen looked down at her hands. "It's a terrible thing to lose your hair."

"And you wore hats when it was coming out? Just like now."

She nodded.

April swallowed. "Who else wears your hats?"

Jo Ellen's face was gray. "It happened a long time ago. More than a decade ago. An accident, explainable. It couldn't happen again. That's it."

She closed her mouth with a snap.

"Who are you talking about?"

"My daughter, Leah, my *adopted* daughter. She wears my hats, but would not hurt anyone again. She promised me. A promise is a promise. It couldn't be her."

April felt sick. "Is she at your house?"

"Of course. She lives there."

Cops don't panic when events start spinning out of control. They just move forward. Ten thousand questions shot into April's head, but she didn't take the time to ask them. She collected Woody from the bull pen and briefed him in a sentence. They ran for the stairs, both reaching for their phones.

Fifty

As soon as she stepped inside the house, Eloise detected a peculiar musty odor The place had an old-house smell and something more complicated—a combination of dead-animal-in-the-walls and rotting-vegetation-in-the-greenhouse smell. It was creepy. The wallpaper was dark with age, and the Oriental runner badly worn, but there was no dust any-where. She scanned the scene. Near the door an umbrella stand was crammed full of canes with or-nate handles. Along one wall a coat and hat rack sported fashions from another era. From above came the dim glow of two Art Deco, gold-tinged glass tulips that barely illuminated the rows of sepia photos adorning the wall of the narrow staircase leading upstairs.

"That's the family," Leah said, pointing to pho-tos of men in top hats and tails, and ladies wearing summer dresses and big hats. "They're famous."

"It smells like they died in here," Eloise remarked.

"That's the smell of old wood. I clean and clean, but I can't do anything about it." The girl stared at her as if she'd made an accusation.

Imagining Gothic horrors, Eloise quickly stepped

aside so the girl could pass in front of her. "Please lead the way," she said gently. The house was unsettling, and the intense expression on the girl's face warned her that she had to go easy.

"You feel it, too, don't you? It's haunted," Leah said. "Woo, woo." She wiggled her fingers.

"No kidding," Eloise murmured uneasily.

"Just kidding. Gotcha, didn't I?"

Eloise laughed. The girl was a little weird, but not very big. She wasn't afraid of her. "What's the layout of the house?" she said.

"The living room, dining room, and powder room are on this floor. The kitchen and pantry are downstairs. Two bedrooms share a bathroom upstairs, and the maids' rooms are on the fourth floor. I live up there. The ghosts are in the basement. Do you want to see them?" she teased.

"Maybe later. Is there anyone else in the house?"

"You already asked me that. We're all alone."

"How about animals? It smells like you have animals."

"We had a cat for a while, but it's gone now."

Leah opened big double doors to the living room and went in.

Eloise slowly followed her into a room crowded with furniture. Heavy sideboards of mahogany lined the walls. Small marble-topped tables and ornate chairs made an obstacle course of the room. It was hard to imagine people gathering and relaxing in such a place. She threaded her way through the maze to the window facing Fiftieth and looked out. From there she had a clear view of the Perkins house across the street. Anybody arriving or leaving there could be seen, and it would be easy to determine when Alison would be alone. She began to feel some trepidation and was glad Barry was on the way.

Ahead of her, Leah pulled open the heavy sliding doors that separated the living room from the dining room, and Eloise was distracted from getting her phone out to call her boss with her location. In the dining room, the furniture was heavily carved, as dark as stain could make it, and too big for the space. Another bay window opened on a back garden that was a tangle of overgrown bushes, weeds, and unpruned trees. Everywhere the surfaces were loaded with stuff—commemoration cups, souvenirs from trips abroad. Beer steins, Dresden, and porcelain—people, animals, parrots. Silver boxes, tortoiseshell boxes, enamel pillboxes. Plates. Objects were stacked everywhere and completely dust free.

"Where did all this stuff come from?"

"Gifts from clients. Things they collected."

Eloise pointed at the sparkly bracelets on her wrist. "What about those?"

"Jo Ellen's favorites." She held them up for display.

Eloise thought about Alison's missing bracelet and started chewing her lipstick off. "Are they real?" she asked.

"Of course they're real. Don't worry, she lets me wear them."

"Where did she get them?"

Leah shrugged, and Eloise thought of Alison's husband.

"How well did you know Mrs. Perkins?" she asked suddenly.

"The lady across the street?" Leah fingered the bracelet.

"You know who I mean."

"I knew her."

"What about Lynn?" Eloise's eyes kept moving around, looking at the boxes and cups. The place was like an antiques warehouse.

"She's my best friend," she said warmly.

Eloise focused on her. "Good, then you can help me with what happened yesterday. Did you see Lynn in the morning?"

Leah put her lips together and shook her head.

"Okay," Eloise turned away and ran her finger over a surface, looked at it, then nodded. "Very good. What is your routine here?" she said casually.

Leah stared at her. "What do you mean?"

"Do you make breakfast for Miss Anderson?"

"No, not really." She stared out of disconcerting blue eyes, one hip cocked against the table.

"What happens then?"

Leah shrugged. "She leaves for work."

"What time would that be?"

"Nine, ten, eleven. Depends on her treatment."

"What treatment?" Eloise lifted an eyebrow.

Leah frowned and moved a few paces away. "I'm not supposed to tell."

"Oh, come on. You can tell me," Eloise said. Leah shook her head again. "No way. Why all the questions?"

"Just curious. Did Miss Anderson have a treatment yesterday?" Eloise picked up a porcelain parrot, all green, studied it for a second, then put it back.

"No, she's finished for now." Leah copied what Eloise had done a moment before. She ran a finger across the highly polished table and showed it to the detective. "See, I'm a good cleaner. I'm the best. That's why Joey has me here at her house. I can do the job." She made a face. "I have to clean up for Lynn though. She's not the best."

Eloise glanced at her watch. Where was every-body? Surely, someone should be calling her by now. "You have to clean up for Lynn?" she said slowly.

"She's lazy. I'm not." The girl laughed.

"You clean across the street?" Eloise asked.

"Oh, sure, but I don't babysit. I'm not supposed to do that."

"Why not? You look like you'd be a very good babysitter."

"You have to go now." Leah went out of the dining room, then down the back stairs, leading the way to the front door.

Eloise hesitated even as her adrenaline kicked in and her training directed her to move. The girl was out of her sight, and she now had put together enough of the pieces to know she'd made a number of tactical errors. She'd heard of the girl from the interviews, but didn't know she lived here. No one had mentioned that, not Alison, not Lynn. And Leah had worked in the Perkins house. That meant she had access, maybe even her own key. They had assumed it was the old lady. Now her heart slammed away in her chest telling her to get the hell out of the house and call for backup. She reached for her phone and realized that it was off. Berating herself for a dozen stupidities, she started down the stairs.

Fifty-one

The rain started again as April and Woody came out of the building and dived into the car. Woody ground the key in the ignition before the door was closed, and the engine roared to life.

"Perkins house," she said, which was close enough.

"I know," he muttered. He pulled out, barely looking as a bus was cruising in. The driver hit the horn. Woody hit the siren and cut him off.

April shut her eyes to the offense and punched the number one on her phone. Mike's voice mail came on immediately. "It's me," she told it. "I've called for backup at the Anderson house. Sergeant Gelo is over there, and she isn't picking up." *Shit.* She didn't want to say she was ticked because her sergeant didn't like being left behind and had taken matters into her own hands. The big no-no could have widespread repercussions for both of them. She ended the call without pointing a finger and muttered angrily to herself as a yellow light slowed the traffic in front of them at Fifty-seventh Street. When the light went red, a hole opened up.

"Go," she said, and he ran the light.

She punched two on her cell. Charlie picked up on the second ring. "Hagedorn," he said.

"Charlie. What happened with Gelo?"

"She stepped out. I've been trying to reach her. I have something on Anderson."

"What do you have?"

"She has a girl living with her."

"I know about that," April said impatiently.

"Did you know her name is Lucy Walters?"

"Is that supposed to mean something to me? Oh, Jesus." April braced as Woody dodged an ambulance.

"You okay?"

"I'm on Lexington with Woody."

"My condolences. Okay, Lucy Walters hit her homeroom teacher in the head with a chair when she was in sixth grade. The woman died of her injuries. That was thirteen years ago. She served eighteen months in juvenile, out of state, and she's been in and out of programs until she moved in with Anderson."

"Call Minnow with that, will you?" April said tersely.

"I already took the liberty. Didn't want to be slow sharing that."

"Good thinking. And Mike?"

"He knows, too."

"Okay. What's the story on Gelo? Don't hold back on me."

"I'm working on it. As soon as I know . . ."

April's stomach heaved. Whenever she was upset, all her nerves went right to her gut. She told herself that everybody was on the way, that it was going to be all right. She wanted to believe that, but she knew she was responsible for her people. Even if no one was hurt, she was still going to have to take the hit for her officer's bad judgment. But more importantly right now, she had no way of knowing whether or not Gelo was in that house and if she was, what was happening there. She started to pray.

where five middle-aged women sat at desks with computers, talking on the phone. They all displayed surprise at seeing visitors.

Josie pointed at the empty chair on the far end. "That one is mine."

"Miss Anderson's office?"

"In there." She pointed to a closed door opposite her desk.

April nodded. They were going to have to talk to all the women. "Let's go to the parlor," she said.

When they got there, Woody whistled at the antiques and decorations on the wall. Josie smiled at his reaction, and her face softened. "Josie, how long have you been here?" April asked.

"A year."

"Do you like your job?"

She hesitated. "I need my job," she said softly, trailing her hand along the inlay on the desk.

"We all need our jobs. Do you get along with Miss Anderson?"

"She's been very nice to me," Josie said guardedly.

"I guess you feel loyal to her then."

"Of course." She glanced at the door longingly as if she wished she were back at her desk.

"You know that two of your clients have been murdered?"

She nodded solemnly and looked frightened.

"Did you know them?"

"Only from taking phone messages. I don't deal with the clients personally. Is it okay if I sit down? I feel a little sick."

April waved her hand at the French chairs. "Of course."

Josie sat in the closest one and hugged her chest. April took the chair near her. "Do you know Miss Anderson's schedule?" she asked.

Josie shook her head. "She keeps that very confidential."

"Do you know where she is at the moment?" April asked.

"No." Josie chewed on the inside of her mouth.

"Does she call you to let you know when she'll be here?" April asked with a raised eyebrow.

"Uh-uh."

"Does she come in every day?" April was pulling teeth.

"Absolutely." Josie knew the answer to that one and nodded vigorously.

"How about yesterday? What time did she come in?" She started doodling.

"Mmmm. Maybe nine thirty, ten. I'm not sure," Josie said.

"What about the day before?"

She looked up at the ceiling, then at April's notebook. "I don't remember," she murmured apologetically.

"That's okay," April assured her. "Tell me about your job. What do you do here?"

"I get coffee. I run errands, take messages. I do background checks on new people," she said slowly.

"Do you get Miss Anderson coffee when she comes in?"

"Yes, and a muffin."

"Do you have to go outside for that?" April kept on.

"We have a coffee machine. I get the muffin on

At the bottom of the stairs was an old-fashioned stainless steel kitchen. A gas stove, dish-washer, and refrigerator were in the usual places against the walls, along with some freestanding glass cabinets filled with china. A large worktable was in the center and a rustic table and chairs by the back window might have been used at one time for staff. There were three doors in the large room. A back door led to the untended garden. A side door opened on the front hall, and a half-glass door faced the street. The floor was the color of old precinct walls.

When Eloise came in, Leah was rubbing a corner of the worktable as if she'd already left. It was then that Eloise noticed the diamond rings on her finger for the first time. Eloise was only a few steps from the little fenced-in area outside the house where garbage cans were kept on the street. A gate from there led to the sidewalk and freedom. Through windows in the kitchen door, she could see that the rain had started again. Once again she hesitated about making her escape.

"Does Lynn come here often?" she asked.

"Nobody comes here. I told you Joey is sick."

"What's wrong with her?" Eloise asked. She thought the girl was mistaken. She was the sick one. She lifted her shoulders in an angry shrug. "I'm getting tired of this," she announced. "People aren't supposed to upset me."

"Are you sick, too, Leah?" she asked gently.

"No, not anymore."

"Are you taking medicine to make you better?"

"You're very pretty," she said. "Mrs. Wilson was pretty, but not as pretty as you."

"Does Joey know you clean for Lynn at the Perkins house?"

"No." She looked away.

"Is she afraid that you would hurt them?"

"No."

"Is that what you're taking medicine for?"

"Don't bug me about meds when I'm telling you you're pretty," she said angrily. "I could hurt you."

Eloise had a gun. She thought she could handle it. "Oh, Leah, you're not going to hurt me. I'm a police officer. We're surrounded here. People all over the place, and Miss Anderson is coming over. She'd be upset if you touched me."

"She doesn't care what I do. I'm her daughter."

Those blue eyes were like marbles.

"Well, I talked to her yesterday. I know she doesn't want her daughter to hurt people," Eloise said calmly. "We're going to help you so you don't do that, okay? You're going to be fine now."

There had been many times in Eloise's life when she'd been frightened, sometimes even terrified, but not when it counted. During 9/11 and the days that followed she was frightened for other people, never for herself. These days she was terrified only in her dreams. To Eloise, a sick young woman in a room equipped with knives and wooden mallets and skewers and forks did not pose a real danger because she had confidence in herself to handle anything. She'd dealt with crazy people before. That was her mistake. She could have walked out that kitchen door, and let somebody else mop up. But she wasn't used to letting other people do her dirty work. She wanted to stay, to conquer Leah herself and make sure nothing happened to her. Call it arrogance or ego—she wanted to be a hero. And Leah seemed to be responding well.

"I'm sorry about Marsha. I didn't mean to hurt her," she said.

"Who's Marsha?" That was a name Eloise hadn't heard before.

"Jo Ellen's assistant. Will you hold my hand? I don't want to go back."

Eloise swallowed. "Where is she?"

"In the basement. Hold my hand."

No, she wasn't going to do that. She was concerned that there might be a living person in the basement who needed help. She moved two steps back. "How long has Marsha been in the basement?" she asked softly.

Leah noted the retreat and didn't answer for a long time. Then she said, "She was pretty."

Eloise licked her lips. Leah had a "pretty complex," among other things. If she were in restraints, Eloise would be happy to talk about it. Who didn't have a "pretty complex"? It sometimes felt like a good reason for murder, but killing the pretty ones wasn't the solution. Sometimes there wasn't a reason. Crazy people did sick things because they couldn't help it.

"Why are you moving away? Are you afraid of me, too?"

"No," Eloise said quickly. "Why would I be afraid of a beautiful girl like you?"

What they did in the academy was practice with a number of contraptions—nets, restraining devices, even stun guns. Sometimes when people were out of control mentally, or high on drugs, police officers had no other choice but to use them. Eloise didn't have any of those devices to keep swinging fists, kicking feet, a battering head—and human teeth—away from her. And she hadn't practiced physical combat in many years. All she had was a firearm she didn't want to use. The gun gave her comfort.

One second she and Leah were having a conversation of sorts; the next second her phone rang. Before she could reach for it, or make a plan, the girl crossed the space between them.

"No phone," she said furiously. "No phone."

She came at her fast as if to grab the phone, and Eloise stepped back again to keep the distance. The phone rang again.

"It's all right. It's just my partner."

Leah shook her head, angrier than the situation called for. "Don't make me hurt you," she said.

It was the very thing that Eloise was thinking herself; she did not want to hurt an EDP (emotionally disturbed person), even one who might be a killer. She had that thought and didn't see the knife. Leah raised one hand above her head. Eloise watched the hand going up so she could get out of the way when it came down. The other one whipped out at her and stabbed her in the stomach before she could dodge it.

"Oh shit," she exclaimed in surprise. "Why did you do that?" She felt the knife burn as it pierced her skin. At first it didn't seem so very much worse than a paper cut. But when it came for her again, she got angry. "Cut that out," she screamed, and reached for her gun.

She didn't get to it. Leah was all over her with that knife. She was an attacking tiger, a wolf, panting and growling as if there were no other form of expression, and Eloise was slipping in her own blood. It was everywhere, on her black and red pants, on the knife, on the floor, and splattered all over the crazy girl trying to kill her.

Blood gushed out of her. She could feel it pulse with every heartbeat as she tried to dodge out of reach. She hit the refrigerator, the stove, the wall, bouncing off of all surfaces as she looked for something to fend off the blows. The kitchen became slick with her blood while the one thing that she'd always relied on, her gun, remained strapped in its holster. She didn't collapse and go down, but she couldn't get at the gun as she struggled to stay on her feet. She found herself moving in closer to the table, forcing Leah to circle with her. That was when Eloise realized that there was something else wrong with her. Leah was so wound up and enraged that she was almost foaming at the mouth. But like a rabid animal, she was not an agile fighter. Her circuits weren't connecting. Her movements were awkward and uncoordinated. She struck at her victim but couldn't bring her down. The phone in Eloise's purse started ringing again. Leah was distracted by it and turned to it, almost as if she thought it was for her.

In the split second when Leah was listening to the phone ring, Eloise grabbed the one lone chair at the worktable. She swung the chair around and pushed it into Leah's knees. It took her by surprise; she lost her balance and fell forward with a scream. Her arms were pinned in front of her as her chest hit the spindles on the chair back. The knife tumbled to the floor and she struggled to untangle herself from the chair. She got free of it and lunged for the knife.

Eloise wanted to kick her, smash her head in, but she was pulsing blood and too weak to lift her leg. Crouched forward in an awkward position, she had only one thing—possession of the chair. She shoved it at the girl again, and Leah flopped down on her stomach. A wild cry rose out of her mouth when Eloise pushed the chair over her, trapped her between its legs, and sat on it so that she couldn't get up. It was then that she finally got the gun out of its holster and shot out the window so she could call for help.

Fifty-three

It was a scene April had played so many times in her life, and one that plagued her dreams. She was in charge of a major investigation that was going terribly wrong, and she couldn't get there to stop it. Someone would die who shouldn't die and as a result she, too, would lose her life or her job, or lose face, which was just as bad. She needed to get out of that car. Same old, same old. The traffic lights were too slow, and cars and trucks blocked the way no matter how aggressively Woody drove, or how loudly he used the horn with the siren to tell people, "Police—get out of the way."

One minute she was in the passenger seat of the black Buick on Second Avenue. The next minute the dispatcher made an all-points bulletin, asking for officers to respond to a report of gunshots fired from a residence on the four hundred block of Fiftieth Street.

"Fuck, that's us," Woody said.

"Call for an ambulance," April told him. Then, as sirens started wailing in the distance, she jumped out of the car and started running down the block in the pelting rain, determined to be the first responder. She didn't feel the rain and nothing went through her mind, not her past life, or her future with her husband or the Skinny Dragon Mother she loved as much as anybody on earth. All that drove her was her instinct and training. Dodge the oncoming traffic and pedestrians with their umbrellas up and get there.

"Police, move back," she screamed at two men standing outside the house as she unholstered her weapon.

"I called 911. He's in there. He has a gun," a man standing outside told her.

"Get back," she said. "Get away."

She went through the gate, sidestepping as she looked through the shattered panes of the kitchen window. She'd seen plenty of bad things in her life, but nothing in all her years in police work prepared her for the blood in the kitchen.

"Oh, shit. Oh, shit." She didn't hear herself whimpering as she raised her weapon and fired into the lock. People were yelling behind her, but she didn't hear what they were saying. Like her own Sergeant Gelo before her, she did the same thing. She entered the house alone, and the horror she saw did not stop her from moving forward into the gore. She was trained to go where the trouble was, and that's what she did. The kitchen was awash with blood. Sergeant Gelo was so drenched with it, she couldn't tell what color her clothes had been. She was sprawled across a kitchen chair, and a female body was pinned under it. Neither moved, and for an awful second April thought both were dead.

"Aw, Jesus, Eloise," she said softly.

Eloise took her hand off her stomach. "She got me."

"Looks like you got her, too. Hang on. We'll get

you out of here." April moved forward to see how bad it was. Eloise yelled.

"Watch out."

April didn't see it in time. The woman on the floor grabbed her foot and yanked hard, trying to pull her down. "No," she said sharply, wrenching her wet boot from the bloody hand. Then she leaned over and tapped her on the back of the head with the butt of her gun. The Glock was not heavy steel the way the old .48s were. But it was hard enough to put her out.

"She did it," Eloise gasped. "She killed those women." She was already in shock, shivering, and couldn't hold her head up. "Please don't be mad. I got her."

"You sure did. Just hang in there, and I won't be mad. I promise." April ripped off her jacket and murmured encouragement. She didn't even know what she was saying. As she waited for the ambulance to arrive, she prayed for a life and offered her own in exchange. She made a vow to whatever gods might be listening. *Let Gelo live, and I'll retire from police work. Just let her live.*

April knew that it was one thing for her to mess up personally and get hurt herself as she had done in the past. Her many failures in this case, starting with Alison's death, and ending with one of her own officers doing the unthinkable, was something else. As Gelo's commanding officer, April felt it was her fault that the sergeant took such a crazy risk, and Chinese face demanded that she be the one to go. Gelo was still breathing when the ambulance arrived. April got in with her, an held her hand all the way to the hospital.

Epilogue

On Friday, April and Mike's honeymoon cruise departed without them, but they were hardly in the mood for rejoicing in paradise and barely noticed. As police officers say when they miss important life events, "Something came up."

In the days that followed Lucy Walters's (aka Leah) internment in Bellevue for psychiatric evaluation, all April could think abut was the fate of her second whip. Fast work by surgeons at New York Hospital—and a miracle—saved Eloise Gelo's life. Doctors on the case said what others in the Department already knew about her: Eloise was as tough as they come; she always beat the odds.

Patching her up, however, took time and more than one surgery. April and Mike were among the many police officers who gave blood for her transfusions, and April was a daily visitor during the weeks that she remained in the hospital. Included in her gifts were some special (and quite disgusting) herbal medicines purchased by Skinny Dragon Mother in Chinatown to cure her. Who knew, maybe they helped.

The only bright light in the very dark story was that Eloise was the sole survivor of Lucy's wrath.

The badly decomposed remains found wrapped in garbage bags and locked in an old steamer trunk in the basement of Jo Ellen's house turned out to be Marsha, the Anderson employee whom Jo Ellen said wasn't with them anymore. Along with her teacher of years ago, Maddy, Alison and her unborn baby, Marsha brought the number of Lucy's victims to five.

Working at Jo Ellen's house brought the troubled young woman in contact with the mothers and their households. Jo Ellen, who'd been stealing from her clients throughout her long career, encouraged Lucy to continue the tradition. If the customers complained about theft or other irregularities, innocent employees were fired and replaced with new ones. The scam had worked until Lucy started killing the employers she despised. Furthermore, she lost all her wiggle room with her attempted murder of a police officer. Jo Ellen was exposed and faced prosecution for her many crimes.

But April weathered the storm; she always did. Her promise to quit the Department if Eloise lived was not forgotten, but in the end no one wanted her to go. Two months later, when the case was fully resolved and the legal system had taken over, she and Mike sailed from San Juan to the West Indies for the vacation of their lives.

New York Times bestselling author

Leslie Glass

**Hit the streets with
NYPD detective April Woo**

THE SILENT BRIDE	0-451-41037-8
JUDGING TIME	0-451-19550-7
TRACKING TIME	0-451-20228-7
STEALING TIME	0-451-19965-0
A KILLING GIFT	0-451-41091-2

**"I'll drop what I'm doing to read
Leslie Glass any time."
—Nevada Barr**

S301